"I want to come with you."

Laura stared up at him.

"Are you afraid of the dark?" Gabe knelt down at her side and stroked her midnight-black hair.

Shaking her head, Laura denied any fear. "For these few days, I want to live in your world. I want to know what it's like to walk in the night with you, to be part of the silence, the moon and the mountains."

Gabe curled his hands into her hair. She had bewitched him. Knowing the dangers of opening his world to her, he still found he couldn't deny her. "Do you know what you're doing to me?"

"Same thing you're doing to me," Laura said shakily. "Filling my world until I wish—" She turned away to hide the sudden tears.

His arm came around her, drawing her against him. "I wanted to give you pleasure, not pain," he said.

Dear Reader,

When two people fall in love, the world is suddenly new and exciting, and it's that same excitement we bring to you in Silhouette Intimate Moments. These are stories with scope, with grandeur. The characters lead the lives we all dream of, and everything they do reflects the wonder of being in love.

This month, Silhouette Intimate Moments has two exciting projects to present to you. First, read *Sea Gate*, by Maura Seger, if you're looking for a romance with a difference. Romantic fantasy has always been a part of these books, but in *Sea Gate*, we go one step farther to fantasy of a different kind. Just for a moment, suppose that the legend of Atlantis had a basis in reality, and that the inhabitants of that watery world had survived into the present day. What if a woman from their world met a man from ours and discovered that love is always the same, no matter where you live?

Bestselling author Heather Graham Pozzessere has a treat in store for you too. She's written an exciting short story called "Shadows on the Nile," and the first chapter is included in all the Silhouette Books titles for this month. But the remaining five chapters will be published only in Silhouette Intimate Moments, and we hope you'll join us next month and every month through March to follow the rocky course of love in the shadow of the Pyramids.

And, as always, we will continue to bring you the best romantic fiction available today, written by authors whose way with words is guaranteed to touch your heart.

Leslie J. Wainger
Senior Editor
Silhouette Books

Sibylle Garrett

Surrender to a Stranger

Silhouette Intimate Moments

Published by Silhouette Books New York

America's Publisher of Contemporary Romance

SILHOUETTE BOOKS
300 East 42nd St., New York, N.Y. 10017

ISBN: 0-373-07211-2

First Silhouette Books printing October 1987

America's Publisher of Contemporary Romance

Printed in the U.S.A.

SIBYLLE GARRETT

was born a Berliner, but considers herself a citizen of the world. After years of moving across the globe, first with her parents, then with her husband of twenty years and their two children, she finally settled down on Long Island. She began writing as a way to pass the time during a lull in her career as a physical therapist. What began as a hobby quickly became a passion to be a published writer.

Chapter 1

The midday sun looked like a ball of fire shrouded in a cloud of haze. Not even the whisper of a breeze fanned any coolness to relieve the oppressive heat. The patches of grass, which had flourished during the summer rains, had long ago turned brown and brittle. The ground was cracked, its surface riddled with a crosshatch of lines. The land stretched to the horizon, an endless, shimmering sea of brown emptiness.

Nothing stirred in the heat. Even the flies had found a cooler place until sundown.

The Jeep's idling motor grated on Laura's nerves. She felt like an intruder, an invader from a place as different from this barren land as night from day, violating this world of silence. New York was crowded and hectic, both opulent and decayed, filled with so many noises but never silence. Only the loneliness was the same.

And the fear.

Laura raised the water bottle to her dry lips and took a few careful sips. Everything had gone according to plan since her arrival in Mexico. No one had questioned her. No one had followed her. During her two days in Acapulco, everyone had accepted her as just another tourist. But her quest was just beginning.

Storing the bottle in the ice chest on the Jeep's passenger seat, she wiped the perspiration off her face and restarted the engine. Dust stirred, following her like a flag. The broken ground was a constant challenge as she tried to keep the vehicle close to the ridge separating the desert from Acapulco Bay. Its gullies and boulders turned her repeatedly from her chosen path, causing her to swerve back and forth.

For almost an hour she had been driving over this obstacle course. She'd covered ten hard, twisting miles since she'd left the smooth highway at Las Cruces. How much farther could it be to the Hacienda de los Leones? Another hour? Two?

She was sure she was on the right track. "Just follow the mountain ridge," the hotel receptionist had said. She had forgotten to mention, and Laura had neglected to ask, just how long she was supposed to follow the ridge or how far the hacienda was from the Mexico-Acapulco highway.

Laura had not yet seen any cattle. She was probably not anywhere near the hacienda. She had never been to Julio's home, but she had seen photos showing the main house surrounded by a mass of green bushes, grass and trees. The photos had shown the house to be a sprawling single-story structure with a center courtyard, heavy oak doors and a red tiled roof. A profusion of oleander, bougainvillea and geraniums surrounded tennis courts, a built-in swimming pool and a helicopter landing pad. The Vasquez family was wealthy and powerful. And Julio was part of that family.

The Jeep rattled in protest as Laura drove over the uneven ground. When she hit a dry basin the tires spun, enveloping her in a cloud of dust. She drew to a stop and covered her face with a scarf until the dust had settled once again.

In New York, the first part of her plan had seemed so simple she had never considered failure. She had thought midday, when man and beast together sought shelter from the desert heat, was the best time to approach the house unnoticed. Her plan had been to park the Jeep some distance away, then walk closer to hide among the bushes and watch the activities. If she was lucky, she'd catch a sight of Peter. But she had not considered the dust.

Julio had never spoken of guards patrolling the place. Now she realized why. There was no need for them. Plumes of brown dust rose high behind approaching visitors and hung in the still air like smoke signals, announcing the presence of strangers from miles away. Sooner or later someone would spot her. She looked back toward Las Cruces. Should she turn around?

Suddenly the air rumbled. Puzzled, Laura looked at the hazy blue sky, searching for clouds. Moments later, the rumble changed to a chopping sound. She saw a helicopter rise high above the ridge, wag its tail to look around, then come straight toward her.

Her fingers clenched around the steering wheel. What should she do? Hide, and let them think that someone had abandoned the Jeep? No, they were sure to land and investigate. There was only one thing she could think to do: brazen it out, play the foolish American tourist who had gotten lost in this desert and hope that Julio—the only man who would recognize her—was not sitting at the controls.

As the helicopter dipped lower, Laura stayed beneath the Jeep's canopy. She pushed back the few strands of dark hair that had escaped the bright red scarf. She cleaned her big sunglasses and covered her eyes. Their deep blue color, and especially the tiny black flecks framing the pupils, was a dead giveaway. Julio might have warned his men to watch out for a woman with her distinctive eyes and long dark hair. They might spot her resemblance to Peter. People had often remarked on the similarities of their features, especially their eyes. She couldn't afford to be recognized. It would destroy all her plans to find her son.

The helicopter slowed, whirling up dust. Then it sped directly at her, its dark glass gleaming like a menacing black eye.

Startled by its rapid approach, Laura sat frozen into immobility. It seemed to envelop the hood of the Jeep. Dirt stung her face and filled her nostrils. Beneath the canopy the dust thickened until she couldn't breathe. Coughing, she ducked and threw herself onto the ground. Scrambling to her feet, she ran a few yards, then burrowed facedown into the hard-baked dirt.

The chopping sound suddenly increased, then leveled off. A stream of air buffeted her clothing and raised up dirt around her as the helicopter seemed to hover directly above. Laura felt her scarf slide off her face. Lifting one hand, she held it in place. Seconds passed like hours before the helicopter moved on. Laura lifted her head, watching it rise into the sky.

Grimly she wiped the dirt off her face, noticing she had lost her sunglasses. Then she swiftly scrambled to her feet. One hand shading her eyes, she watched the bubble turn. They were coming back.

Run. Run. Her first thought was to escape out into the desert. But open spaces were dangerous. There she would be an easy mark for the men. She looked at the ridge rising at the other side of the Jeep. She could climb up there. Perhaps she would find a boulder large enough to hide behind.

The helicopter dipped lower, making directly for her again.

"Get under the Jeep!"

Laura started at the sound of the voice. Had she imagined it? She looked around wildly. All she saw was desert and rocks, and the helicopter coming closer. She ran back to the Jeep.

"Get down!" The voice was barely audible above the noise of the helicopter. Blindly Laura obeyed. She threw herself to the ground and crawled under the Jeep, scraping her hands as she hid in its shade.

The thundering noise the chopper made became deafening. Shaking, Laura covered her ears. They wouldn't dare ram the Jeep, she told herself, trying to calm her fears. Their helicopter could crash and burst into flames from the impact.

As the air twisted and stirred, she moved to the farthest edge beneath the Jeep. Then the runners of the chopper came into her view, hovering above the ground.

It was going to land.

"Run!"

Was it panic yelling inside her head? Or was it the mysterious voice of her guardian angel again? Laura scuttled from beneath the Jeep toward the foot of the ridge. As the helicopter settled down, Laura was up and running, clawing at the rocks, pulling, leaping, skidding, sliding. Up, down, and up again. She didn't stop to look over her shoulder, even when the sounds of Spanish curses began to follow her. She climbed higher and higher until her breath came in short, loud gasps. Finally, wheezing and choking, she had to stop. A glimpse down showed her that her pursuers were not far behind.

The two men were moving slowly but steadily, deliberately pacing themselves. Even as they shouted at her, they did not pause. Slowly Laura took a few deep breaths, and with a shaky hand pushed some strands of hair out of her eyes.

For one instant she wondered if she should stop and face them. She carried no purse, no ID with her. It hadn't been an easy decision to leave her passport and driver's license at the hotel. Without them she had felt curiously defenseless. Now, watching the men come closer and closer, she was glad that she had taken the precaution. But she wasn't caught yet.

She kicked some loose rocks at the men below. The Mexican closest to her cried out, twisted and slid down a few paces. Laura turned and began climbing again, forcing herself to adopt a steadier pace. Soon her movements became less erratic. With fluid grace she moved from rock to rock, breathing evenly. Another glimpse over her shoulder showed her that she had now gained some distance. Hope gave her added strength. With luck, she might escape after all.

Suddenly a rock face loomed above her. She stood up in a space barely wide enough for two people and stared at the overhang in dismay. By jumping, she might catch the ledge, but she knew she was not strong enough to pull herself up over it. A drop of several feet cut the area off from the rest of the ridge. She saw no way around the barrier.

Wildly she looked over her shoulder. The men were gaining. The front one grinned at her, his teeth flashing triumphantly under a dark mustache. "Give up, *señorita*," he called in Spanish. "There's no escape." He pulled himself upward, his strong muscles bulging with the effort.

Laura understood the words. After she had married Julio, she had decided to take Spanish lessons. Julio's English was perfect, but when excited or angry he reverted to his mother tongue. After the first year of their marriage the knowledge had been useful. At least she had understood his muttered threats, although she had been too innocent to believe he would act upon them. She was no longer that naive.

Now she decided to play dumb. *"No comprendo,"* she said haltingly, bending down to pick up another handful of rocks. "Why are you chasing me?" she demanded in furious English.

"The *señorita* is American?" The man had finally reached level ground. Getting to his feet, he stepped closer. He was of medium height and built like an ox, with flat, dark Indian features.

"Yes, I'm an American," she said firmly, trying to keep her tremors of fear under control. "Why are you chasing me?"

"This is private property," he said in heavily accented English. "You are invading." His dark eyes ran over her slender form, an appreciative gleam coming into his eyes. "We got ourselves a nice bird, Juan," he threw over his shoulder in Spanish.

"Es muy linda," Juan agreed. He was a slimmer version of the first man.

The words sent a shiver of apprehension down her spine. Convulsively her hand tightened around the rocks until they bit into her palm. "I didn't know this was private property," Laura stated firmly. She hated the looks the two men exchanged. "I apologize for trespassing."

"That's okay, *chica*," he grinned, stepping closer.

"Stop right there," she warned coldly. "If you let me go back to my Jeep, I'll leave your property."

"*Si, como no, señorita*. We play nice little game, yes?"

Closing the gap between them, he reached for her chin. When she tried to shake off his hand, his fingers cruelly bit into her skin. For a moment her eyes widened with fear.

The man stared at her, amusement slowly changing to disbelief. "*Dios mio,*" he muttered, shaken.

"*Qué pasó, Jorge?*" Juan asked, stepping closer to look over his friend's shoulder.

Laura knew what had shaken Jorge. He had caught a good look of her eyes. Panic welled up in her. She had come so close. Too close to let these men take her to the hacienda. She wouldn't go without a fight.

"The eyes, Juan. Look at her. They are the same blue as the Señorito Pedro's. And see those dark spots? The boss says the boy's mother has the same eyes." His hand bit into her flesh, turning her face to give Juan a better view. The younger Mexican grunted his surprise. "You his mother," Jorge accused in English.

"Whose mother?" Laura asked. It took all her self-control not to shout that Peter was her son. But she could not yet admit that fact—not until she held Peter again in her arms.

"You have no little one?" Jorge asked, studying her features. His hand went to the scarf covering her hair.

Laura took advantage of his weakened hold, twisted away and took a step backward along the narrow space. "No," she shouted, her voice sharp with the pain of her loss. Julio had stolen her son. For one long, lonely year, he had kept them apart. But not much longer, she vowed.

For twelve months she had existed on hope while her lawyer had written letters to congressmen, senators and the State Department. For fifty-two weeks she had dusted off toys that no one played with and changed the sheets on a bed no one slept in. For three hundred and sixty-five days his empty chair at the kitchen table had been her only companion during the skimpy meals. Her apartment was a dark and silent place, waiting for Peter to return.

Laura was tired of ineffective legal games. When her lawyer had finally admitted last week that he had come to a dead end, she had almost welcomed his words. She longed for action and wanted her son back before he stopped remembering her. The young forgot so swiftly, and Peter was only five.

The desperation she recalled now lent her strength. She leaped forward, pushing Jorge backward. The Mexican's expression turned to surprise. He grunted, stumbled and lost his balance. Arms flailing, he collided with his partner, pushing him down the slope. Juan skidded, slipped and slid down the rubble. A few yards down they caught themselves, got to their feet and charged like bulls back up the ridge.

With all her force Laura threw the rocks at Jorge. He roared in fury and pain. Laura backed along the rock where the space became narrow, too narrow for two to walk on, looking for a stick or anything else to hold him off.

Suddenly someone jumped from the overhang, landing smoothly in the spot Laura had occupied moments earlier.

Openmouthed, she stared at the apparition, blinking in disbelief. It was no figment of her imagination. A six-foot wall of sinew and muscle stood between her and her assailants.

Her guardian angel.

Silently he reached for her, strong hands grasping her waist. He lifted her until her face was level with the overhang. Laura grasped the rock firmly. With a quick boost by the legs from the stranger, she scrambled easily over the top. Lying flat on her stomach she gulped in air, stunned as much by the unexpected arrival as by her strenuous climb. Then she scooted back to the edge, looking down at the man who had saved her.

Tawny hair streaked with gold glinted in the sunlight. His khaki-clad shoulders were broad and powerful. In spite of his height, he moved with singular grace. He had accomplished the six-foot leap with the graceful coordination of a mountain cat. She remembered the ease with which he had lifted her. Her waist still felt the impression of his strength.

He stood silently, with supreme confidence, facing the two angry men.

"Who are you?" Jorge challenged angrily in Spanish. "What are you doing here? This is private property."

The stranger stared silently at him.

"Don't interfere," Jorge warned, measuring the man's size through slitted eyes.

"Perhaps he is a gringo, too," Juan suggested, trying to stand beside his friend. But the space was too small for both of them. After balancing for a moment, Juan had to step down.

"You are American?" Jorge repeated, his mustache twitching nervously. When the man did not answer, he muttered over his shoulder, "We have to get the woman. The *patron* will kill us if we lose her."

"We don't have to tell him we saw her," argued Juan.

Frowning, Jorge considered the words, then shook his head. "If she is the one the boss is looking for, he will find out sooner or later that she was here. And what about the Jeep? I say we take her now." He took a cautious step closer.

Juan moved sideways, muttering, "What if she is the wrong one?"

"Then we let her go." Jorge shrugged his shoulders, taking another wary step.

Laura could see the stranger's powerful shoulders tense. They were two against one, yet he was taller and stronger. He also had the advantage of solid ground beneath his feet, and the narrow footing prevented his foes from approaching him simultaneously. Laura guessed that the stranger would be the winner in the uneven fight.

Jorge apparently was no fool. He, too, must have recognized the threatening stance. For several seconds he glared at the man. Then he abruptly retreated. *"Vamonos, amigo,"* he muttered, sliding down the slope. "We will catch her later."

With one last glare at Laura, Juan followed.

The stranger did not move until they were halfway down the slope. Then he turned and looked up at Laura. "Do you want to come down?'' He spoke English, his voice a gently soothing drawl.

Laura's head was but a foot away from him. She stared into the bronzed, hard face. Tawny brows shaded deep-set eyes that glowed like topaz through thick, gold-tipped lashes. His square jaw was covered with a sheen of gold, as if he had shaved many hours ago. His thick, unruly hair fell onto his forehead. Looking at her, he brushed it away with a careless hand.

''I think I'll stay here until they're gone.'' She looked down the slope and saw that the Mexicans had reached level ground. Somehow she doubted they were going to leave.

''They won't give up,'' he said quietly, confirming Laura's fear. Looking back, he watched the smaller man climb into the helicopter while the bigger man searched the Jeep. ''They're calling for reinforcements.''

For one weak moment, Laura closed her eyes in defeat. What chance did she stand fighting the powerful Vasquez family? If she walked down the slope and let the men take her to Julio, she might be able to work out some deal with her husband to allow her access to her son. But visiting rights would never be enough for her.

With an exclamation of disgust, Laura discarded the idea. She was still free and intended to remain so. Getting to her feet, she said with grim determination, ''Then I'll have to walk back to Acapulco. I'm glad I wore sneakers.'' How long a walk was it back to civilization? How far would she get with the helicopter shadowing her? She had no water, no map. Somehow she'd make it, she vowed. For Peter's sake.

''It's a long walk,'' he said quietly, admiring her courage. ''You won't make it before sundown.'' He knew she didn't have a snowball's chance in hell of making it back to Acapulco. Not with reinforcements on the way. She was one small woman, alone and on foot, against helicopters and men who knew this land. Perhaps he should even the odds.

Don't be a fool, he told himself, trying to dismiss the thought. This woman was nothing to him. He had enough troubles of his own without becoming involved in hers. He'd give her a bottle of water and detailed directions. That should relieve his conscience.

He looked up into her delicate heart-shaped face, tight with courage and defiance, and knew he couldn't walk away. She deserved better than to be hunted down like a coyote. Without his help, her capture was a certainty—if she didn't break her neck or die of heatstroke first. Before he could check himself, he reached for the ledge.

Laura started when she saw two big hands appear at her feet. With a swift, powerful surge the man hoisted himself up. The smooth play of hard muscles beneath the bronzed skin was both fascinating and alarming. When the stranger rose to his full height, she stepped back involuntarily. Facing six feet of dangerous toughness, she could understand why the Mexicans had backed off without a fight.

His shoulders were broad, tapering down to a slim waist. His partially unbuttoned shirt showed lean muscles of whipcord strength. He held his head in arrogant confidence. Not a man to back out of a fight, she guessed. He would be swift and lethal.

What was he doing in these mountains? Looking at the sweat-stained shirt, the dusty, unkempt appearance of the stranger, Laura feared she had escaped from one dangerous situation only to face another one.

"I'd better be on my way," she said briskly.

"Do you know which way you're going?" he asked quietly, his hand reaching for the water bottle hanging from the back of his belt. This was his last chance to back out gracefully. But he had already made his decision. He could no more leave her stranded than he had been able to watch the cruel game the two Mexicans had played with her.

"North," Laura said, looking down the slope to where the Mexicans were searching her ice chest. "Eventually these mountains lead back to Acapulco."

His eyes narrowed as he sensed the fear and desperation she tried to hide.

"Eventually," he agreed dryly, uncapping the water bottle and handing it to her.

With a grateful look, Laura raised it to her mouth. She took a big gulp and swilled it in her mouth before slowly swallowing. "Thanks," she said, handing it back to him. "And thank you for helping me. I hope I didn't get you into trouble."

"Nothing I can't handle," he said smoothly. Abruptly he looked over his shoulder. The two men had taken bottles from the cooler and were leaning against the Jeep with their eyes on the ridge. Apparently they had been told to wait for help before taking the helicopter up again.

Vasquez seemed to be searching for a woman with her looks. Was this a case of mistaken identity, or was she the one? Thoughtfully he probed her face. He had never seen eyes like hers, the shade of bluebonnets dotted with dark specks of dust. A grim smile curved his lips. He could use a break in his war against Julio. "Let me show you a way out of here."

"Is there one?" For an instant Laura's eyes brightened with hope, only to narrow suspiciously seconds later. "Why are you offering to help me?"

"I don't like uneven odds," the man said calmly, waiting patiently for her decision.

Laura knew she did not have a real choice. She could either trust the stranger or chance getting caught. "Let's go," she said, placing her confidence in his quiet strength. If anyone could get her back to Acapulco, she sensed it was this man.

He watched her for another moment, his eyebrows raised in silent query. Then he turned abruptly and led the way. His questions could wait until they had reached a safer place.

Laura followed him up the slope. With admiration she observed his easy rhythm, his arms and legs moving from handhold to foothold without dislodging any rubble. It explained to her one unanswered question—how he had appeared so suddenly without any warning.

Laura tried to imitate his style. Her arms were too short to reach some of the boulders. Once or twice she slipped on the rubble but caught herself immediately. When she reached for the last rock at the top of ridge, his hand closed around her wrist, easily hauling her up the rest of the way.

"The worst is over," he said, waiting for her to catch her breath. "You're in pretty good shape."

"For a woman?" Laura countered, smiling, grateful for the many hours she had spent exercising during the last year. The aerobics classes had served a dual purpose: they had kept her away from the empty apartment and had tired her enough for her to get a few hours much-needed sleep.

His brows shot up in amusement. "No. For a city dweller," he corrected, his drawl more pronounced.

"How can you tell?" Laura asked curiously. She wore serviceable jeans, a simple blouse, no makeup or jewelry.

His eyes slid down her long slim legs. "No boots," he said. "Sneakers are no protection against the snakes around here."

Laura stored that bit of useful information. "And where do you come from? Texas? Oklahoma?" she guessed from his drawl.

"Texas." His eyes narrowed against the sun, he looked toward the foot of the ridge. "Reinforcements are coming."

Following his glance, Laura spotted a cloud of dust in the distance. "How far away are they?" she asked, her voice tight.

"Ten minutes," he guessed calmly.

The answer sent shivers of fear down her spine. Only ten minutes before the hunt began. Why were they standing here? Why weren't they trying to put as much distance between them as possible?

"We can't outrun them," he gently answered her silent question. After one more look at the land below, he turned and walked along the top of the ridge, still in clear view of the Mexicans.

Laura followed him, her attention divided between the uneven ground and the back of the stranger. He moved easily, as if he was used to rough country, blending into the rocks. Laura doubted that the Mexicans could still see him from the foot of the hill.

They could easily spot her, though. Her blue-and-white striped shirt stood out against the earth tones like a bright buoy, and the red flag of her scarf was easily trackable. She slowed her steps and freed her hair, using the cloth to wipe the perspiration off her face.

When she looked at the stranger, she found him watching her, a smile of approval curving his lips. Reaching into his pocket, he withdrew a large clean handkerchief and handed it to her. "Use this instead."

With quick, practiced movements Laura coiled her waist-long mane on top of her head, then held out her hand for the handkerchief.

As he folded it into a large triangle, he thought that it was a shame to cover her hair. He had never seen such a cloud of dark, vibrant silk in combination with creamy white skin and huge blue eyes. Ignoring her hand, he stepped behind her, placing the triangle on her head, tying it at the back of her neck.

The moment his fingers touched her neck, Laura tensed. It had been years since she had felt a man's hand on that intimate part of her body. No man had been allowed to come closer than shaking her hand—not since that awful night she had fled from Julio.

He felt the sudden tension as his fingers brushed her nape. His eyes narrowed as he continued to tie the knot, but he was careful not to touch her again. "It's a pity we can't do anything about your shirt," he said, his voice deliberately low-pitched to calm her. "But we don't have much further to go." The handkerchief securely tied, he lowered his hands and stepped ahead of her.

"Thanks." Laura flashed him a weak smile. Testing the hold of the cloth, she followed him down the other side of the ridge. She had never met a man with such a combination of dangerous toughness and gentle strength. He moved through the wilderness without hesitation. Again she wondered where he had come from and what he was doing on Vasquez land. Whatever the reason, she was grateful for his interference.

Because she had been concentrating on the man, she did not notice immediately that he had turned south. When she did, Laura stopped in consternation. "Isn't this the wrong direction?" she asked. Acapulco lay to the north.

He looked over his shoulder. "Trust me," he drawled, and walked on.

With a hiss of exasperation, Laura watched him duck beneath a ledge, never looking back. He could have given her some kind of explanation. Life in New York City had taught her caution from early childhood. "Don't talk to strangers," had been her mother's constant advice. In the city jungle the phrase "blind trust" was a synonym for foolishness. An unwilling grin spread across her face. "Perhaps I'm a fool," she muttered, "but trust him I do." She walked after him, creeping below the overhang.

Suddenly she heard the distinctive rumble of the helicopter. She hurried after the stranger. When she reached him he flattened himself against the rocks. "Walk ahead of me now," he said, unbuttoning his shirt. Shrugging out of it, he laid it across her shoulders. "It's too hot, but it's the best I can do to camouflage you."

Laura slipped into the sleeves, walking on as she buttoned the shirt. A cloud of masculine scents enveloped her. He smelled of fresh air and clean sweat, different from the cologne-drenched men she usually met.

The noise of the engine became louder until it seemed to hover above them. "Don't look up," the stranger said close to her ear, "and don't make any sudden moves. Just inch along and lean toward the rocks."

He walked so close behind her that his breath fanned her neck. Slowly they moved on, each of their steps synchronized. Dust stirred around them, shrouding them in a protective cloud.

It was torture to move along blindly when her mind screamed at her to look up and run. Perspiration dripped down her face. Suddenly she felt his hands on her shoulders, turning her toward the rocks. Then his body covered hers, pressing her into the stones.

Laura stiffened. For one dark moment the past rose, terrifying her. Wildly she shook her head, her hands pressing against the stone face to shake him off. A sob broke from her lips, "Let me go."

Then she felt large, rough hands covering her own, exerting a gentle pressure without hurting her. A deep voice whispered assurances into her ear. Panic receded, leaving her weak and trembling but alert. The helicopter hovered above them while minutes seemed like hours.

Caught between the sunbaked cliffs and the stranger's body, she was stifled by the heat. Sharp rocks dug into her flesh, hurting her. She wanted to shift her position, but she dared not move. She listened to the deep hypnotic voice assuring her that she was doing fine, telling her to hold on for a little longer. He promised her escape. He promised her water and rest. Laura felt her fears subside long before the helicopter moved away.

When he finally lifted his body from hers, she breathed a sigh of relief. Turning, she looked at him.

His bronzed chest gleamed with sweat, damp curls clinging to his skin. Strong, sinewy muscles rippled, honed to perfection as if by a sculptor's hand. With his head thrown back, he followed the helicopter's path, revealing the strong column of his neck.

Laura felt a strange stirring within, like the whisper of a breeze touching her heated skin. It had been so long since she had looked at any man with pleasure that she did not recognize her body's reaction.

"They're gone," he said. Turning to her, he noticed that she was still pale beneath the streaked film of dust. Her huge blue eyes, however, held none of the fear that had made her body tremble moments ago. He recognized the spark of interest in their depth, the slow awakening she seemed as yet unaware of. Enveloped in his stained and wrinkled shirt, she looked like a teenager on the brink of womanhood.

"For now," Laura agreed, pushing herself away from the wall. "I don't know how to thank you."

He shook his head. "You owe me nothing." A slow smile spread across his face. Creases deepened on his lean cheeks.

His eyes narrowed and brightened, forming small crescents of laughter lines at the edges. "Except my shirt."

She grinned, her hands working the buttons. "I would offer to wash it, but—"

"We can't waste good water," he agreed, reaching for the water bottle and handing it to her in exchange for his shirt. "I promised you a drink." He watched her raise it to her lips, approving, as he had earlier, of the careful sip she took. She did not waste any water, but savored it instead, wetting her mouth before swallowing it. The tip of her tongue brushed across her dry lips. Did she know how provocative the gesture was?

When she returned the flask, her eyes were filled only with innocent gratitude. "Until now I never knew water could taste so good."

"We never appreciate what we take for granted," he agreed, raising the bottle to his lips and taking a small swallow.

Fascinated, Laura watched the smooth movements of his throat. There was something curiously intimate about watching the stranger drink from the same spot she had touched only moments ago. This time she was aware of the strange tightening of her body. Her reaction both pleased and scared her. She tried to take her eyes off him, but found that she could not.

He lowered the bottle, screwed the top on and hooked it on his belt. Lifting his eyes, he found her staring at him. He smiled, as if he knew what she was thinking and was pleased about it.

"I'd better leave before the helicopter returns," she said quickly. "Perhaps you could show me the best way."

"Lady, this isn't the city. There are no maps. Out here you won't find street names telling you where to go."

He saw her face tighten with the same odd mixture of defiance and courage. "I'm going to make it," she said firmly.

"You'll be lost before you know it. You're better off staying with me. I promise to deliver you to your hotel in time for dinner."

Laura had never felt so tempted to accept a stranger's help, but innate honesty made her hesitate. "I can't involve you in my troubles."

"I'm already involved," he pointed out quietly. "Those men saw me as clearly as they saw you. We're in this together."

Troubled, Laura stared at the hard, confident face. "It's only fair to warn you that I'm in quite a mess."

He shrugged his shoulders. Suddenly he tilted his head and tensed, as if he heard something. "You can tell me about it later," he said. "First let's find some shelter before the helicopter returns."

Not waiting for a response, he walked ahead of her, still heading southward and slightly downhill. In the distance Laura could hear the rumble of the helicopter. It was so faint that she wouldn't have heard it had the stranger's actions not alerted her to it. Watching him, she almost could believe that they might have a chance of evading Julio.

The stranger led her around a huge rock, its surface cracked and crumbling with age. Below, a canyon opened, its walls straight and smooth. "About ten feet down there's a ledge," he said when Laura stared at the drop apprehensively. "Don't look down," he warned, and went over the edge. "Wait until I tell you to follow."

Laura was used to skyscrapers and heights. Her Manhattan apartment was on the eighteenth floor. She'd looked down many times to the streets below, but never with the idea of climbing to the floor beneath. Her stomach tightened as his head disappeared. When he gave her the signal to follow, her mouth felt as dry as the desert. She hesitated briefly. The sound of the helicopter coming closer decided her. She got to her knees and eased herself backward over the edge.

For one anxious moment, her legs dangled. Then she felt his hands on her feet, guiding her to footholds. Lowering herself, she found small outcrops of rock to grasp. Slowly she climbed down, until she felt his strong arm circling her waist.

He took her weight easily. She turned, and with her hands on his shoulders she could feel the powerful strength. She slid down his body, and their eyes locked. Breathless, Laura thought he was going to kiss her. It was the first time in years she had not shied away from a man, and the idea did not threaten her. When he stood her on solid ground, she felt a strange disappointment. "Another few steps and we've made it," he said, his hand guiding her over the crumbling rocks. To her right the canyon gaped like a dark, bottomless pit. Around a bend it suddenly widened, the walls receding.

An oasis of lush green spread before her eyes. Tall oak trees shaded the house from below. Laura saw only a glimpse of a red tiled roof.

Abruptly she froze. Wide-eyed, she stared at the scene below. She had come so close. So damn close. Another fifteen minutes and she would have made it.

At her feet, about thirty yards below, lay the Hacienda de los Leones.

Chapter 2

Laura swayed, frustration and desperation shaking her.

Instantly the stranger's arm tightened around her waist. Low-voiced, he reassured her. "Don't look down. Just put one foot in front of the other."

She could feel his leg nudge hers forward as he guided her along the narrow ledge. "That's it. Just another few steps," he encouraged her. One step after another, they inched their way forward until they reached the mouth of a shallow cave.

"Are you all right?" the stranger asked, his eyes probing her pale face.

"Yes," Laura answered with a grateful sigh. Then she stepped forward, slumping against the rough, cool wall of the cave.

Her eyes burned with unshed tears. In the year since Peter's abduction, her ability to control her emotions had slowly eroded. Until now she had not realized just how fragile her control had become, how close her feelings were to breaking free to reveal her most private secrets to a rough stranger. This man seemed to have the uncanny ability to touch those feelings.

Her eyes swept over the shallow cave in an attempt to evade his stare. Sloping up from the cave's back, about ten feet away, walls of rock rose in broad layers, folding over to form a wide domelike ceiling above the stranger's head. The farther area was sprinkled with loose rocks and some odd white shapes Laura was reluctant to investigate.

Near the opening, however, the floor had been cleared of rubble. Resting against the far wall was a backpack of the type climbers used. She turned back to the stranger and found him still watching her.

"Sit down and rest," he said, ignoring the question in her eyes. He briefly raised one hand as if to help her sit down, then withdrew it. "You've had quite a scare."

"Without you I couldn't have made it," Laura thanked him. She slid to the ground and stretched her legs.

"The walk along the ledge is rather frightening," he said quietly, shrugging off her gratitude. "Why didn't you warn me you hated heights?"

Laura had expected criticism, or anger that she had risked not only her own life but his. Instead he was trying to understand her actions. His gentleness was her undoing.

Before she could check herself, she blurted out, "Heights have never bothered me. I live in an eighteenth-floor apartment in New York. I—" Helplessly she waved her hands.

How could she explain the despair, the utter hopelessness that had gripped her at the sight of the hacienda? Standing high above the place that had housed Peter all these months, she had felt her plans crumble like the loose rocks beneath her feet. The house was too well shielded for her to ever get close to it. Peter seemed as far out of her reach as ever.

The stranger smiled faintly, one eyebrow raised, as if he had known all along that it had not been fear that had caused her to stumble.

"I—I guess it was the heat and the climb. And I've never had a helicopter chase me before." She smiled tightly. "I don't even know your name. I'm Laura Foster." She had dropped Julio's name five years ago when she had run from his apartment and their marriage.

"Gabe Borga."

"Gabe as in Gabriel?" A flash of amusement crossed her face. "How appropriate," she said softly. "The archangel in person come to rescue me."

A gleam lit his eyes, sparkling but certainly not celestial. "My father insisted that he could trace our family back to the Borgias," he said.

Laura chuckled, liking the dry sense of humor. But her smile froze as the sudden roar of a helicopter right overhead shook the walls of the cave, loosening a few pebbles. Looking up, she wondered if the cave would hold up under the vibrations.

The helicopter flew past the opening, dropping lower. Gabe walked to the cave's mouth, following the helicopter's descent, his body outlined against the sunlight beyond. The steady roar slowed to a rhythmic chop, then died completely.

"Looks like they're giving up the search," Gabe said, turning back to her.

"I can't believe it," Laura muttered. The Julio she had known would have searched until sundown, chasing her relentlessly until he had found her. From bitter experience she knew just how persistent he could be. Julio simply did not know the meaning of the word no. She doubted he could have changed so much during the last year.

At twenty-one she had mistaken Julio's persistence for strength. Too late, she had found not a man but a cruel, spoiled boy behind his intriguingly foreign, worldly facade. As a child, he'd never been denied a toy and had never learned generosity or kindness. She had paid a high price for her mistake.

She had paid an even higher price for underestimating Julio's capacity for hatred. Laura had thought him too shallow to wait years for his revenge. It was a mistake she would never repeat.

"What's going to happen to my Jeep?" she asked thoughtfully.

"Guess someone will return it to the hotel," Gabe said harshly. The Jeep's use was included in the rent of the more expensive bungalows where Laura had been staying. Since it told Vasquez where Laura was lodged, all he had to do was wait for her to return to the cottage that could no longer be a refuge.

"What does Vasquez want from you?" he asked, walking toward the backpack leaning against the wall.

Laura wondered how much she should tell him. It wasn't that she didn't want to trust him. How could she do otherwise after what he had done for her? But the less anyone knew about her, the better. Over the years she had learned to keep her own counsel. Peter's fate was too important to her to take any chances. "He wants me out of Mexico," she said, her voice flat.

Gabe saw several emotions cross her face; fear and distaste, as well as that defiant courage he was coming to know so well.

"Then why stay?"

"He has something of mine." Laura's voice was rough and determined. "I'm not leaving Mexico until I have it back."

Gabe's eyes narrowed thoughtfully. "Must be pretty valuable," he drawled. "Few things are worth risking your life for."

Laura's body stiffened, her eyes searching his face. How much trust could she place in his quiet strength? The tired part of her wanted to allow him into her confidence, but a hard core of suspicion, forged to tempered steel by Julio's cruelty and deceit, warned her to confide in no one.

"It's not my life that Vasquez is interested in," Laura pointed out, her lips twisting cynically. Julio would love to lay his hands on her and punish her for having scorned him.

"Is he the one who taught you to fear men?" he asked roughly, his face hard and dangerous. He remembered her panic and the way she had flinched at his touch.

With wide, startled eyes, Laura reevaluated the man. "You see too much, Gabe Borga," she said quietly. "I don't fear men, just their brutal dominance."

"Men don't prey on women. Cowards do," he stated quietly. He turned, squatting, searching among the contents of his backpack, his thighs straining against the khaki pants, his shirt molding to the width of his shoulders.

Laura felt a strange weakness rushing through her. She smiled slightly as she realized that he had reassured her more with those few words than others could have in a lifetime. Gabe was all man.

Suddenly she wished that she was all woman. Unscarred, free to respond to Gabe's strong sexuality.

The thought surprised her. For the first time in years she felt no distaste when she thought of a physical relationship. Perhaps there was hope yet. "How did you find this cave?"

"I stumbled into it. Literally." He stood and came to her side. "We may as well eat while we wait. We can't leave in this heat." Handing her the paper bag, he sat down next to her, deliberately leaving a small space between them.

Laura's eyes moved from the bag to the man, then to the pack leaning against the opposite wall. "You obviously came prepared," she said dryly. "I never did ask you what you were doing here."

"Same thing you planned," Gabe said calmly. "Spying on Vasquez." Actually, he had done his spying weeks ago. The last few days he had roamed the ridge to familiarize himself with the land, to watch the comings and goings at the hacienda, using the cave as a convenient resting place.

Stunned, Laura shook her head. The back of her neck tingled with apprehension. This was not the first time Gabe seemed to have read her thoughts. She would have to be more careful if she wanted to keep her secret.

Taking the bag from her hands, he opened it. "Later, after we've eaten, I'll show a spot from which you can watch the house."

"Why do you think I came here to spy?"

Gabe looked at her steadily. "Didn't you?"

"Yes," she agreed reluctantly. Out here there were no ruins, no tourist attractions, just burned-out grass, rocks and the hacienda. She opened her mouth to ask him for his reasons, then thought better of it. If he answered her, she would have to reveal her own purpose—and she didn't yet trust him that far.

He reached into the bag and brought out a roll sprinkled with sugar. "You ought to try one of these." Calmly he handed the bag to her. "One thing I like about Mexico is the variety of breads it has. It's a residual from Maximilian's reign. The French brought bakers over with the soldiers and guns." He smiled wryly. "I wish they'd also sent over some chefs."

With a mixture of exasperation and amusement, Laura glanced inside the brown bag. He had changed the subject so smoothly. "So far, I like the Mexican food I've tasted here. It's different from the Mexican stuff they serve in New York."

"You can't have tasted chicken mole yet." He bit into his roll.

Laura watched the roll almost disappear between his long-fingered hands and remembered their strength and gentleness. The calluses on his palms spoke of physical labor. "What is chicken mole?"

"Chicken cooked in peppers and chocolate sauce," he said, his face so expressionless that Laura thought he was teasing her.

"Sounds interesting," she said, grinning. "Do they top the dish with whipped cream?"

He liked the flash of humor brightening her face. "That's not a bad idea," he chuckled. "It might soften its sharp bite. The chicken is so hot it takes the skin off your tongue."

"I thought Texans liked spicy food," Laura said, remembering the hot chili she had been served in a western steak house.

He raised his eyebrows. "Ever been to Texas?"

"No." She had been to the British Isles and most of Europe, but in the States she had not traveled farther than Washington. "Some day I'd like to drive all over America. So far, there hasn't been an opportunity." Her father, an Irish immigrant, had been too busy building up a business. With the proverbial luck of an Irishman and a thorough knowledge of the stock market, he had prospered within a few short years. He had died before he could take the time to enjoy the fortune he had made. Her mother had always returned home to Ireland whenever she could, and soon after her husband's death had moved back to the old country permanently. A short time later, Laura had met Julio. Since their separation, she had been too busy to think about vacations.

After receiving her business degree at New York University, she had joined her father's investment firm. Her father's partner was of the old school. He had kindly told her that there was no need for her to work. It had taken months of long hours and dogged persistence to prove to him that women were more than mere ornaments. Now she vowed that when Peter returned to her, she would make time to see the country.

Gabe looked at her, touched by the wistful sadness in her eyes. For a few minutes, while he had talked about food, she had relaxed. Now her eyes darkened once again with pain, and her hands clenched the bag with nervous tension. Before he could check himself, he reached out to her, covering her fingers.

"Eat a roll. Things always look better on a full stomach."

Laura shot him a startled look. Her first impulse was to withdraw her hand, but the warmth of his touch had an odd effect. Her skin tingled, sending a pleasant fire up her arm. His slow smile was reassuring rather than predatory. She relaxed. "I believe I will."

"Let me choose one for you," he said easily. He reached in and withdrew a raisin-studded braid. "This is one of my favorites."

Laura eyed the crusty roll. "You have a sweet tooth," she said teasingly. The moment she bit into it, she realized just how hungry she had been. At breakfast she had been so nervous she had only nibbled at her food. With good reason, she thought grimly.

Abruptly she stopped chewing. "Why are you spying on the hacienda?" Until now she had been so wrapped up in her own dilemma she had barely given a thought to why he was watching the house.

"Gathering information." His chin jutted ruthlessly. "I need Vasquez's cooperation. I'm trying to find out what I can offer to persuade him to deal with me."

Laura opened her mouth to ask for clarification. Was it a business venture? She knew that Mexican laws prohibited the sole ownership of any enterprise by foreigners. Whether in real estate or factories, fifty-one percent had to be owned by Mexican nationals. Julio had once tried to interest her in some land in Mexico City. For Laura, the risks involved had been too high. She disliked the odds of forty-nine percent in a country that only tolerated foreigners. She knew, better than most, just how difficult it was to get justice in a Mexican court of law. She also knew how those laws could be bent and twisted by the Vasquez family. Should she warn Gabe not to become involved with them?

But with one look at his tough, closed face she abandoned the thought. Gabe Borga was not a man who would be taken in lightly.

"And have you found a way?" she asked slowly.

"Yes." Gabe looked at her with hard, cold eyes.

Laura couldn't suppress a sudden shiver of fear. Gabe's gentleness had given way to the dangerous ruthlessness with which he had faced the ranch hands earlier. Whatever the nature of this deal, it was not friendly. He knew the type of men he was dealing with. She almost pitied Julio and his father Don Emilio.

"Care to share your secrets with me?" she asked, trying to keep the tone of her voice carefully neutral. Today's fiasco had shown her that she would need help if she wanted to hold her son again. With a man like Gabe by her side, she might succeed.

Gabe looked at her long and searchingly. Apart from Herb Miller, a longtime friend, no one knew what had brought him to Mexico. "The same way you share your secrets with me?" he finally said mockingly.

He could have told her that he already knew why she had come to the hacienda. For the last five days he had watched the little boy Pedro swim, ride and throw temper tantrums. From a distance he looked like a typical Mexican child, deeply tanned and with a shock of dark hair. But he didn't need to see the child's blue eyes to draw his own conclusions. Only a mother's love would drive a woman within reach of the man whose name alone brought fear to her eyes.

He wanted her to open up to him of her own free will. Instinctively he knew that it had been a long time since she'd trusted any man. Vasquez's doing, he thought grimly. He'd spoiled more than one life. He thought of his nephew Gino and the utter hopelessness in his eyes, a look that was past fear. Vasquez was responsible for that, too. But he was going to pay.

The deadly coldness in Gabe's face frightened Laura. If Gabe had overheard Jorge's words, he didn't have far to look for bait for his "business deal." Julio would do almost anything to get her back within his grasp. Slowly she inched away from him.

The movement attracted Gabe's attention. When he saw her wariness, he said roughly, "You have nothing to fear from me." Slowly he reached out for her, cupping her dust-streaked face.

The rough skin of his palm was soothingly familiar, reminding her of the moments when he had shielded her with his hard body. For an instant she was tempted to reveal everything. But something held her back. Perhaps it was that he had told her nothing of himself.

"What exactly is your business?" she said briskly.

Pulling his hand back, Gabe smiled coldly. "Revenge."

Stunned, Laura turned to face him. The grim set of his mouth was frightening. Now she knew why he had helped her. Not because he was some knight in shining armor. Having overheard Jorge's words, he had ruthlessly grasped the opportunity to hit back at Julio. Unwittingly she had become a tool in a dangerous game, a handy object to be used and discarded. If she'd known how to get back to Acapulco, she would have run from the cave and Gabe.

"I don't like being used," she said coldly.

Puzzled, Gabe frowned. "What are you talking about?" he asked.

"Oh, come on, Gabe Borga. I'm not a fool. I know why you helped me." Angrily she shot to her feet, facing him with fury shaking her.

Slowly Gabe tilted back his head, insolently running his eyes over her long legs, the slender curve of her hips, estimating the span of her tiny waist. Raising his eyes, he drawled mockingly, "Why did I help you, Laura?"

"Because you overheard Jorge and grasped at the opportunity to hit back at Vasquez," Laura accused.

His eyes suddenly blazed. "I don't need you to hurt Vasquez," he said, his voice clipped. "If you'd been a goat instead of a woman, I'd have done the same."

Laura searched his face, reading the truth in his eyes. Slowly the corners of her mouth began to twitch. "A goat?" she asked, laughter bubbling in her voice. "Couldn't you've come up with a better example?"

"Cow? Dog? A chicken?" Gabe offered alternatives, the lazy drawl back in his voice. He watched her clap her hand in front of her mouth, stifling the sound of laughter. She looked vibrantly alive and utterly beautiful. Desire and something else, something so elusive he could not put a name to it, stirred deep within him. Abruptly he tore his gaze away from her.

Laura swallowed her laughter. "I'm sorry," she said softly, sliding down beside him again. What was it about this man that stirred such conflicting emotions inside her? Usually she was quite adept at reading men but only in a business capacity. She knew she could hold her own in the male-dominated field of finance. Here she had to depend on a man she couldn't figure out. That knowledge left her vulnerable and afraid.

Nodding, Gabe picked up the piece of roll she had dropped when she had jumped to her feet. "Do you want another one?" he asked.

Slowly Laura shook her head. "Perhaps we could make a deal. I, too, want to see Vasquez on his knees." At least long enough to get my son back, Laura thought grimly. "Perhaps we could pool our information. There are things I know about him no investigator would report."

"What makes you think I depended on anyone to gather facts for me?" Gabe asked curiously.

"Unless you spent weeks in New York and Washington, Miami and Las Vegas, Julio's favorite hangouts, you must have had someone else do your legwork for you," Laura pointed out.

"What makes you think I didn't?" Gabe's eyes narrowed suspiciously. His friend Herb had actually supplied most of his information. As head of the Drug Enforcement Agency at the American embassy in Mexico City, he had access to information Gabe could not tap. For the sake of their long friendship, and because of a certain amount of guilt, Herb was doing everything to help.

"Camouflage, or rather the lack of it," Laura pointed out, smiling. "Here, you're part of the land. In the city, you'd be easily spotted. You just don't fit the mold of polished businessmen."

"A savage among civilized people?" Gabe said with amusement.

"No." Laura rejected the idea firmly, placing her hand on his hair-roughened arm for emphasis. He was a man used to wild country and wide-open spaces. It showed in everything, even in his deeply tanned, tough skin. But there was nothing savage, nothing coarse about Gabe. He had shown her more kindness than most of the smoothly polished men she worked with. "Do we have a deal?" she asked, returning to her original suggestion.

For a moment, Laura thought he might reject her offer. Then he got to his feet. Going to his backpack, he took a bottle from it. "Shall we have a drink to seal the bargain?" Unscrewing the top, he returned and handed her the bottle.

Laura looked at the clear liquid suspiciously, shaking it. A worm rose from the bottom, making her shudder. She disliked the taste of mescal. Mexicans might consider the worm a delicacy, but the sight of it always made her stomach turn.

The dubious expression with which she examined the bottle made him grin. "There's another way," he said softly, staring pointedly at her mouth. "A kiss."

Laura's eyes flew to his firm lips. What would they feel like pressed against her own? A longing to find out if his mouth was as gentle as his touch claimed her. Would it erase the brutal memory of Julio she had carried for more than five years?

Abruptly she lowered her eyes to the bottle. She was drawn more to Gabe than to any other man, and the temptation to find out if he could heal the wounds her husband had inflicted was great. But her fear that even this man's kiss might leave her cold was greater than her distaste for the worm. She raised the bottle to her lips and drank swiftly so the worm wouldn't fall into the neck.

The strong liquid made her shudder. After one small swallow she handed the mescal back to Gabe with a grimace. "Give me wine any time," she said, watching him turn the bottle and raise it to his lips.

He poured the clear liquid down his throat, wiping his mouth with the back of his hand. "Wine wasn't one of the choices," he said dryly, closing the bottle.

"No," Laura coolly agreed, refusing to let him bait her.

He gave her a level look before turning to restore the bottle to the backpack. "Not all men are beasts," he said quietly over his shoulder. Closing the flap, he straightened, covering the space between them. Squatting down in front of her, he continued softly, "A kiss should give pleasure, not fear."

His eyes held her own, refusing to let her withdraw once again behind the wall of fear. Laura found she couldn't look away. Slowly he raised his hand, giving her the chance to move her head. "You're a beautiful woman, Laura. And I want very much to kiss you."

His low, seductive voice sent shivers of anticipation down her spine. His rough palm cupped her chin, tilting her head up to his. His touch was gentle yet firm, spreading heat from her chin in ever-widening circles. With the tip of her tongue she moistened her suddenly dry lips.

He arrested the movement with his thumb, bent his head and lowered his mouth until his lips rested against hers, dry and cool. He did not move. He gave her time to become accustomed to his touch and his taste, asking nothing that she wasn't willing to give.

Deeply, he inhaled the scent of her. When her lips moved hesitantly beneath his, opening slightly, he was tempted to accept her invitation. But he knew it was too soon. Gently he rubbed his mouth across hers in a tender caress before reluctantly drawing back.

With satisfaction he noticed the flare of disappointment in her eyes. It was not easy to ignore her invitation. She had no idea how much restraint it cost him to let her go. The sudden desire he felt for her surprised even him. Grimly he reflected that he had not bargained on becoming involved with her. He could not afford the distraction of an affair, and neither could Laura.

Laura raised her fingers to her lips to capture the lingering sweetness of his touch. No one had ever kissed her like that. Unselfishly giving. Without the need to conquer. His mouth had been at once soothing and stirring. She had felt at peace, pleasure seeping through her like the heat of a fire on a cold winter day. At no time had she wanted to withdraw. Instinctively her lips had softened, surrendered and opened in invitation. Why had Gabe ignored her desire for a deeper contact?

She looked at the grimly set face and sighed. Gabe was a man in his mid-thirties. Too old to play childish games, and too experienced, she guessed, to find satisfaction in a small gesture meant to comfort her.

She watched him rise to his full, powerful height and move to the mouth of the cave. Slowly Laura became aware of the changes around her. Sounds of activity echoed up the canyon walls. Voices mingled with the noise of engines and the whinnies of horses. The siesta was over.

Getting to her feet, Laura joined Gabe. One hand holding on to the cave wall, she leaned forward for a better look through the canopy of oak leaves gently stirring in the mild afternoon breeze. To her right she could make out the deep blue of the swimming pool. She heard a splash as someone dived into the water, but she could not see who it was.

Perhaps it was Peter. Her son was a water baby. Laura had taken him to swimming lessons since before he was six months old. In New York, with beaches surrounding them, learning to swim was a necessity.

"Where's this lookout you promised to show me?" she asked, her voice husky with excitement.

"Over there." Gabe pointed past her to where the ledge they had walked on earlier narrowed to less than two feet.

Laura's eyes widened with apprehension. The path was made for mountain goats, not for humans. "You're kidding," she said.

"It's only a small stretch. Further on, it widens." He returned to his backpack and took out a pair of binoculars. "I won't let you fall," he said reassuringly, slinging the strap over his neck.

Laura hesitated. "What if someone finds the cave?" It seemed perfectly plausible that people at the hacienda knew of it. As boys, Julio or some of the ranch hands might have chanced upon it in much the same way Gabe had.

Gabe shook his head. "Until recently, this cave was used as a den by a family of mountain lions. The signs of habitation were everywhere. It took me quite some time to clear the grisly remains of their meals."

Laura frowned, not sure if he was teasing her. But someone had cleared the front of the cave of rubble. "What if they come back?" she asked. "I wouldn't want to be trapped between the canyon and the fangs of an angry mountain lion."

"Wild cats don't like the smell of humans. Our scent is enough warning to chase them away." His guess was that they had been shot at until they had been killed or had looked for a safer place. During the five days he had roamed the ridge, he had seen no recent signs of them anywhere.

The sound of splashing water decided her. "I'm ready," she said. She wanted to get to the lookout before whoever was swimming left the pool. Her eyes sparkled with hope and eagerness to catch a possible glimpse of her son.

Gabe could read the expression on her face. He wondered how she would react if she saw her son. He hoped that she had enough sense not to cry out. He would have to stay close to her to muffle the sound in case she did. If someone spotted them at the lookout, they would be trapped. Gabe had no intention of getting caught.

"Stay close behind me," he warned. "If you feel dizzy, grab my belt." When Laura nodded he stepped out of the cave and, facing the rocks, moved along the ledge.

Laura followed close behind, her fingers reaching for his handholds the moment he moved on. A few feet farther the ledge widened, just as he had promised, until it came to an end. "We have to climb down now. Wait until I tell you to follow. Then just slide over the edge. I'll catch you."

Laura watched him climb down about eight feet with the powerful grace that made everything look so easy. She could see a ledge jutting out over the canyon walls, giving them a clear view of the red tiled roof below. Perhaps, Laura thought, they should have waited until later in the year. Without the protection of the trees, a person below would only have to look up to notice them.

When Gabe tilted his head and raised his arms in invitation, Laura sat down on the edge, turned and lowered herself until she could feel his hands on her feet, guiding her steps until she was down.

"Whatever happens, don't make a sound," Gabe warned in a whisper when she stood next to him. She nodded, and he pointed to the end of the platform. Soundlessly Laura moved toward it, knelt and lay on her stomach. With a smile of approval Gabe joined her. City-bred she might be, but she adapted swiftly to her surroundings.

Laura scooted to the edge and looked over it. Excitement welled up in her at the almost unobstructed view of the pool. As in the photos, it was surrounded by masses of red and white flowers. Groups of tables and lounges dotted the terrace leading to the house. One of the chairs was occupied by a slim woman with gray hair, reading a newspaper.

Laura recognized her immediately from the pictures Julio had shown her. Dona Elena had seemed like a warm-hearted woman, the only family member who had acknowledged their marriage. Don Emilio had been furious when Julio had called him after the ceremony.

Sometimes Laura suspected that Julio had married her to get back at his father for sending him out of Mexico. Just why Don Emilio had arranged for Julio to work at the Mexican consulate in New York, Laura had never been told. But from innuendos made by his colleagues she had guessed that he had seduced a respectable girl whose parents were insisting on a marriage.

"Abuela, ajuda me." At the clear sound of a child's imperious voice, Laura's gaze shifted. With narrowed eyes she searched the pool, willing her son to swim into the area where she could see him.

Dona Elena slowly rose to her feet and walked toward the sound. Moments later, the sound of splashes floated through the air. Laura held her breath and gripped the rocks so tightly that her knuckles turned white. Suddenly a rough, bronzed hand covered her fingers, squeezing them.

"Relax," Gabe whispered into her ear. With his hand he pointed toward another woman stepping out of the house. Obviously one of the maids, she wore an apron over a simple dress. Her arms were filled with floating toys, which she threw into the pool. With a shriek of delight a nut-brown boy came into view. Running along the terrace, he dived like a seal into the water.

Gabe felt Laura's body tense. Her fingers gripped his hand tightly. No sound escaped her. Yet he could feel her silent pain. His eyes darkened with compassion.

Laura watched Peter swim to a bright green floating dolphin and climb on its back. Splashing with his feet, he propelled himself forward. How healthy he looked. Hungrily she followed his every move. What she wouldn't have given to be down there with him, to play as they had done so many times before.

Tears filled her eyes. Angrily she blinked them away. She didn't want to miss one instant of his play. She strained to get a better look at his face, but he was too far away for her to make out his features. If only she could move closer or had a pair of binoculars.

That was when she remembered Gabe.

She stiffened and turned her head, a startled, frightened look on her face.

The hand covering her own tightened reassuringly. "Don't worry, Laura," he said gently. "Your secret is safe with me."

Slowly Laura felt fear leave her like a sigh released. Earlier she had placed her life in his hands. Now she added the happiness of her child to the burden thrust upon him. Yet she saw no resentment in his eyes. Only compassion, and questions she knew she would have to answer sooner or later.

A sudden splash, followed by silence, drew Laura's eyes back to the pool. Peter had fallen off his dolphin. Moments later his head surfaced again. He reached for a big blue-and-white ring, propelling it forward.

"Hand me the binoculars," Laura whispered.

Gabe hesitated. The afternoon sun stood behind the pool, directly opposite them. If someone looked up the canyon, the reflection off the lenses would announce their presence as surely as a beacon of light.

Turning her head, Laura saw him pointing at the sun. A sigh of disappointment escaped her, but she didn't argue. She might have risked her own safety for one good look at Peter's face, but she could not endanger Gabe's plans.

Together they watched Peter play with each of the floats. After a while he abandoned them to swim lazily around the pool before finally getting out of the water. He sat at the pool's edge, kicking his legs. Laura's heart ached for him.

How lonely he seemed. He had a big pool and expensive toys, but no one to play with, no one to share his pleasures or to laugh with. Even the ice cream the maid brought out a few minutes later did not lift his spirits. Joining his grandmother at the table, he ate little more than a few spoonfuls.

Since Mexicans still had remnants of a feudal society, she guessed that Peter was rarely allowed to mingle with the children of the ranch hands. Even the attempted land reform in the late sixties had not been able to close the wide gap between the classes.

How different his life had been a year ago. Because she had been a sheltered only child, she knew what it was like not to have playmates. So Laura had taken every opportunity to let Peter mingle with children. She had enrolled him in a private nursery school and had encouraged him constantly to invite his friends over. Had he forgotten his life in New York during that long year? Did he miss his best friend Mark? The two had been inseparable.

She followed Peter's lonely figure as he walked around the pool. On the other side of it he bent over a bush and began picking the flowers off, tearing them apart.

"Stop that, Pedro," Dona Elena called.

Peter ignored her words. He picked more blossoms and threw them into the pool, his head tilted defiantly in her direction.

"Pedro, look at the mess you're making," his grandmother shouted.

"Why doesn't she get up and stop him," Laura muttered, exasperated.

Instead Dona Elena picked up a little bell on the table and rang for the maid. Moments later the woman appeared, walked over to Peter and took his hand. Laura could not understand the woman's words, but the soothing singsong of her voice drifted up the canyon walls as she tried to draw the boy toward the house.

Peter screamed, kicked and threw himself on the ground, resisting the maid's attempts to remove him from the patio. Then, to Laura's utter amazement, the woman knelt and hugged the brat. Lifting the boy in her arms, she placed him on a swan floating near the edge of the pool and pulled him through the water until squeals of delight had replaced his anger.

Laura's eyes filled with angry tears. What had happened to the cheerful child she remembered? They were turning her son into a little monster, catering to his wishes. Unchecked, he would become another Julio.

Muffled sobs shook her slender frame. Lowering her face to her arms, she gave in to her tears. A year of pent-up emotions finally broke down the wall of discipline she had erected around herself. Silently the tears rolled in an ever-increasing torrent, like water dammed and finally released. Even the dim knowledge that Gabe was witnessing her breakdown could not change the tide of grief.

Gabe watched her cry, her slim body racked by pain. Rarely had he felt so helpless as now, confronted by her loss. Slowly he moved closer, until his body touched hers. Rolling onto his back, he reached for her and pulled her into his arms. As he cradled her head against his chest, her tears mingled with beads of perspiration.

"They took my son," she whispered forlornly, her hands clenching in the folds of his open shirt. "Stole him from the kindergarten, while I was at work."

"We'll get him back," Gabe murmured into her ear. His strong arms wrapped around her, and his hands soothingly ran over her. Holding her slight body pressed against his, he could feel the sharp contours of her bones. When was the last time she'd eaten a decent meal? Not since the loss of her son, he guessed. Didn't she have any family to take care of her? Was she alone in this world?

She wasn't alone anymore, Gabe thought grimly, icy rage filling him. He would take care of her now. Gently he raised her face and brushed away the tears until they finally stopped falling.

His face was hard and unreadable. Yet Laura was not frightened of his grim expression. Whoever his anger was directed at, she knew it was not at her. Slowly she reached out and stroked the hard line of his jaw, trying to soothe his tension.

"Feel better now?" he asked her.

Silently Laura nodded. Unashamed, she had leaned on him for support, drawing strength from the immense store of power he seemed to offer so freely.

A blush stained her face as she became aware of their position. She was lying half on top of him, her breasts pushing against his bare chest. She did not experience any fear, only a surge of curiosity about what it would feel like to be really kissed by him. The thought startled her, and she began to move away.

Before she could, Gabe's arm wrapped around her waist, holding her in place. His hand caressed her neck and drew her head down to his, giving her time to evade his kiss.

His touch was like the gentle afternoon breeze rising from the desert. She heard his sigh of relief when she did not freeze. Gently his lips lingered against her own, waiting for her to make the first move. Without hesitation her mouth softened in surrender and invitation, opening eagerly to the gently probing tip of his tongue. He kissed her sweetly, without pressure or force.

Warmth spread through her. The small flickering flame of curiosity turned brighter, growing steadily. She wanted more than solace and sweetness. Desire pulsed through her in ever-increasing strength. She was no child to be comforted but a woman with newly awakened longings. Her hands touched his cheeks, the pressure of her lips increasing.

For one moment Gabe did not move. Then he broke away and tilted her head up, staring at her searchingly. The blue of her eyes had darkened, her fine nostrils flaring with desire and impatience.

With a groan he drew her head down, his tongue thrusting deeply into her mouth. He kissed her with the thirst of a man long denied water.

Laura clung to him, shaken equally by her release from fear and the heat of his desire, responding to him with an abandon she had never experienced before.

Gabe felt the change. The body beneath his hands relaxed. Warning signals flashed through him. It had been one thing to comfort a lost, frightened woman. He had wanted to free her from her fears. But now she was seeping into his blood like raindrops into parched earth.

If he didn't stop, the gentle rain would turn into a flash flood, untamable, uncontrollable, leaving in its wake nothing but destruction and the bitter taste of loss.

Gently he withdrew from her, cradling her, absorbing the aftershocks racking her body until she lay quiet and spent in his arms.

When her breathing returned to normal, Gabe shifted her with firm hands. She was too drained to even lift her head. Gently he cushioned her face on her arms. Then he moved to the farthest corner of the plateau, putting as much distance between himself and temptation as possible.

Chapter 3

Not since her father died nine years ago had Laura fallen to such despair. Even then she'd had to be strong for her mother's sake and had tempered her sorrow with duty. Later, her brief marriage to Julio might have destroyed her, but the small life growing inside her had given her the strength to go on.

Today, though, she thought with wry self-mockery, after nine years of fighting alone, of winning her periodic battles with loneliness and frustration, she had come apart in Gabe's arms.

Gabe had treated her the same way she'd coddled her son after he'd scraped his knee—with hugs, kisses and soothing promises. But his hugs and kisses had sent messages of desire as well as of comfort.

Laura's hand went to her lips. They still carried the taste of him. Her body still tingled from his touch. Even now she could feel the hard sinew and strong muscles beneath her, the powerful arms wrapped around her. She felt pleasure and a strange emptiness. She turned her head and looked across the space at the long lean body that had cushioned her.

Strange that within the span of a day one man could change so many things. That morning she had awakened to fear and doubts, almost certain that she was tilting at windmills. Now she had a tough and resourceful man as an ally. She knew almost nothing about him, but trusted him nevertheless.

"Did you mean it?" she asked, looking across the width of the small plateau to where Gabe had moved earlier.

"Mean what?" he said, never taking his eyes from the scene below.

"That you'd help me get my son," Laura said. Was he already regretting his words? Had the promise been given only to stem the flow of her tears?

Abruptly he turned his head. Did Laura have any idea just how difficult it would be to kidnap a child constantly surrounded by family and servants? Even if they managed to get past those barriers, they would have the Mexican police force on their tails all the way to the Texas border. One thousand miles of roadblocks, helicopters and search planes.

Getting Gino out of jail and out of the country would be child's play compared to that. Until today his plans to free his nephew had developed with smooth precision. He had Vasquez exactly where he wanted him, backed up against a wall. Helping Laura might jeopardize his own mission instead of aiding it. Was he risking Gino's freedom for a pair of blue eyes?

"Maybe," he said noncommittally. He wasn't a man to renege on his promises, but neither was he foolish enough to go blindfolded into a trap. He wanted answers. A lot of them. The moment they got back to his truck, Laura would supply them. Then he could decide how to help her. The idea of hitting out at Vasquez from another angle appealed to him more and more. Trying to rescue the boy would divide Vasquez's attention between the twin attacks. But he'd make his decision later, when he knew all the facts. He turned to observe the activities below.

Laura's eyes narrowed as she watched his face, her conscience and her need for this man's strength warring within her. Her need won. She couldn't afford to throw his offer away. Gabe was the only chance she had to get her son back.

The fact that she had been given legal custody of her son at the time of her divorce was worthless. It meant nothing to the Mexican authorities, especially since the powerful Vasquez family was involved. In a country where a wife still needed her husband's notarized permission to take her child out of the country, Julio's action was a justified move.

Laura had tried to hire professionals, but every one of the detectives had refused to help her. They had listened to her story and shaken their heads. None had wanted to become involved in a kidnapping, especially not one that meant tangling with Mexican laws. Even when she had offered a small fortune, they had not been tempted to risk their necks.

The last man she had begged to take on her case had suggested she hire someone who had neither license nor scruples. Laura had shrunk away from seeking help from one of society's predators. She wanted an honest man, a man she could trust. A man who could not be bought by Julio.

Gabe was exactly the man she had been looking for. One way or another, she would keep him to his promise. Crouching low, she crossed the plateau and lay down beside him.

From this position she could look down into the yard at the back of the house. It was bustling with activity. One man was wetting the hard-baked ground with a watering hose while several laughing children tried to dodge the spray. Two women sat in the shade of the terrace, cleaning vegetables. Several men loaded watermelons onto a truck while ranch hands saddled horses.

A beautiful palomino stallion was tethered to a mounting block near the rear entrance to the house. From time to time he'd flick his pale gold tail to brush off irritant flies, his muscles rippling with a bronze sheen. Laura's breath caught in appreciation. "He's magnificent," she whispered.

"I'd like to breed one of my mares to him," Gabe said softly. Turning his head, he looked at her curiously. "Do you ride?"

"I love it." Her eyes brightened with enthusiasm. As a child, on her trips to Ireland, she'd had plenty of opportunities to learn about horses. With her father's help, his brother had established a small but well-known stable of thoroughbreds. Uncle Sean had taught her to appreciate and handle beautiful animals. Laura didn't enjoy riding the downtrodden horses that were for hire by the hour at the city stables. But the sight of the prancing palomino made her fingers itch to hold the reins. "What kind of horses do you breed? Quarter horses? Arabians? Thoroughbreds?"

"Quarter horses." Gabe wondered where she had learned about quarter horses and Arabians.

At that moment the rear door of the house was thrown open, and a man of medium height, dressed in black pants and tall, gleaming boots emerged and strode toward the palomino. Gray hair, gleaming like silver, framed his face. Placing his sombrero on his head, he swung himself into the saddle with the smoothness of a much younger man. At sixty, Laura thought, watching the easy way he handled the fractious stallion, Don Emilio appeared to be in better shape than his son had been at thirty.

Don Emilio shouted a few orders. Within seconds the ranch hands were mounted, following their *patron* out of the courtyard.

Gabe stirred restlessly. "Time to leave," he said abruptly, scooting backward before getting to his feet.

Laura didn't move. She wanted to hang around in the hope of catching another glimpse of her son. Turning, she looked at Gabe, opening her lips to plead for another few minutes.

Reading her thoughts, he shook his head. Had he been alone, he would have waited until the sinking sun cast shadows over the ridge. He could find his way down the rocks in total darkness. But Laura was not an experienced climber, and she was tired. Beneath the layer of dust her face was tightly drawn, her exhaustion held at bay by willpower alone. "It's a long way back to Acapulco," he pointed out quietly.

"All right." Laura crawled away from the ledge. When she felt certain that no one would see her from below, she rose. She swayed, black dots dancing before her eyes. Too much heat, she thought, fighting the weakness. She felt her knees tremble and locked them in place. She couldn't afford to pass out.

Slowly she closed her eyes and willed the world to stop spinning in circles. Then she felt strong hands steadying her. Laura wanted to lean against Gabe, to absorb his power, but she was afraid that the tattered ends of her strength would slide beyond recapture.

"I should have worn a hat," she said, opening her eyes cautiously, trying to focus on the layers of rocks in front of her. After a moment she succeeded.

"Why didn't you?" Gabe asked, fighting the urge to lift her over his shoulders and carry her. The ledge above them was too narrow.

"I didn't plan to sunbathe in this heat," she said dryly, testing her control of her legs by pulling away from him. They still quivered, but didn't buckle. Turning back to Gabe, she looked at his bare head pointedly. "What excuse do you have?"

His grin was a flash of white in his bronzed face. "I don't get sunburned."

Laura's gaze slid from his face, down his strong neck to his broad chest, bronzed by the strong southern sun. "I thought Texans always wore hats," she said teasingly, "even in bed."

His eyes crinkled at the corners, turning to liquid gold. "Do they sleep with their boots on, too?" he drawled.

Laughter welled up in her, bubbling free. It felt good to be able to laugh with a man without caution. It had been so long since she had felt that exhilaration which only sparring with men could spark to life.

The freedom was too new for her to ask the next obvious question: did they sleep in their clothes? She lowered her lids, her eyes once again straying to his bronzed chest, staring pointedly.

Gabe laughed softly, knowingly. "I think we better start climbing," he said. "You go first." He folded his hands into a stirrup for her to step into. "I'll be right behind you."

Laura reached for a handhold, accepting the boost. When her toes found a steady surface, she clawed for the ledge. She swore when her fingers slipped. She should have joined gymnastics instead of aerobics, she thought grimly. With sheer determination she pulled herself over the edge. She did not wait for Gabe to come up to her level. Carefully she moved toward the cave, her body curving into the rocks.

Gabe followed behind her, watchful, prepared to catch her should she sway again. She reached the cave with the same determination that had given her the strength to climb up the ridge. Once inside the cooler shade, she leaned against the wall.

"Sit down and rest," Gabe said gently. Bending over his backpack, he reached for the bag of rolls and handed it to her. The look of disgust on her face made him smile.

"Eat," he said, waiting until she had taken her first reluctant bite. Then he took a bottle of water from the pack. "And drink at least half of that. Once we start climbing down there's no place to rest."

Taking the bottle, Laura promised quietly, "I won't slow you down."

With narrowed eyes, Gabe watched her raise the bottle to her lips. Her knees trembled from the climb and her dust-streaked face was drawn into a tight mask of exhaustion, but her eyes were firm with resolve. No, she wouldn't slow him down. She would push herself until she collapsed.

His unwilling admiration for her deepened to tenderness. "Take your time," he said softly. This time she drank eagerly, letting the liquid run down her parched throat. His gaze slid down the graceful and oddly vulnerable curve of her slender neck. Her breasts strained against the damp material of her blouse.

Gabe took a swift, silent breath. What was it about this woman that affected him so strongly? In the brief time he had been with her, he had seen her shocked and torn apart by grief. He had seen the first stirring of passion darken her eyes, had held her when she had cried. He had watched her hold off two men twice her size, had seen her fight and overcome her body's weakness. He had met no one like her in all his thirty-eight years. She drew him like no other women he had known. Abruptly he turned away and walked to the mouth of the cave.

If the situation had been different, he might have given in to temptation. Few places were more romantic for a holiday affair than Acapulco. Except he was not on vacation, and neither was Laura. The sooner they left here the better.

Thoughtfully Laura chewed on the dry bread, washing it down with the last portion of water she had allotted herself. With scrupulous fairness she drank exactly half of it. She looked from the bottle to the dark, tall shadow blocking most of the light, wondering if she should hand it to him or simply store it in his backpack.

Gabe stood like a rock, silent and immobile. Yet Laura could sense the waves of restless tension. Recapping the bottle, she stood. Gabe did not move when she walked across the cave. He did not stir when she replaced the water bottle in the backpack.

"I'm ready," she said quietly, walking toward the mouth of the cave.

Gabe turned, his eyes running appraisingly over her. The food and water had done the trick. She looked stronger and more relaxed. "When was the last time you've had a decent meal?" he asked quietly.

"Last night," Laura said, raising her eyes questioningly to his face. She had ordered *carne asada*, marinated broiled steak, French fries and an assortment of steamed vegetables. Laura had eaten less than half of it.

"From now on, you'll eat three good meals a day," he said firmly. "It's one condition if you want my help."

"And the others?" Laura asked coolly.

"I'll decide that after you've answered a few questions." He turned and reached for his pack, swinging it onto his back. "You go first," he told her, ignoring the mutinous set of her mouth.

With a fiery look, Laura stepped out on the ledge. Anger pumped adrenaline through her, sharpening her senses, infusing her with strength. She moved easily, swiftly, quietly. Not once did she falter. Without hesitation or fear, she passed the spot where she had almost fallen earlier. With a grin of satisfaction, Gabe followed her.

Dusk was settling over the ridge by the time they reached Gabe's concealed pickup truck. During the long descent and the even longer walk, Laura's anger had changed to admiration of Gabe's tireless strength and disgust at her own weakness.

Now, every muscle screaming for rest, she leaned against a nearby tree and watched Gabe uncover the truck. Despite her weariness, her eyes glowed with satisfaction. She had kept up with Gabe.

She knew that he had slowed his pace, that he could have reached his truck before the sun went down behind the ridge. But few people could match his stamina and strength.

Laura stared at the truck with its camper top, hidden cunningly beneath a net studded with maguey plants. "I would have walked right past it." Her eyes swept over the area, which was dotted with the same spiky growth.

"That's the stuff they make mescal from," Gabe said, fingering one of the sharp-pointed, fleshy leaves. "Among other things," he added, plucking plants from the net's hold.

Laura pushed herself away from the tree and picked up one end of the net, stretching it tight between her arms to make Gabe's job easier. "What else is there?"

"For one, rope. Once they've pressed every ounce of juice out of the leaves, the fibers are beaten and dried, twisted and spun. After corn, maguey is the most versatile plant in Mexico."

Laura looked around her with interest. Maguey of every size thrived around them on the dry, hard-baked ground. "And it's easy to grow," she observed.

Discarding the last of the camouflage, Gabe turned to look at her. "It's virtually carefree," he said, surprised once again by her quick grasp of things. "Once a year the blooms have to be cut back. Otherwise the plants will die."

Life's circle, Laura thought soberly, feeling the ever-present pain swamp her. She blinked her eyes, distracting herself by watching his strong hands fold the ends of the net. He unlocked the camper's door and laid it inside. Moments later, drinking from a bottle of beer, he returned and handed her a bottle of cola.

"We can drink these on the way," he said, walking to the cab.

"Just where are we?" Laura had lost her sense of direction after the first ten twists and turns. She had no idea how close they were to Acapulco or how far from the hacienda.

Opening the door, Gabe gave her a swift, searching look. "Don't try to find the cave by yourself," he warned quietly. "Not unless you want to move in with your son."

"Is that why you led me through a maze?" Laura asked dryly. The slow smile in his eyes confirmed her suspicion. "Don't worry, Gabe," she said, exasperation filling her voice. "I never make the same mistake twice. I know now that trying to sneak into the hacienda is impossible. There has to be some other way to get to Peter."

The last words were said with such quiet desperation that Gabe reached out for her, drawing her against him. "If there is, we'll find it," he told her gently.

"And if there isn't?" Laura tilted her head back to stare into his face. She needed to hear his confirmation that he would try to help her against all odds. Once they reached Acapulco, there was nothing to stop him from dropping her off the way a mailman dropped a parcel and simply forgetting about her problems.

"Laura." Gabe's arm tightened around her shoulder reassuringly. "You have my promise. I'm not going to break it."

Slowly she smiled. In a world where contracts were not worth the paper they were printed on, Gabe's honor was a rarity. "I didn't know that men like you still existed," she said softly.

Seeing the trust in her eyes, Gabe swore softly. "I'm no damned saint," he warned her harshly. The pliant pressure of her body tested his self-control. He wanted to forget about caution and the business that had brought him here. For one moment he wanted to be a man without responsibilities and kiss those lips.

Laura could feel his body tense with desire. For a moment she hesitated, listening for the echoes of fear. She heard nothing but warm whispers of a kiss as hot as the afternoon sun and a strange yearning to test her newfound freedom.

"Saints make me feel uncomfortable," she said softly. "You make me feel . . . good."

With a groan, Gabe lowered his mouth. He took her lips with a mixture of hunger and gentleness that was devastating. He pulled on the handkerchief covering her head until it dropped to the ground. His fingers caught the heavy silk of her hair, freeing it from its coil. With a ripple it dropped down her back, caressing the heated skin of his arm.

Laura felt the tip of his tongue tease her lips until she sighed and opened up to him. His hungry intensity startled her. She tried to turn her head, but the hand buried in her hair would not let her shy away. Her fingers moved between their bodies, pushing at his chest. It was hard, as powerful and as unyielding as forged steel. But beneath the solid wall she could feel the strong, rapid beat of his heart, telling her how much he wanted her.

She realized the restraint he imposed upon himself. He could have demanded rather than asked. But instead he held her in his arms, waiting until she had made up her mind.

His tongue teased her teeth, running over the edges, tempting her, but he did not invade her mouth. With a burst of pleasure, Laura realized that he gave her a choice. She could stop now, before a kiss changed their relationship. She could accept the pleasure of being held in the security of his arms without giving anything in return.

But once she had let him past the barrier, he would not allow her to withdraw into her shell. Laura had never been handed a more precious gift—the power to decide her own destiny.

"Oh, Gabe," she whispered, cupping his chin, rubbing her hand over the bristles tenderly. Her arm went around his neck, drawing his head down to hers. She opened herself to him, her tongue twining around his own.

The rough velvet of his tongue stroked her own in a dance of desire. Laura closed her eyes as sensation swept over her, hot and weakening and strengthening at the same time. She felt his arm tighten, bringing her closer against his male hardness.

His mouth tasted of beer, strong, bitter and utterly male. Once again she was enveloped in his scent. Then the sensations whirled together, raising her to a cloud where nothing existed but the pleasure he gave.

With a soft curse, Gabe finally put her away from him. He could not believe he had almost lost control. The last time he had felt this way had been so long ago he couldn't remember a specific incident. He probably had been Gino's age, young, idealistic and full of dreams.

Laura stared at his face, wishing she could read him as easily as he seemed to read her. But a man like Gabe was outside her experience. She guessed that very few people truly knew him.

"We'd better get going," Gabe said softly, stroking her cheek with the knuckles of his hand. "It's still quite a drive to Acapulco." He opened the cab door and motioned her inside, helping her climb into the truck.

Laura had to push aside the hat that lay on the bench. With a small smile she watched Gabe reach for it and put it on the moment he joined her. "Now I know you're a Texan," she teased him.

One brow raised questioningly, he looked at her. "My hat?" he asked, his lips twitching. "A hat doesn't make a Texan."

"No, but the automatic gesture with which you reached for it does. Why did you leave it behind?" she asked when he started the truck.

"Didn't want to lose it," he said, backing the pickup out of its hiding spot. "You can't buy a decent Stetson here in Mexico." Slowly he eased the truck over the uneven terrain, leaning forward to peer through the windshield. He didn't turn on the lights.

Laura grabbed the bottle of beer he had put in front of the air-conditioning vent to keep it from toppling over. For the next five minutes, silence reigned while Gabe steered the truck through the swiftly falling dusk. They passed a small house surrounded by tall corn, the bright turquoise paint peeling off the adobe walls.

A little farther on, they reached a narrow track. Gabe turned on the headlights and increased the speed of the truck, then held out his hand for the beer.

"Thanks," he said, raising it to his lips. "You're an unusual woman, Laura. You know when to be quiet."

"I didn't want you to land us in one of those deep ruts," Laura said dryly. "I've done enough walking for one day." She watched him drink, then asked, "I always thought that Texans didn't walk a lot."

Replacing the bottle in front of the vent, Gabe wiped his mouth with the back of his hand. "They don't," he said, "not if they can avoid it. There are places, however, where cars and horses won't go. I've done my share of walking and climbing, catching calves and goats."

"You raise goats? I thought you bred horses and cattle."

"I do. The goats are Gino's project." Abruptly he stopped. She was so easy to talk to that Gino's name had slipped out before he was aware of it.

"Who's Gino?" Laura asked curiously. She saw his mouth harden into a thin line in response.

"My nephew," Gabe answered her in a tone of finality that told her not to pursue that particular subject. "Tell me about your son," he said.

Laura wondered where to begin. There were so many things she wanted to tell him. Peter was bright and inquisitive. He was very clever with his hands. His room was filled with Lego planes, cars and houses he had built. He liked chocolate but hated raisins. His favorite ice cream was chocolate fudge swirl. He knew no strangers because he knew the names of most of the people he came in contact with day after day. From the moment he got out of bed he attacked life with a whirlwind of energy. In the evening he dropped off to sleep swiftly and suddenly. But those were not the things Gabe wanted to know. He wanted statistics.

"He was five years old in May. His name is Peter Ian Foster. Ian Foster was my father's name."

"And Julio Vasquez is his father," Gabe said coolly. Somehow he couldn't see Laura getting mixed up with a man like Vasquez.

"I was twenty-one going on nineteen when I met Julio," Laura said, her voice tightly controlled. "I was a student at NYU. Julio was attached to the Mexican consulate. I was attracted to the glamour, not the man, only I was too young to know it at the time. When I found out, it was too late."

"What about your parents? Didn't they warn you?" Gabe asked tersely.

"My father died two years before I met Julio. My mother was in Ireland."

Colleen Foster had come to the wedding, though. In the few short days preceding the ceremony, she had tried to warn Laura that Julio was not the right man for her. Charming but empty, she had called him. And thoroughly spoiled. She also had disliked the fact that Julio had not notified his parents of his forthcoming marriage. Laura had brushed aside her mother's intuitive warnings. Where Julio was concerned she'd had tunnel vision.

Frowning, Gabe drove through the falling dusk, mulling over the information she had just given him. There were things she was keeping to herself. He felt that there were discrepancies, but could not put his finger on them. "Why did Vasquez kidnap your son?" he asked bluntly.

Sensing what was coming, Laura countered evasively, "Why does any father want his son?" Newspapers were full of instances of parents abducting their children. The State Department was swamped with requests to help return kidnapped children from foreign countries. To most people, love would seem a plausible reason. But Gabe was not most people. If he knew Julio only half as well as she suspected, he must know that he was not a loving father.

Laura's hands clenched into her jeans. Grimly she waited for the ax to fall. What would she do when Gabe told her, like all the others, that he would not interfere in divorce squabbles? Would she look for a man with no license and no scruples?

Abruptly Gabe stopped the truck. Both arms folded over the steering wheel, he looked at her silently. His gaze raked her face. "I've been watching the ranch for five days. I've seen no affection between Julio and Pedro. Until today I thought that the boy was a nephew, one of his sister's sons."

He stared at her face, wondering why he had not guessed at the truth before. Men like Vasquez did not bring their bastards to their homes. Dammit, she had lied to him, by omission if not with words. "You're Vasquez's wife," he challenged her in a cold, hard voice.

And what had Herb been doing? Sleeping? Why hadn't he uncovered the information about Vasquez's marriage?

Laura stared at the dark, menacing shadow, fear and hopelessness tightening her throat. "No. I *was* married to him, but I divorced him shortly after Peter was born," she admitted hoarsely. "The courts gave me full custody of my son."

The ring of truth was in her whispered words, but could he dare trust her again? Gino's life was too precious to take chances. Abruptly he turned the light on. "Dammit, I thought Peter was illegitimate."

"I never said so," Laura protested, despair roughening her voice.

"No. But you weren't exactly truthful, either." With an oath Gabe pushed away from the steering wheel, reaching for the light switch. "Just when were you going to tell me the facts? When Vasquez had me arrested for kidnapping his heir?"

Laura closed her eyes against the sudden brightness. When she opened them again she found Gabe staring at her with such a hard, dangerous glitter that her skin prickled with fear. Darkness descended. Nightmares of another time, another place closed over her. Of another man with eyes that glittered with rage. Of fury lashing out at her.

Of blows. Punches. Kicks. Then paralyzing horror when rage turned to lust.

She blinked, and the darkness faded. Fear gave way to a surge of raw courage and cold determination. She would never be a victim again. Her hand inched behind her back, curling around the door handle. She would rather die than suffer the same cruel fate again.

Her naked fear was like cold well water on hot skin. Gabe waited, counting seconds, swearing silently. One wrong move and she would run into the swiftly falling darkness.

Unblinking, he willed her eyes to meet his steady gaze. When they did he slowly shifted his arms, folding them across his chest, releasing his breath with a sigh of relief when her tension eased. He wasted no words reassuring her that she had nothing to fear from him. She would toss them aside like a bag of empty lies. Softly, slowly, he repeated his question, ''Why didn't you tell me?''

Laura slowly eased her grip on the door handle. ''I am desperate. I've tried the legal way. I've begged congressmen and senators for help. Without success. I've been turned down by every respectable detective agency in the country. You're my last hope.''

She swallowed, then added quietly, ''I filed for divorce on grounds of physical cruelty. I was nursing my baby for the first time when Julio called. It wasn't a loving visit. He threatened to take my child away from me if I tried to divorce him.'' Bitterness seeped into her voice. ''I went ahead anyway, though I often wish I hadn't.''

She took her fingers off the handle and spread them in front of her. Catching his eyes, she said, ''I suppose I should have told you at once. But I was afraid that you'd refuse to help me if you knew the whole truth.'' She paused, then added harshly, ''I don't know what I'm going to do if you, too, walk away.''

''No,'' he said roughly, his anger tightly leashed. ''No, I won't turn you down.'' He shook his head, adding quietly, ''Even if you had stayed married to him, he would have

taken the child. A weasel like Vasquez doesn't respect
promises or laws. He uses them, twists and turns them and
frames innocent people with them. He sends women and
kids to a hellhole they call prison for doing nothing more
than bloodying a nose. Yours is not the only life he's tried
to ruin.''

Laura reeled beneath the brutality of his revelations. She
gasped, staring at him with helpless horror. Pain and frustration darkened his eyes. Like her, he had lost someone he
loved. She didn't know who it was. He would tell her when
and if he ever trusted her enough.

Instinctively she knew that it was not Gabe's woman
Vasquez had mistreated and finally thrown into prison.
Gabe would not have kissed her with desire shaking his body
if he felt committed to someone else.

Slowly she reached out to him and touched his face, forgetting the lessons of the past in her desire to share his grief
as he had held her through her bout of tears.

Gabe stiffened under the gentle touch. Already he regretted letting her see a glimpse of his private hell. His hands
fastened around her wrist to stop her, but her eyes pleaded
with him to let her share his pain as she had accepted his
help. With a groan he drew her forward until she lay on top
of him.

The kiss was as soothing as night, gentle warmth flowing
from lips to lips. There was no haste, no pressure, only a
strange sensation of sharing and peace.

His mouth opened on hers, and her lips parted for him.
She felt his tongue tease her mouth and outline the edges of
her teeth. A trembling need spread down her throat and beyond, warmth changing to heat. Laura closed her eyes and
shivered at the sensations rushing through her.

She felt the strong muscles of his chest beneath her, the
lean waist and the taut muscles of his thighs. As his arms
tightened around her, she felt a sensation of being drawn
into him, of losing herself within him.

Her hands moved to his shoulders to steady herself. She
felt off balance, her world spinning beyond control. With
his gentle touch, Gabe had unleashed feelings she had not

known she was capable of. The depth of her need exhilarated and scared her at the same time.

She heard the groan of protest with which Gabe raised his head, showing her that the kiss had affected him as much as it had shaken her. He stared at her searchingly for long seconds. Her wide-eyed, startled gaze brought a small smile to his lips.

Laura had enjoyed and wanted the kiss as much as he had.

Chapter 4

The night was clear. Stars studded the sky. The moon seemed to hang at the edge of the world, a huge lantern brushing the calm waters of the Pacific Ocean. Rising from the sea, the night breeze gently fanned palm leaves with moist salt air.

From the balcony of Gabe's tenth-floor room Laura had an unrestricted view of the shimmering sea. Wrapped in the large folds of his white bathrobe, she watched a string of fishing boats vanish behind the rocks forming a natural protected basin for yachts and cruise ships.

The beach was almost deserted. A few couples walked hand in hand along the gently rolling sea. From the terrace below, faint laughter, children's voices and mariachi music drifted up. As Laura sipped at a glass of dry white wine, she felt very much alone.

Her eyes searched out the jutting peninsula to her left where a brightly lit cross reached for the sky. Below, scattered pinpoints of light flickered off and on, lights from the bungalows shining through swaying plants.

Was Julio at the bungalow, waiting for her? At the thought of her narrow escape, she shivered. Since her divorce she had lived in daily fear of his revenge. But as time passed and he made no move, her nightmares had become less frequent. Her biggest mistake had been to ignore his activities. If she had known a year ago that he was leaving New York and returning to Mexico, she would have sent Peter to her mother in Ireland. She should have known that a man like Julio would not leave the United States without his son. He might have no love for him, but Peter was his heir. From the reaction of the two ranch hands, it was clear that he had expected her to follow her son to Mexico. Could he, in his twisted way, want her back? The thought made her stomach turn.

Where was Gabe? She looked at her watch and sighed with impatience. More than an hour had passed since he had left without explanation.

Turning back to the room, she thought about his leave-taking. "Don't answer the phone," he had told her. At the door he had paused and reached out to brush a strand of hair from her face. "Try to get some sleep. We'll have dinner when I come back."

She looked at the wide bed where Gabe had dropped a pair of brand new stone-washed jeans and a snap-buttoned blue western shirt. Placing her glass on the nightstand, she examined the clothing. The jeans had a thirty-inch waist. Not Gabe's size, she thought. The shirt was a medium. Too small to cover the powerful width of Gabe's shoulders. Who had he bought those clothes for?

He had taken them from the camper before they had entered the hotel, along with a toothbrush and a comb. Laura tried to imagine the man who would fit into the jeans. Long legs, gangly rather than muscular. A young man before his prime, or an old man well past. No. Old men did not fight and give bloody noses. Young men did. Who was the person Julio had framed? Was he Gabe's son, brother, cousin, nephew, friend? The possibilities were many. All she knew for sure was that Gabe cared for him deeply.

Frustrated, she shrugged her shoulders. Gabe would tell her when and if he trusted her, and that day might never come. Trust had so many shades and variations. Not even the very young gave it without reservation—and life experience taught them even more caution.

With another look at the closed door, Laura reached for the belt of the robe. She had forgotten to mention to Gabe that she would have to call her friend and lawyer, Al Wilkins. If she didn't, he would be on the first flight out of Kennedy tomorrow morning.

Laura stared thoughtfully at the phone, wishing she could use it. She wondered if the switchboard kept records of collect calls, then discarded the thought. Gabe had been emphatic, so she wasn't going to take any chances. She'd have to use one of the many pay phones in the hotel lobby.

Swiftly she slipped into the clean clothes. Using her belt to hold up the pants, she rolled the cuffs up to her ankles. When she put on the shirt it fell in loose folds to her thighs. She looked at her sneakers with disgust. They were filthy, the insides damp with perspiration and caked with dust. The thought of wearing them made her shudder. She pushed them out of sight, preferring to go barefoot. Reaching for her billfold, she went to the door and locked it behind her.

The hallway was deserted. At this time of night, most people were out eating and dancing, and only a few stragglers were riding the elevator. To Laura's relief, though, the lobby was crowded. Swiftly she slid between groups of people to one of the phone booths.

With her back to the lobby, she dialed the operator and asked for a collect call to New York. Moments later she heard Al's familiar, precise voice.

"Wilkins."

"Hi, it's me," Laura said softly. Then she held the receiver at arm's length to avoid hearing a string of choice words about inconsiderate behavior.

"Were you worried about me?" she asked when he ran out of steam.

"I just reserved a ticket to Mexico," Al said dryly.

Laura laughed softly. "Cancel it."

There was a pause. "You sound very cheerful. The last time I heard you laugh was a year ago. Don't tell me you've done the impossible."

"Not yet. But it looks promising. I want you to do me a favor. Check out a man named Gabriel Borga."

She heard the rustle of paper, then Al's voice, sharp and precise: "Gabe Borga. Male. Age and address?"

"Late thirties. Somewhere in Texas. Drives a Ford pickup with license number—"

"Darling, are you for real?" Al interrupted. "I'm a lawyer, not a detective. Give me a New York number, and I'll get you the driver's name and address and the number of kids, cats and dogs that go with it. But you're talking about the Wild West."

Laura knew from experience that Al's appearance and behavior were deceptive. Slim and always impeccably groomed, he had a bored, languid manner which had almost deceived Laura into running out of his office on their first meeting. But behind the thin, pallid face and baby-blue eyes hid a razor-sharp mind and a dogged persistence. Unperturbed, Laura gave him the number. "Cash in on some favors," she advised softly.

Al groaned. "I don't know why I ever agreed to take you on. I must have grown a gray hair for every day I've known you."

Laura grinned, thinking of his jet-black, carefully styled hair. "Because I make your life interesting. I won't mention the fact that I've doubled the profits on your investments."

"I know my wife loves you, but my ulcer doesn't. What's so special about this cowboy?"

"He saved you a trip to Mexico," Laura said quietly.

Al swore under his breath. "Come home, Laura," he pleaded quietly. "I'll find someone. Some ex-army guy, or an ex-marine. I just heard of a guy in the boondocks who runs a survival camp and who does little jobs for big bucks. No questions asked."

Laura's hand tightened on the phone. "I think I've already found an ex-military man," she said slowly. She recalled Gabe facing the two Mexicans, standing utterly controlled. She recalled his discipline, the shirt he had thrown over her to camouflage her blouse, his order to move slowly but steadily while the helicopter hovered above them, and the net, studded with maguey plants, hiding his truck. She had seen similar maneuvers countless times in war movies but had not made the connection until Al had mentioned the word army.

"That's easy to check out," Al grunted with satisfaction. "Give me more particulars."

Laura grinned wryly. "I should think a simple check into license plates would be easy. Checking military files should be difficult. Sure you didn't get the two mixed up?"

"Darling, they don't have martini lunches in the Wild West. What does this cowboy look like?"

"Six feet of solid muscle, tawny hair, hard face. Cat's eyes." And a slow, beautiful smile, she thought. If she said that aloud, Al would be in Acapulco tomorrow. "Moves with the stealth and swiftness of a mountain lion."

"Cats scare me, Laura. They're so unpredictable." He paused, then added quietly, "I once read that wild cats can't be tamed."

Laura drew in her breath. She should have known that Al would sense the difference in her. "I'll remember that," she said quietly. "Give my love to Helen and the kids. I'll call you tomorrow night."

"Be careful."

Laura hung up without answering and stared at the phone for a long time. She remembered Gabe's gentleness and the strength of his arms around her when she had cried. She savored the memory of the different tastes and sensations of his kisses—wiping out fear, evoking tenderness, stirring desire and providing the comfort of shared grief. Al's warning had come too late. She wanted Gabe with a passion that both scared and excited her.

She had to get back to their room before Gabe returned. He would be worried if he found her gone. She searched the lobby through the booth's glass window before leaving it, but found nothing suspicious. On her way to the elevators she passed several boutiques. Her steps slowed as she looked at the smart, brightly colored fashions displayed in the windows. Looking down at the ill-fitting jeans, Laura wished that she had something more stylish to wear.

Somehow she sensed that even if she dressed up Gabe would be unimpressed. She had guessed earlier that he was used to beautiful women and had known for sure when they'd walked into the hotel. Despite his dusty, sweat-stained appearance, the eyes of every female between twenty and eighty had followed him.

With a last regretful look at a white jumpsuit with a wide black belt, Laura made her way to the elevator.

Party sounds came from one of the bungalows—subdued laughter, the clinking of glasses, disco music. Gabe slid silently through the vegetation outside, his senses alert, his movements slow but smooth.

Separating himself from the cloying scent of oleander bushes, he passed along the edge of the brightly lit area separating Laura's bungalow from the party place. His toe hit a round, ball-sized object. He froze, watching a green coconut roll into the light. Holding his breath, he listened, his eyes piercing the night's shadows.

Luck, he thought grimly when no one stirred. Luck, and dealing with amateurs. Ten years ago that little mistake might have cost him his life. But a decade ago he would not have tripped over that coconut. He had been younger and in constant training in the jungles of Vietnam.

Now his skills were rusty. But Vasquez's men were not the Vietcong. Yet Gabe did not make the mistake of underestimating Vasquez and his men. They were dangerous because they were unpredictable.

He moved around the dark building in a wide circle. There was no sign of Vasquez or his men, but he knew that they were here. He had seen Laura's Jeep in the parking lot, and sitting next to it the black Ford Galaxie belonging to the hacienda.

Silently he moved to the back of the house. There was a small window, designed to allow cross-ventilation during the cooler winter months when air-conditioning could be dispensed with. Tonight it was closed. Crouching low, Gabe moved nearer. With his ear pressed against the painted concrete blocks, he listened for sounds from within. Silence. He raised himself to his full height, peering through the glass into what must be the living room. Through the front window the moon shone into the room, casting shadows and light over three men sprawled in chairs.

He recognized Jorge and Juan easily. The third man sat too far in the darkness to reveal his face. His legs were crossed, and the tip of one highly polished shoe swung like a pendulum, measuring impatience. Did it belong to father or son? Both were meticulous dressers. Then the man leaned forward to stub out a cigarette. Pale moonlight danced over the blue-black sheen of Julio's hair.

A welcoming committee of three strong men waiting for one small woman. White-hot rage coursed through Gabe. For an instant he thought of bursting into the room and teaching those cowards not to prey on women and children. But now was not the time. Not tonight. He would be risking too much for a few seconds of satisfaction. Soon he would, he promised himself grimly. Very soon.

He retraced his steps to the parking lot with equal care. The retrieval of Laura's clothes would have to wait until the morning. Before sliding between the cars, he checked the area just in case Vasquez had been cautious enough to station another man near his car.

The area was empty—and so was the Ford Galaxie.

Its doors were locked, but Gabe had expected that. Within seconds he slid inside the plush interior, a grim smile on his lips. He had not lost his skill of getting past simple barriers. Reaching into his shirt, he took out a small manila envelope containing two photos and a note and placed it on the driver's seat.

The photos had been shot at night with infrared film. One showed the delivery of a Colombian shipment, the plane's model and number clearly visible. The other showed Julio Vasquez handing the pilot a paper bag. Gabe doubted that it held the pilot's breakfast. The note stated a time and location, suggesting a meeting to discuss demands.

At this early stage of the game, Gabe had no intention of showing his face. When Vasquez turned up, he would find only another envelope with its set of pictures and new instructions. Each envelope led to another, each message a little more threatening than the last, each set of pictures more incriminating than the previous. Out of the hundreds of photos Gabe had accumulated over the last few months, he had chosen seven sets showing Vasquez and the other men involved in every stage of their filthy operation. A time bomb ticking away relentlessly.

Over the past few days Gabe had carefully and precisely planted six of those envelopes all over Vasquez's land. This most important notice he had saved for last, waiting for the right opportunity to place it. Laura had provided him with the perfect time and place to set the bomb ticking.

Gabe knew the effectiveness of psychological warfare. He'd had the best teachers. Faceless, nameless shadows turning peaceful rice paddies and gently swaying bamboo into places like hell. He knew that one nameless, faceless man could do more damage than a troop of well-trained soldiers.

This first notice would do little more than frighten the bastard. The second envelope would deepen fright into fear mixed with fury. By the third day, Vasquez would be looking over his shoulder constantly. His nerves would be raw. He would flinch at every sound, wondering when the bomb would explode, frantically looking for a way to defuse it. By the seventh day he'd be a squirming, sweating worm. That was when Gabe planned to establish contact and make a bargain with the man: Gino's freedom for the negatives. But he didn't have a plan regarding Laura's son.

Silently he slid from the car and locked the doors. With the same tool he had used to pick the lock, he deflated the two front tires. Imagining Vasquez's curses, he grinned. The man had a long, frustrating night ahead of him.

The coastal road was busy at this time of night as people flocked into Acapulco for dinner and shows. Gabe had little difficulty flagging down a taxi. Fifteen minutes later he entered the hotel lobby.

Instead of making for the elevators, Gabe turned to one of the many phone booths on one side of the spacious hall. He ducked into the first and dialed a number in Mexico City. He let it ring five times, hung up, redialed and let it ring three times, then redialed again.

After the seventh ring, a man's voice answered. "Dammit, you're late," Herb Miller barked. "You know how many Scotches I've drunk waiting for your call?"

"In that altitude, too many," Gabe said. "You never could hold your liquor, even at sea level."

"That, my friend, was ten years ago. Things change. I've developed a certain tolerance with practice."

"You've also gotten careless. Your report was incomplete."

"Run into trouble?" The voice on the other end became quiet and alert.

"I'm not sure yet," Gabe said. "Remember the boy I was telling you about? Well, he's Junior's son. He was kidnapped from New York a year ago. I just met his mother. She's trying to get him back. How come you missed the little bit of information about Vasquez being married to a woman named Laura Foster?"

Herb swore long and viciously. "I'll kill those guys," he swore. "They don't like us poking around their files, especially those marked Diplomatic Immunity! How much easier my life would be if they canned that status. I'll rip them up good."

"Forget it," Gabe said, impatience tightening his voice. He didn't want to listen to departmental jealousies. He knew all about the petty tricks various groups used to protect their territories. Once he too had played their games. Now time was too limited to waste. "Just get me a personal on Laura Foster. It must be collecting dust somewhere in the embassy." Swiftly he repeated what Laura had told him about her legal efforts.

"Affirmative." There was a pause. "Hope you're not planning to get involved in that mess. Unless—" Herb paused, then asked slowly, "Can we use her?"

"Helping her get back her son will make a perfect smoke screen. But there her usefulness ends," Gabe said firmly. He had no intention of endangering Laura. The mere thought of Vasquez laying his hands on her made him shudder.

"You always were a gallant fool," Herb sighed. "Look where that got you. Talking to cows and horses and no one to laugh with. All because your mother taught you that women are too weak to survive the heat and loneliness of the ranch. Today's women are tough."

Gabe thought of Laura's softness and warmth and shook his head. "You have a one-track mind." He sighed wearily.

"Edith and I care about you," Herb said gruffly.

Gabe did not answer. He had given up long ago trying to stop Herb and his wife to find him a mate. They were both city people who enjoyed the occasional visit to his ranch. They had never lived through a dust storm when visibility was nil and fine grains of dirt invaded everything: the clothes, the house, the food. They had never experienced a blizzard that turned the airplane runway into a sheet of ice, or endured the occasional flash floods that tore down bridges and swept away roads. They didn't understand how heat and drought grated on the nerves until they were raw and bleeding.

Gabe had watched his mother's love for his father wither and die like the rose garden she had planted with so much care. Even his sister, who loved the ranch, had moved to the city eventually. No, he hadn't met a woman yet who would settle on thirty thousand acres halfway between Lubbock and New Mexico, at least none he wanted to share his life with.

Unbidden, he thought of a pair of huge blue eyes, midnight-black hair and skin the color of fresh snow. He saw Laura's passion and felt her slim body curving into his.

He wanted her. He wanted to give her pleasure, to free her from fears and watch her turn into the warm and sensual woman she promised to be. Unforgettable. Destroying his peace. Forever leaving him yearning, like the desert for rain.

"How is Gino?" he asked tersely.

"As usual. I brought him some money today and paid off the guards. Should make his life easier for a week or so. Don't be foolish and become involved in that woman's mess. Hell, once we've nailed Vasquez you can pick up the child as easily as a shell on the beach if that's what's bothering you."

"I'll handle it my way," Gabe said firmly, knowing that in his position Herb would have acted the same way. Herb blamed himself for Gino's imprisonment because Gino had run into Vasquez while staying at his home.

"Stubborn old fool," Herb muttered. "What's she like?"

"I won't make any more phone calls. So turn on the radio," Gabe said, ignoring the question. For tonight, while Vasquez still waited at the bungalow, Laura was safe. But tomorrow the hunt for her—and for him—would begin. Sooner or later Vasquez would find them. High-rise hotels were great for anonymity, but too easy to get trapped in. He wondered if Laura liked camping.

"I don't like your change of plans," Herb protested.

"Too bad, my friend," Gabe drawled. "Kiss Edith for me."

"The hell I will," Herb countered, a reluctant smile in his voice. "Be careful."

"I will." Gabe hung up. During the next few days he expected little development. One of the advantages of surprise was that his prey didn't know whom he was dealing with. The threats could be coming from Colombia or from the local mob, from Mexican drug enforcement or any number of other sources. Vasquez would be fighting shadows.

All Gabe had to do was monitor the pickup of the envelopes from their various hiding places, contact Herb once a day and keep a low profile. At least that had been the plan before today.

Wearily Gabe brushed his hair away from his forehead. The solution to Laura's problem was more difficult. Perhaps with both Don Emilio and Vasquez otherwise occupied, he might have a chance to enter the hacienda.

The house was not as impregnable as Laura thought. But getting in was not the problem—leaving was. If the boy kicked and screamed he would have the whole household on his tail within seconds. He could drug the child, but he doubted that Laura would approve it. Besides, children reacted differently to drugs than adults did. The logical solution to this problem would be to take Laura with him.

He abandoned the idea almost before it occurred to him. He had seen the results of Julio Vasquez venting his anger. Never again on Laura, he swore.

But what if she was already within the bastard's grasp? What if Don Emilio had been searching this hotel while his son sat waiting at the bungalow?

Ice-cold fear settled in the pit of his stomach. His eyes narrowed, searching the crowd of suntanned bodies coming and going. Soft-footed, with a stride that was deceptively slow, he wound his way through the groups of men and women clad in everything from cotton shorts to sequined silk dresses. His eyes were cold and expressionless. Like the lens of a camera, he saw everything. She wasn't there.

The elevator was crowded but empty. He was the only one getting off on the tenth floor. His stride lengthened almost to a run. Nearing his room, he slowed. Holding his breath, he pressed his ear against the door of room 1056. And heard nothing.

His hand reached for a square of tough plastic to open the lock with. Then he thought better of it. If Laura was asleep, he did not want to scare her. He knocked twice. Silence was his only response. Even before he slipped the plastic into place, he knew that the room was empty. No Laura. No threats. Just emptiness.

With one sweeping look he took stock of the room. The open terrace door. An empty glass. The smooth bedspread. She had not slept. A hint of warm moisture still hung in the air. She had taken a shower and used his robe. Gino's clothes were gone. Where was she?

He examined the lock. No sign of forced entry. Had she gone down to the shops? Perhaps she was buying makeup.

His tension eased a little at the thought of that possibility. He looked around, his expression softening as he registered the mess. Her dirty clothes lay in a heap on the floor. His robe had been flung across the bed. He picked it up and took it into the bathroom. The towels she had used hung straight and neat. She had even washed the water spots off the sink. Frowning, he returned to the room.

Then he saw her sneakers, pushed halfway under the bed.

He stood and stared at the tips of the shoes pointing toward him while nightmares flashed before his eyes.

Easy, easy, he told himself. She could be anywhere. Walking on the beach. Sitting around the pool.

Or halfway to the hacienda.

He moved to the door, flung it open—and stopped.

Halfway down the hall, Laura was coming toward him. Even dressed in Gino's ill-fitting clothes, she looked beautiful. The wide shirt hinted at curves and valleys, long legs and alabaster skin. Her hair was shining like highly polished ebony, rippling with each step, swinging across her shoulders like a satiny cape. She moved with confidence in surroundings familiar to her.

Gabe registered all of these things in an instant, registered too his body's response. He was burning with anger. Adrenaline was pumping, sharpening his senses. He wanted to shake her for giving him one of the worst moments of fear he'd ever gone through. He wanted to kiss and hold her until his world stopped spinning.

Trying to bring his rage and his desire under control, he leaned against the doorframe. Folding his arms across his chest, he waited for the moment she lifted her head.

Clutching the key in her hand, Laura raised her eyes to the door. "Gabe," she said, smiling, her eyes shining with a mixture of pleasure and relief that he had returned safely. "When did you come back?"

"A while ago," Gabe said, staring at her face. She was beautiful. Her skin glowed like pink gold, her eyes sparkling like precious jewels. Those ridiculously long lashes added a touch of mystery. But no matter how good she looked she still had some explaining to do.

The change was subtle, but Laura noticed it. With a flicker of apprehension, she stopped in front of him. "I hope you weren't worried," she said. Something stirred beneath his calmness, something dangerous.

"Where were you?" he asked.

"You didn't tell me to stay put." Laura walked past him, leaning against the small desk.

"Where did you go? You should have left me a note," Gabe said softly.

"I went downstairs to make a phone call," she said quietly, trying to control the swift surge of anger and guilt flashing through her. She knew she should have left a note telling him where she had gone, but she had thought that she would be back before he returned.

"A phone call?" Gabe's eyes narrowed dangerously. How come he hadn't seen her when he'd made his call? Of course, he had not searched each booth. Laura might have been in one at the opposite end.

Laura met his eyes coolly. "To New York. You didn't want me to use this phone, so I had to go downstairs to the lobby. Gabe, I'm not a complete fool. I've dealt with risks and calculated percentages all my life. I know when to take chances and when to play it safe. I didn't leave New York without anyone knowing where I went. If I don't check in each day, my lawyer will be on the next plane to Mexico."

No, she wasn't a fool, but perhaps she was too damn clever! Briefly he wondered if he had walked into a trap. Despite his tight security, a leak could have happened. Someone might have tipped Vasquez off. The scene at the ridge could have been staged. "Why did you keep it a secret?" he asked, watching her reactions carefully.

Anger exploded, swift and hot. "And where did *you* disappear to tonight?" she countered, replacing his question with one of her own. Her eyes were bright with anger, her voice raised. "Where are your explanations, your reassurances? I'm tired of the silent treatment," she snapped. Then she stopped, getting her anger under control. "I was worried," she added quietly.

"You didn't ask," Gabe said calmly, pushing himself away from the door. His spark of suspicion had been swiftly quenched. Her surge of anger had been too real. Quietly he added, "When I couldn't find you, I imagined the worst." He swiftly covered the distance between them. Staring down at her, he said soberly, "You scared the hell out of me."

His words startled her. She looked up into his face and saw fleeting, haunted shadows. "I'm sorry," she whispered, reaching out to touch his cheek. "I didn't mean to worry you." She ran her hand over his bristly chin. "Would you have told me where you were going?" she asked, enjoying the rough sensation under her fingertips.

Gabe caught her hand, kissing its palm. "I went to check out your room. I thought you might want your clothes." He saw her eyes darken with pleasure, a question in their depths. "Julio was there, waiting for you. With Juan and Jorge." With the tip of his tongue he teased the soft palm and felt her pulse quicken. "Tell me, what's all this about percentages and risks?"

Heat ran up her arm. The sweet caress made her feel oddly light-headed. She wanted to lean closer, to touch his broad chest and rake her fingers through the golden curls. She wanted to forget about Julio's dark shadow threatening her.

But for the first time since they'd met, Gabe was answering her questions with words instead of silence. "Investments. That's what I do for a living." Slowly she tugged at his hand. "What else happened?"

Surprised, Gabe raised his head, releasing her hand. He couldn't picture her poring over annual reports or studying price-earnings ratios. She was too full of vitality to be stuck in an office. "Nothing. I couldn't get into the suite. They were sitting in the living room."

"They must have bribed someone to get in," Laura said thoughtfully, "because I have the key." Then she remembered another key, the one to this room. "How did you manage to open the door?"

"All it takes is one strong push, and the lock gives."

With a mixture of amusement and exasperation, Laura shook her head. "Gabe. I want some answers. I know less about you than any company I've bought shares in. I've never invested so blindly." Nor risked so much, she thought soberly.

He put one finger over her lips, silencing her. "We'll talk later," he promised gently, stroking the soft flesh. "I need a shower and a shave."

Slowly he circled her mouth. The soft flesh of her bottom lip contracted beneath his touch, tantalizing him. With a groan he bent his head and kissed her. Her lips tasted fresh and sweet. He wanted to draw her against him and deepen the kiss, but he knew that once he put his arms around her desire would replace common sense.

He lifted his head and stepped back. Swiftly he walked to the closet and took out a change of clothes. "Don't disappear," he said softly before entering the bathroom.

Chapter 5

The restaurant Gabe took her to was small, with plastic furniture, red checkered tablecloths and open skies. Ruby-red and bright orange glass containers protected flickering candle flames against the mild breeze. Palm leaves rustled overhead. A few feet away, gentle waves lapped ashore, their continuous sound background music to laughter and excitedly raised Spanish voices.

Laura had met Gabe's suggestion that they go out for a meal with conflicting feelings. She had worried that Julio might discover them should they leave their room, yet was equally apprehensive about staying. Her emotions for Gabe were too new, and frightened her with their intensity. Gabe had explained that the restaurant he had in mind was too far off the beaten track for Vasquez to discover them. It was miles from Acapulco, even past Puerto Marquez, the nearest village to the south. Laura decided she welcomed the diversion.

Now she watched Gabe order their food, occasionally looking at her for confirmation. What a difference a shave and a change of clothes made, she thought. He appeared as smooth and sophisticated as any man of her acquaintance.

As long as one didn't look beneath the surface of the well-cut white shirt, tan slacks and the smooth bronze face, he seemed just like any other tourist.

As he leaned back in his chair, seemingly relaxed, Laura could see his powerful muscles ripple beneath his shirt. His eyes probed everything, the shadows beneath the palm trees, the faces of the other patrons. Even while giving their orders to the waiter, his head was tilted toward the sounds surrounding them.

To encourage the tourist trade the menu was in both Spanish and English. It offered a wide range of choices, from typical Mexican dishes to hamburgers and fries. They chose broiled shrimp as an appetizer, tacos with beef and chicken with avocados as the main course, and a bottle of white wine, which their waiter brought almost immediately.

With a smile, Gabe tested the small amount poured into the glass for his approval. "It's dry, but smooth," he observed.

"Fine," Laura said, watching Gabe dismiss the waiter and pour the wine himself. She wanted to slide her fingers over the golden curls of the hair-roughened skin of his forearm and feel the pulsing warmth beneath.

Abruptly she stopped staring and accepted the glass he offered. To allow herself to fall in love with this man would be as foolish as investing her life's savings in commodities about which she knew very little. She could lose so much. But she could gain more, so much more, a small voice inside her said, tempting her.

"Have you ever gone camping?" Gabe asked her, leaning back lazily in his chair and twirling the wineglass in his hand.

"Camping? Like in a tent? Or like in your truck out in the wilderness? No." She sipped her wine while her heart lurched with excitement. This is it, she thought. Action. No more sitting back, nor more waiting for another legal avenue to come to a dead end.

"I guess I'm about to broaden my education," she said with outward calm. Why hadn't she thought about getting a van and camping out instead of wasting money renting rooms?

It was an easy question to answer. She knew nothing about camping or cars. Oh, she could change a flat tire. But if the engine stalled she would be lost, stranded in a world as new to her as it was familiar to Gabe.

"Yes." He liked the way she accepted the idea, her eyes sparkling with suppressed excitement. "No questions?"

"Lots of them," Laura answered lightly. "Let's start with where we are going."

"To several of the small villages bordering Vasquez's land. We need some more information about the layout of the house, where Peter's room is situated in relationship to the rest of the family and the servants' quarters. There's one woman in particular I have in mind who might give us some useful tips."

"What about sleeping arrangements?" Laura asked. In her excitement she had forgotten to consider the intimacy of living in close quarters. "How many beds are in the camper?"

Gabe's brows shot up in amusement. "Two small ones or one big one," he said. "You can have your pick."

"And where are you going to sleep?"

"In this weather? Outside." He put the glass on the table and reached for her hand, caressing the soft skin of her palm with his thumb. "Laura, you have nothing to fear from me. I want to make love with you, but only if you want it as much as I. The choice is yours. Tonight, or any other night."

A strange ache spread through her body. Ignoring it, she said softly, "It wouldn't be very wise to become involved."

"Wise? No." But inevitable, Gabe thought. He knew what could happen when excitement and danger became part of the situation. He had seen it happen time and again, even without the chemistry sparking between them. "Denying desire won't make it disappear. I think we both would enjoy sharing a sleeping bag. As long as we both know the rules."

The rules of the game were never to become emotionally involved. To enjoy sex, but not to dream. To let a man touch your skin but not your heart. How often had she listened to such advice from well-meaning friends? She had always known that such games were not for her.

Her heart contracted with angry pain. She realized that already she had begun to dream. "Thanks for the warning," she said coolly.

With relief she turned toward the waiter approaching their table with two big platters of shrimp decorated with pineapple, orange slices and wedges of lime. She withdrew her hand and reached for her napkin.

The moment he had issued his warning, Gabe had wanted to retract it. Even to his own ears it sounded cold-blooded and cruel. Silently he cursed the waiter's timing. The warning had been more for himself than for Laura. Laura was like a sleeping princess awakening from a nightmare, new to love and very vulnerable. If she came to him, he would only hurt her. He could only give her a few days, and she was a woman who deserved a lifetime of love.

By the time the waiter had finished placing the plates in front of them, the moment for words had passed. Perhaps, Gabe thought grimly, it was better this way. But he felt no satisfaction, only a vague emptiness.

Despite her anger, Laura could not resist the tempting aroma of butter-and-garlic-broiled shrimp. They were sweeter, crisper and juicier than any she'd ever eaten. "These must have been caught today," she said after her third bite. She reached for her napkin to catch a drop of butter running down her chin. Lifting her head, she saw Gabe watching her with a smile.

"Want me to find out?" he asked.

The warmth of his smile soothed her pain. "No," she said, spearing another shrimp with her fork. "Whose clothes did you give me earlier?"

He hesitated briefly, then said roughly, "I bought them for Gino."

"Gino? The nephew who is raising goats?"

"No." His voice was as hard and grim as his eyes. The carefree boy who had played with those goats did not exist anymore. "The one who is spending his youth in a Mexican prison, sentenced to ten years on trumped-up charges of drug smuggling."

"The same one Julio framed?" she whispered, her eyes wide with shock. A few years back there had been a series of articles about Americans in Mexican prisons. The newspapers had been full of accounts of their abuse and the extortions bankrupting the families who were trying to keep them alive.

"He witnessed Vasquez roughing up a woman, and interfered."

Laura saw his hand clench around the fork and wished she had waited with her questions until the meal was over. "I'm sorry," she whispered. "I wonder how you can stand even the sight of me."

Gabe dismissed those words with a shake of his head. "You have nothing to do with it. The guilt is mine, because I raised Gino to be a man. He should have turned away like the rest of the crowd."

"You don't mean that." Quietly protesting, Laura reached across the table and covered his fist, remembering Gabe dropping from the ledge, shielding her with his powerful body. "You did the same thing for me. You interfered. And if the men hadn't backed off, you would have fought."

Laying down the fork, he curled his fingers around hers and drew them to his lips. "You were worth it," he said with quiet bitterness, "this woman wasn't. I found out that she makes her living pressing young, innocent kids into the hellholes of drugs and prostitution."

"That was for Gino to decide," Laura said softly. "How are you getting him out of prison?" As far as she knew, only one American had ever managed to break out of a Mexican prison. But she doubted that breaching the walls was what Gabe had in mind. The risk of injury would be too high. Hadn't he mentioned a business deal?

Gabe shook his head firmly. "It's safer for you not to know," he said quietly. "Let's eat before everything gets cold."

When Laura didn't pick up her fork, he speared one of his shrimp and fed it to her. "Three square meals a day," he reminded her gently.

"Are you going to feed me every one of them?" With a ghost of a smile, Laura began eating, but her enjoyment was gone. The shrimp suddenly tasted like straw.

"If you want me to," Gabe said simply, spearing another and holding it to her lips.

Laura took it between her teeth, remembering the last time she had been fed. "Peter used to have me lick his ice cream," she said, memories of shared laughter haunting her. She swallowed and added quietly, "Sometimes I have nightmares that I will fail, that Peter might grow up to become the image of his father. I have to get him away from the hacienda." She looked at Gabe with eyes that were dark with desperation and fear. "Have you any idea how—"

Gabe's eyes darkened with suppressed anger. "We'll get him out of there," he promised her harshly.

"Won't helping me jeopardize your own plans?" Laura asked quietly.

Gabe's face tightened ruthlessly. "Nothing is going to interfere with Gino's freedom," he said grimly. He hoped he wouldn't have to make a choice of whom to rescue and whom to leave behind. He remembered another time and another decision. He had brought ten men out of the jungle alive and left one to die. He had gone back, but by then it had been too late. Rationally he knew that the man would have died of his wounds long before they reached camp. But the man had been his responsibility and Gabe had failed him. He was not going to fail again.

"How difficult can it be to abduct one little boy from the hacienda?" he said lightly.

More difficult than getting into a prison, Laura thought, fear almost choking her. High canyon walls, helicopters, an army of loyal servants and desert and mountain ranges offered more obstacles than any prison wall. Desperation roughened her voice as she said, "There has to be another way to get to Peter. He must leave the ranch sometimes."

Her despair tore at him. Gabe wanted to take her into his arms and reassure her. "Yes," he agreed gently, knowing that it would be easier to enter the hacienda in the dead of night than to abduct Peter on an open street. "We'll talk about it later," he said, turning back to his food.

With a grimace, Laura picked up her fork and speared another shrimp, not because she still was hungry but because food was fuel.

"How come you raised Gino? What happened to his parents?" she asked when only pineapple and orange peel remained on her plate.

"His father died when he was ten. My sister Irene, his mother, remarried a year later. Gino didn't get along with her new husband. He's been living with me since he became a teenager."

"So your sister gave him up to you?" she asked, her eyes wide and haunted.

Gabe scowled, remembering the nights he had spent searching for the lost angry boy whose life had fallen apart. A new father he did not care for, friends he had to leave, a city instead of the wide open spaces that were as much a part of him as they were of Gabe. "His father was my foreman. Gino grew up on the ranch. When my sister moved to Dallas, he couldn't breathe."

"So he was better off with you," Laura said.

"He used to say so."

Laura shook her head. Like many strong men, Gabe blamed himself for the actions of others. Laura wished she could help cleanse him of his bitterness. But she knew that nothing she did or said could diminish his guilt and anger. Strong men also walked alone.

For the rest of the meal they made light conversation, touching none of the subjects that moved them most. "Do you like your work?" Gabe asked. "Somehow I can't see you buried in an office."

"It's a constant challenge and rarely boring." Laura raised the cup of coffee to her lips, wondering at his perceptiveness. "But you're right. There are times when the walls close in on me. That's when I get on a plane and fly to Ireland. My uncle Sean raises thoroughbreds. When I'm there, I help around the stables." She wrinkled her nose. "After a month of mucking out stalls, I'm usually ready to return to New York."

"So that's where you got your knowledge of horses."

Nodding, Laura went on, "As a young girl I dreamed of riding in steeplechases and cross-country races. But my mother wouldn't hear of it. Too dangerous, she said. That's one of the drawbacks of being an only child."

Gabe nodded thoughtfully. Until now he'd had difficulty understanding how she could show such courage and determination and yet had waited a year to come into Mexico. But her words helped explain some of the discrepancies in Laura's behavior. Since childhood, her mother's fear had instilled extensive caution in her, quenching her spirit. As a surrogate father, he could understand her mother's view. He had often refused to let Gino ride the range alone. But too much caution was damaging to a child's development. It had taken her son's abduction to rekindle the innate spirit in Laura.

The waiter appeared at their side, handing Gabe the check. "Want to walk on the beach for a while or go straight back to the hotel?" Gabe asked after paying it.

"Walk."

Leaving the restaurant, they turned to the beach. When they reached the sand, Gabe steadied Laura while she took off her sneakers.

Barefoot, she waited for him to do the same.

Taking her shoes, he grinned. "I'm wearing boots."

"Don't tell me Texans also swim in them," Laura said mockingly, running down to the water's edge.

Gabe watched her, a slim figure dancing in the moonlight, rolling her jeans up to her knees and balancing in the waves. She was beautiful, soft and warm. He wanted her. More than he had ever wanted a woman. Slowly he followed her to the water's edge.

"Take your boots off and join me, Gabe," she called softly. "The water is absolutely beautiful."

"You know what happens when Texans take their boots off?"

She turned her laughing face toward him, the water gently lapping around her calves. Something in his voice stilled her laughter. Deep, like a sensuous caress, it floated through the night. Desire shot through her, hot and piercing, stunning her with its sudden force. She had never known what it meant to want a man. Not like this, with this mixture of tenderness and heat. It was a heady sensation that left her rooted in the sea, the warm water gently swirling around her.

She watched him come to the water's edge, dropping her sneakers in the sand. He walked softly, his hard face softened by pale moonlight. The pounding of her heart merged with the lapping sound of the waves. "They wash their feet," she taunted him, waiting.

Gabe's laughter was a low growl. She looked as alluring as a mermaid. He reached for her swiftly, touching her shirt. At the last moment Laura twisted, barely evading his grasp.

She faced him with several feet of water between them. At the taut look of desire tightening his face, her laughter stilled. She swayed, took two steps forward and then stopped.

She moved warily, her head tilted as if she were testing him and herself. The fierce power of her attraction drew her to him. With each breath, with each retreating wave, reason flowed out to sea, erosive, stripping her of excuses and pretenses.

She wanted Gabe with a deep, aching need that left no room for caution. Today he had saved her and shielded her with his strength. Tonight she wanted to become a woman in his arms.

Silently Gabe held out his hand, willing her to come to him. Trust me, he said silently. Let me show you and give you pleasure.

As if drawn by that silent voice, Laura moved until she stood just outside his reach. She stared at the tall quiet man who had come to mean so much to her. "There's something you ought to know about me," she said, her voice hoarse. "I'm not very good at sticking to rules."

Gabe reached for her. "It doesn't matter," he said roughly, brushing her lips with fire. The rules of this game had been set a long time ago. Within a week at the most, two thousand miles and two worlds as different from each other as drought and rain would separate them. One week, he promised himself, drawing her closer.

She curved into him with a trust that caught his breath in his throat. Wisps of dark hair, curling in the damp salt air, framed her face. Slowly he reached for her curls, watching them run in shimmering waves through his hands. Gently he tilted her head up. Then he lost himself in the softness of her mouth.

His lips were as warm and gentle as moonlight. Laura sighed his name and let her hands slide up his arms. His hair felt rough beneath her fingertips. The clean smell of shaving cream and male scents mingled with the night air, surrounding her.

Slowly she answered his kiss, her lips opening, her tongue tempting. She pressed herself against his hard body while her hands slid to his neck, drawing his head closer. I'll take it one day at a time, she thought. How many days did they have? How many nights? Never enough, she thought, shivering, offering more of her lips.

Gabe made a sound of pleasure in his throat. He felt as if he could not hold her close enough and kiss her deeply enough. Wild passion ran through him, threatening to break free.

With an effort that left him shaking, Gabe raised his head. His hands trembled as he tried to restrain himself. "Don't trust me too much," he warned her huskily, staring down at her luminous eyes, her soft lips swollen with his kiss. "Your sweet passion could tempt a saint. I'm only a man."

Laura turned her face into his hand, kissing his rough palm. "I want to tempt you, Gabe, not a saint," she said with devastating frankness. She saw him frown at her words. "I want you to show me how beautiful love between a man and woman can be. That's all I'm asking of you. I'm not asking for promises you can't keep, just sweet memories instead of nightmares." And dreams, she thought, to keep her warm during the lifetime of lonely nights to follow.

Laura knew the price she would have to pay. The years ahead stretched endlessly. For one panicked moment she wondered if the asking price was not too high, if dreams would carry her through the nights. Then she remembered the last years, years filled with nightmares and fears, and swayed against Gabe.

Gabe wrapped his arms around her. Bending his head, he kissed her with tenderness. Somewhere in the back of his mind, a voice warned him that Laura was different from any of the other women he had made love to over the years, that he would not be able to wash off her memory with a shower and a change of clothes. Within the space of a few hours, she had slipped through his defenses. But his hunger was greater than the voice warning him.

"Let's go back to the hotel," he murmured against her lips, running his hands through her silky hair. Her lips parted in a helpless acquiescence that he welcomed with a deep sound of need. His tongue caressed the softness of her mouth, drinking of her sweet response until desire ripped through his powerful body in strong, hungry waves, eroding his restraint.

He groaned, his arms tightening around her slim body in an effort to gain control. "Tell me to stop, Laura, or I'll take you here on the beach."

Slowly her eyes opened. "I want you, Gabe," she whispered, her breath caressing him with warm mist.

Gabe gasped at the complete trust, the all-consuming need tightening her face. Too much trust, he thought, too much emotion. Too soon for her, and too late for himself. If he had been younger he might have braved the flash flood of longing without a thought to survival. But he was wiser now, older and infinitely more experienced. Flash floods killed. They left only destruction in their wake. Gabe had learned the art of survival a lifetime ago.

He held her in his arms, his mouth buried in her hair, waiting for the waves of desire to wash ashore. When she leaned against him, he guided her toward the parking lot. With one arm securely settled across her back, he picked up the sneakers at his feet. They passed lovers seeking solitude, parents taking their children for a last stroll before bedtime and teenagers holding hands.

They didn't talk on the long, leisurely walk. Laura was grateful for the soothing darkness and the easy silence between them. She should have felt embarrassed. She had just propositioned a virtual stranger, a man she had known less than twenty-four hours. But she did not feel any shame at her lack of control, only gratitude for Gabe's hold on sanity.

Any other man would have been shocked, delighted or crude. Gabe had understood her desire as he accepted all natural forces. There was no room for embarrassment in nature's cycle.

On the drive back to Acapulco Laura noticed that Gabe checked his rearview mirrors constantly to make sure that no one followed them. Laura breathed a sigh of relief when they reached their hotel without incident.

Opening the door to their room, Gabe searched it swiftly. Only when he knew that no one had disturbed its privacy did he allow Laura to join him.

"Just a precaution," he said when she looked at him questioningly. "Never underestimate Vasquez. He's not stupid."

Julio was a brute and a coward, but he wasn't a fool. "You think he's looking for me here?" she asked soberly.

"When you don't turn up at the bungalow, he's going to turn this town inside out."

"Do you want us to leave tonight?" she asked, fear roughening her voice.

Instinct told Gabe that it might be best to leave the hotel this night. But after five days out in the field, supplies in his camper were running low. All he had left was a bag of stale rolls and less than a half a tank of water. At this time of night, supermarkets and bakeries were closed.

However, it wasn't the lack of supplies that decided him against leaving in the middle of the night. Gabe almost relished the idea of finally confronting his enemy. He had waited for months, stalking his prey, planning and watching but never getting close enough to the man to bloody his nose. Gabe wanted this confrontation with Vasquez almost as much as he wanted Gino's freedom.

Laura had given him the perfect opportunity to do so without endangering his plans. Vasquez would be burning with jealousy and impotent fury but unable to do anything about it. Even Julio Vasquez would shrink from the public scandal a brawl in a well-known hotel mostly filled with American tourists would cause.

"We'll leave in the morning," Gabe said firmly, watching Laura with narrowed eyes. The brief flash of fear crossing her face almost, but not quite, changed his mind.

Gabe knew that Laura needed to confront Vasquez as much as he did, perhaps even more so. For years her life had been ruled by the fear he had instilled in her. Her nightmares had turned the playboy into a monster, omnipotent and indestructible. Vasquez was nothing but a poor apology of a man, cruel and weak. Laura had more courage in her little finger than the man did in his entire body. Only when she realized that fact would she be free of him.

Laura watched the ruthless expression on Gabe's face. "You want him to find us," she said, her voice low and tight. Fear was freezing her blood, and numbness fogged her brain. Even with Gabe at her side, the thought of facing Julio was choking her.

"I'm not going to post a sign to lead him here," Gabe said evenly, watching her closely, his body tensing. Like a cornered animal fighting for survival, she was poised, ready to run. "But yes, I almost wish he would find us here," he continued in that same emotionless, matter-of-fact voice. "I promise you, he won't get close enough to lay a finger on you."

"And how are you going to prevent that?" Laura snapped. "You know as well as I do that he's not going to come alone. I won't wait around to find out what's going to happen.'' She whirled around and flew to the door.

Gabe was right behind her. With both arms pushing against the door on either side of her, he caged her loosely but securely. ''How much longer are you going to let him control your life?'' he asked softly.

''I control my own life,'' she protested weakly. With Gabe's arms around her, she felt secure. But beyond the broad shoulders darkness lurked, watching, waiting.

''Rot,'' Gabe said firmly. ''He's manipulated you through fear, like a puppet dancing by remote control.'' He could feel her body trembling. Gabe wanted to cradle her against him and promise her that she would never have to confront Vasquez again. But creating a temporary illusion of false security was dangerous and irresponsible.

Gently his thumbs stroked her cheeks. ''You will have to face him sometime. If not now, then later, in New York, Ireland or anywhere else you run. Because he's going to follow you, waiting for you to panic. And the more you panic, the less careful you'll become. If you want to keep Peter with you, you have to see the man as he is: weak, sly and cowardly.''

He bent his head and softly kissed her lips. ''You are a brave and courageous woman, and a match for him any day. But words cannot reassure you. Only facing him will give you confidence.'' Gently his breath fanned across her cheeks. ''I want to see his face when you tell him to go to hell.''

The first glimmer of a smile lurked in her eyes. ''You make it sound so simple. You're good for me, Gabe.''

With a groan he drew her closer and captured her mouth. His lips were warm and tender, sliding like sunshine over her flesh, dispersing the dark clouds.

Beneath the firm strokes of his hands, her body became pliant. She sighed while her hands moved searchingly over the material of his shirt, seeking his warm flesh, raking the golden curls.

Gabe shuddered beneath the assault of her fingertips. He fought for control. ''Still want to leave?'' he whispered, the heat of his breath fanning her face. "If you do, we have to stop now."

Surprised, Laura stared at him, the tantalizing movements of her hands stilling. With a mixture of exasperation and amusement, she shook her head. He had done it again, handing her the freedom of choice. Time after time he forced her to examine her fears, then retreated to await her decision.

"You're not playing fair," she protested huskily. "Right now, with your arms wrapped around me, I can think only of reasons to stay."

"Then follow your instincts," he drawled softly, caressing her face with eyes that glowed with desire and need.

Laura felt herself respond to his need. She forgot about choices and instincts and gave in to the irresistible forces drawing her to him. Her hands slid from his chest and drew his head down. She moved her lips and tongue across his lips, instinctively seeking the points of greatest pleasure.

Gabe's arms tightened around her, understanding more than she did about the gift of trust she had just handed to him. He could feel fine tremors of desire running through her, a desire stronger than her fear of Vasquez. Slowly his kiss deepened, his need held tightly in check.

Laura felt his body shift, the tension of his restraint rippling through his body. Never in her life had she felt so wanted and so desirable. A strange sense of power surged through her, heady and intoxicating, obliterating any latent traces of caution.

Finally, unable to stand the pressure building inside him any longer, Gabe raised his head. With a strong, powerful surge he lifted her and crossed to the bed. He sat down, drawing her inside his spread knees. "Sure you won't change your mind?" he asked in his deep voice.

Laura's hands went to the belt cinching her waist, unbuckling it, letting her action answer his question. "The only thing I'm sure about is wanting to make love with you," she said unsteadily while her hands fumbled with the buttons of her shirt.

Desire ripped through him, breaking free of iron restraint. His hands covered hers, swiftly dealing with the remaining buttons. With infinite gentleness he eased the material off her shoulders and down her arms until it fell in a pool around her feet. "I'm glad," he groaned, pressing his lips against her breast, the soft creamy skin shimmering like white satin through the filmy lace. "I don't think I could let you go now."

His tongue teased her for a moment before drawing her inside the moist heat of his mouth. Laura shivered under the unexpected sensation, swaying with the sudden hot need. When his teeth gently nipped at her, she arched closer with a low cry of pleasure.

The gesture was so innocently provocative that Gabe felt the last of his control slipping. She was so utterly beautiful, and so damn vulnerable. His conscience told him to go slow, to ease her gently into passion. To let her set the pace.

"Easy, darlin'." He reached for the front clasp with slow movements. "We've all the time in the world to love."

Laura stared at him, her eyes dark with desire. She watched the hands ease the straps down her shoulders, shuddering at his touch. "Easy?" she gasped, shivering at his touch. She was burning with fire, shaking with unfulfilled longings. "Oh Gabe, I don't think I can. I want all of you. Please don't hold back."

It took all of Gabe's restraint to ease her away from him. He had no intention of holding back. He couldn't, even had he wanted to. She was like a fire in his blood, hot and threatening to break free. He wanted to slide into her softness now, fully clothed and still in his boots.

"I won't hold back," he promised her unsteadily. "But I don't want to hurt you either." Capturing her hands, he drew them against his chest. "Undress me," he said, smiling tautly. "I refuse to make love to you with my boots on."

"So Texans do take them off," Laura said with a laugh. Her fingers were shaking as she reached for the buttons of his shirt.

"This Texan does." He wondered how much he could stand of the slow torture her hands inflicted while she fumbled with the buttons.

He couldn't remember the last time he had felt such an all-consuming need. Even in his youth he'd been able to keep a part of himself separate. He'd shied away from total involvement, because he'd always known that the price he'd have to pay for such folly would be too high. He valued his contentment too much to risk losing it.

Abruptly his hand closed over Laura's fingers, stilling the movement as she tried to unbuckle his belt. Stop her now, he told himself. Stop her or you'll regret it for the rest of your life. If you don't walk away from this woman, you'll spend the next forty years craving the impossible. A lifetime of wanting and aching. And unfulfilled dreams.

His hands reached for her small waist, lifting her to her feet. Dimly he heard the small cry of surprised protest. Against his will, his mouth closed over her lips, stifling her cry and silencing the voices of caution.

Gently he laid her on the bed, sliding out of his boots and dropping the rest of his clothes with a few swift motions. He knew he had passed the point of no return. Even if he left her now the picture of her pale beauty, covered with nothing but her cloud of dark hair, would haunt him forever.

"God, you're beautiful," he breathed, sitting down on the side of the bed.

Laura barely heard the words. Her eyes slid over his powerful shoulders, the broad sculptured chest, following the line of golden curls down his flat stomach and slim hips. Her hands reached for him, the desire to let her hands run over his masculine perfection making her tremble.

"Can I touch you?" she asked, her voice husky and low, drawing him down to her.

"I want you to," Gabe growled, covering her mouth in a kiss hard with repressed desire. The eager warmth of her mouth invited him while her hands stroked his shoulders, moving against his skin in a sensual caress. Before the kiss ended, Gabe knew that he couldn't wait much longer to savor all of her warmth. He covered her smoothly with his weight.

His heat and hardness sent shivers of desire down her spine. Shaking her head from side to side, Laura tried to relieve some of the pressure building up inside her. "Wait," she groaned. She wanted to touch him, before it was too late, before he rolled away in the aftermath of passion.

"I don't think I can," Gabe breathed against her mouth. "Don't fight me, darlin'. Don't be afraid of me."

"I'm not afraid of you," Laura protested fiercely. "I've never wanted . . . this as much. But I need touching you more."

Hearing the distress in her voice, Gabe raised his head. "I don't think I understand. Tell me what you want."

"I want to touch you, explore you with my hands. If we make love now . . . later, you won't want me to."

Understanding tightened Gabe's face with disgust. "Are you afraid I won't want you to once it's over?" he asked her gently. When she nodded, he shook his head, silently cursing the man who had hurt her so. Abruptly he rolled away from her, folding his hands behind his head. "Then touch me," he gritted against clenched teeth, praying he had the strength to withstand the torture.

And torture it was feeling her fingers slide over him, stimulating his already heated flesh almost past endurance. He caught his breath, holding it, while she caressed every part of him.

Her face taut with intensity, she traced the strong column of his throat, wondering at the small cavity formed by his shoulder muscles and clavicles. She marveled at the clean lines of his chest. His nipples responded like her own when she caressed the dark brown aureoles. "Are they as sensitive as a woman's?" she asked huskily, gently teasing them into hard brown knobs.

"Yes," he gasped between clenched teeth, while he watched her kneeling by his side, the silky cloud of dark hair falling wildly around her.

Her gentle exploration continued, down his stomach, tracing the line of hair until it fanned out. A groan broke from his tight lips. Reaching for her, he shifted suddenly until she lay beneath him.

He had enough restraint left to enter her slowly, waiting until she relaxed enough to take his hardness and heat into her. Then he took possession of every soft part of her in an ever-swelling rhythm, their bodies riding the cresting waves of mutual need and absolute pleasure. When the wave broke, a cry tore from Laura's throat. Gabe gathered her to him, holding her tightly while she fell apart in his arms.

Later, when her body stopped trembling and her breathing returned to normal, Laura rolled over. With soft, tender strokes she brushed his damp hair off his forehead. Wonder slowly brightened her deep blue eyes. "I feel...new and free," she whispered raggedly. "I can't explain."

"You don't have to," he said, his lips curving with tenderness. Reaching for her, he positioned her head in the crook of his neck. Rhythmically he stroked the mane of midnight-black hair flowing over him.

Chapter 6

Gray early-morning light filtered through the window. Laura blinked, groaned in silent dismay and turned her face into the pillow. She had at least one more hour before she had to face another day. Drowsily she tried to think of any pressing appointments in her schedule, but could not remember a single one. Nothing important, she thought contentedly, stretching her legs. The movement brought another groan to her lips.

She hadn't felt this sore since her first aerobics class. Cautiously she tested the other parts of her body. Her arms were aching. When she moved her shoulders, she felt twinges of shooting pain. How many classes had she taken last night? Two or three?

Her memory worked as lethargically as her muscles. It took a few seconds more to remember yesterday, to realize that this was not New York but Acapulco, that this was not her bed but Gabe's.

Abruptly she turned her head, ignoring the aches. Her eyes only confirmed what her senses had told her already. She was alone in the bed. She was alone in the room. Her eyes widened in alarm.

Where was Gabe?

Wide awake now, she sat up and looked around. The room was silent with emptiness. Her clothes were folded over the back of a chair. Gabe's things were gone. Everything looked neat—except for the bed. Its rumpled state was a potent reminder of the hours they had spent making love.

Sensations rushed through her body: heat, a feeling of lassitude and a longing for Gabe's arms around her. Laura wanted to curl up and close her eyes and relive the most beautifully fulfilling experience of her life. But the silent emptiness surrounding her was naggingly persistent. She slid off the bed and went into the bathroom. Fresh water drops on the sink showed that Gabe had washed and shaved. Laura reached for a washcloth and wet her face and neck with cold water. Dabbing her face dry, she looked into the mirror.

Her face glowed, a result of too much sun, cold water and Gabe's golden stubble chafing her face. Her lips were fuller, pulsing with life. Her body tingled with new sensuous awareness. Despite her muscle aches, she had never felt stronger, more alive, more utterly complete. She knew she was falling in love with Gabe.

Swiftly she drew the comb through the tangled mess Gabe's hands had created until it fell in a long silky curtain down her back. With a look of indecision she returned to the bedroom and reached for Gino's clothes, wishing for her own things. Perhaps Gabe had gone to the bungalow to get her suitcases. She looked for the key she had left on the nightstand. It was gone.

Her hands clenched in sudden apprehension. What if Julio was still waiting in her room and Gabe had been caught in his trap? With shaking hands, she reached for her clothes.

And then she heard the knock on the door.

She sagged with relief for a moment. Recovering, she ran to the door. "You should have awakened me," she said. "I was—"

Abruptly she stopped, staring at the violently twisting and turning knob. Gabe must have locked the door on his way out. Her breath caught in her throat when she realized that he would have the key, which meant that the person who was trying to get inside certainly was not him.

Clutching her robe tightly, she stared at the shaking door. In terrified fascination she heard the wood groan as someone rammed against it. She ran to the phone to call for help. Before she could reach it, the door burst open. Laura stifled the scream rising to her lips as Juan and Jorge catapulted into the room and stormed past her. All blood rushing from her face, she faced the man who had haunted her nights and clouded her days for years. Julio.

Frozen with horror, Laura stared at the father of her son. His white shirt was sweat-stained, his black pants creased and his usually highly polished shoes covered with dust.

He had changed in the five years since she had left him. Streaks of silver winged his temples. The clear, aristocratic lines of his face had softened and blurred. At one time, his mouth had been fixed in shallow smiles. Now it was caught in a permanent sneer. The blue shadow of his beard emphasized the sallow and dissipated shade of his skin. Red-rimmed by lack of sleep, his eyes stared at her with a mixture of triumph and hate. But her fears were not for herself but for Gabe.

Where was he? Had Julio hurt him?

Behind her, Laura could hear Julio's men searching the room. Then Jorge muttered, "He's not here."

The words penetrated the fog of fear. Laura lowered her lashes to hide the flash of relief brightening her eyes. Unwittingly Julio had weakened his position. The knowledge that Gabe was free and safe infused her with confidence and strength. She considered knocking into Julio, taking him by surprise. Once in the hall she could scream.

Then she heard the slight tapping Julio made on the floor. At the sign of his nervousness, Laura raised her head.

"Hello, Julio," Laura said, facing him with outward calm. "You're up early."

Her quiet words obviously startled him. Black eyes narrowed, he stared at her. "I waited for you in your room last night."

"Were you worried when I didn't turn up?" Laura asked, a sharp edge to her voice. "Is that why you've come looking for me here?"

A furious flush crept into his face. *"Puta,"* he spat, raking her body, clad in Gabe's robe, with contempt. Looking past her to the bed, his lips tightened angrily.

Laura's body stiffened at the insult, but her face showed none of the anger she felt at being labeled a whore. "Name calling?" she asked softly, raising one brow with a slow smile. "Really, Julio. Even Peter is past that stage. Or was, before you kidnapped him. How is my son?"

Black brows drawn, Julio stared at her. "You've changed, Laura," he said, his expression telling her that he was not pleased with the difference in her behavior.

"How? Because I don't cringe and cower before you?" Laura said, her voice hard and cold. "You don't frighten me any longer. The day you kidnapped Peter, you set me free." She realized suddenly that those words were not sheer bravado but the simple truth. He had done everything a man could do to a woman. He had beaten her. He had forced her. He had taken her child. But somehow she had survived each ordeal.

She was still afraid of the pain he might inflict. And the thought that she might never see her son again terrified her. But the omnipotent image of him that had paralyzed her for years had disappeared. Julio was only a man, and a weak one at that.

With an ugly twist to his mouth, Julio stepped closer, kicking the door shut with his foot. "Then it's time to teach you differently." He grasped her shoulders. His lean fingers bit into her flesh. "You made one big mistake, Laura," he jeered, drawing her closer. "You should never have come to Mexico. Here the law is on my side. No one is going to interfere if I teach you a lesson for trying to take my son away from me." With calculated cruelty he grasped her chin, forcing her face up to his.

Laura's stomach lurched with sudden fear. The breath fanning her skin made nausea well up in her. From behind her, the two ranch hands encouraged Julio with vile suggestions. The words made her cringe—and become furious.

Abruptly she raised one hand and slapped Julio's face as hard as she could. Taken by surprise, he slackened his grip. With a twist and a turn, Laura spun away from him. "Has the great lover lost his touch? Is beating the only way a woman will come to you?" she said, her voice filled with biting contempt.

Julio's eyes flashed with rage. Raising his hand, he stepped toward her. For an instant Laura thought he would retaliate. Instead he smiled nastily, fingering the welts appearing on his skin. "Hold her," he said to his henchmen.

This time Laura could not hide the sudden flash of fear darkening her eyes. He noted it with a satisfied smirk. "Not so cool after all," he jeered.

"Coward," Laura spat at him. She felt herself grabbed from behind, her arms bent and twisted upward. With a groan she leaned forward to ease the pain, jerking back immediately when she noticed the lapels of her robe gaping open.

Grinning cruelly, Julio slipped his hand into the opening of her robe, letting it rest possessively on her flesh.

Fury shot through her. Her head shot forward, her teeth striking his wrist. Cursing in Spanish, her tormentor grabbed a handful of her hair and jerked her head back until she cried out with pain and released his arm.

"You bloodthirsty little bitch," Julio swore, staring at the red imprints of her teeth. "You'll pay for that."

"*Señor*, we have to get out of here," Jorge muttered in Spanish. "Let's take the woman and question her later."

Julio's eyes narrowed thoughtfully. "Would you like to see your son, Laura?" he asked, his eyes running down the long slim line of her throat. "I'd like to tame the aggressive slut you've become."

Laura swallowed to dislodge the lump of fear choking her. Where was Gabe? For one panic-stricken moment she wondered if he had deserted her. No, she had to believe that Gabe would return. If only she could delay them, Gabe might arrive in time to stop Julio from abducting her. "It takes a man to do that, not a cruel boy,'' she spat at him defiantly.

"Like that gringo you've been sleeping with?'' Julio sneered. "Seems he wasn't man enough for you. Scared him off, didn't you?'' he jeered. "Who is he?''

Tears of agony filling her eyes, Laura stared at him. "I don't know,'' she gasped, panic welling up in her. "I met him on the flight from New York.''

"And he offered to go with you to the hacienda yesterday,'' Julio snarled, clearly doubting her.

"Yes,'' Laura whispered hoarsely.

"Then why wasn't he in the Jeep when my men spotted you?''

"Because he—'' She cried out as Julio tightened his grip. She stared past him, trying to blot out his cruel face.

Suddenly she thought that the door opened slightly. She twisted abruptly, kicking out at Julio, drawing the men's attention to her and away from the door. She saw Gabe rush into the room, throwing one arm across Julio's throat, jerking him backwards. With a startled cry Julio released her to claw at the arm choking him.

"I left the Jeep to have a look around.'' Gabe finished the sentence for her, his voice hard and cold, more terrifying in its quietness than Julio's loudmouthed threats. Dressed in khaki, he loomed above Julio. His eyes were like flaming coals.

"Let her go,'' Gabe said with deadly calm, his arm tightening pointedly over the windpipe, waiting for Jorge and Juan to drop her arms. When they hesitated, a knife flashed in his hand. Placing it on the bared throat, he said with a softness that caused shivers on Laura's skin, "Take your hands off her.''

Abruptly the men loosened their hold. Wrenching her arms forward, Laura stepped aside.

"Are you all right?'' Gabe asked her, hot eyes running over her for any sign of injury.

"Fine. Only a little shaken,'' she said, rubbing the tender skin of her wrists, already bright red from the tight grip.

After one more penetrating look, Gabe shifted his attention back to the men. "Against the wall, amigos," he ordered harshly. "Hands up, legs spread." With a nod of his head, he reinforced his order. Swearing, the men followed it.

Julio ranted at them. "Cowards," he whispered. "It's only one gringo."

"Es un gringo muy macho," Jorge muttered pointedly. "And he has a knife at your throat, *señor*. We get him later, *Patron*, and the woman, too."

"You lay another hand on my woman and I'll kill you," Gabe warned with deadly calm. "Laura, take the rope from the right-hand drawer and tie their hands behind their backs."

The rope was sturdy, new and stiff. Laura hissed with exasperation as the knots slipped time and time again from her shaking hands. But finally the bonds were tight and firm. To test their strength, she tugged at them with all her weight, then turned to Gabe for confirmation. "Good enough?"

His eyes smiled approvingly at her. "Turn around and sit down," he ordered. The men obeyed instantly, shuffling awkwardly. With their bound hands facing the wall, they stared at Laura with hate-filled eyes. This was the second time the ranch hands had retreated without a fight, the second time Gabe had humiliated them. The next time, their eyes seemed to warn, they would get even. Laura felt her skin prickle with apprehension. How much longer before her luck ran out?

"Laura, go into the bathroom and get dressed," Gabe said, his voice firm yet soothing, as if he understood her fears.

Flashing him a grateful look, Laura swiftly gathered her clothes and went into the bathroom. Once behind closed doors, she leaned weakly against the cool wall. Reaction was setting in. Her body trembled, her teeth chattering. She couldn't understand a word that was being said in the other room. All she could hear was Gabe's voice, cold and low. Laura clenched her teeth and started dressing.

She was standing in front of the mirror running her fingers through her hair when Gabe came in. "I'm sorry," he murmured. "I shouldn't have left you this morning."

"Why did you?" she asked, searching his eyes in the mirror. "When you weren't beside me, I was worried."

"I went to the bungalow and packed your things. Then I filled up the tank of the truck. The hotel water is clean. You won't get Montezuma's revenge drinking it."

"You might have left a note," Laura pointed out softly.

"I planned to be back before you woke up. You were dead to the world when I left. I know I wanted you to face the bastard. But not alone. Someone must have recognized us and tipped Vasquez off."

"You were there when it counted," she said firmly. "You were right about the confrontation. I was scared, but I didn't freeze with fear." She did not know when the change had occurred. Her perceptions had altered so gradually that she had not been aware of the change. Until yesterday. She had finally met a man with real strength—a man who did not need to rely on the power diplomatic immunity and family wealth provided.

"What are we going to do now?" she asked. For the first time it occurred to her what holding Julio prisoner might mean for both Gabe and herself.

The possibilities were promising. "Can we keep the men here and demand Peter and Gino's freedom in exchange?" she asked, excitement flushing her face.

A sparkle of amusement gleamed in Gabe's eyes. "You've seen too many movies," he teased her softly. Sobering, he said, "In real life, taking hostages is a tricky business where both sides can lose. Even if the kidnappers are willing to sacrifice everything, even their own lives, to gain their ends, they can't always depend on the other side to yield or to be less brutal in their efforts to bend the hostage-takers to their will. What are you going to do, for example, if the police rough up Gino or your son outside this door?"

Laura shook her head, biting her lip. "Surely the police wouldn't do that?"

Gabe laughed harshly. "Laura, this is a country where the magazines are censored and sold with pages missing."

"You want to let them go," Laura said in a flat voice.

"I think it's best. If Vasquez turns up missing, we risk having both the police and the military on our heels. If it had been only him, we might've been able to hide him somewhere. But not the three of them."

Laura shook her head in frustration. She could see why Gabe was reluctant to hold the men hostage. But for the first time in all these years, Julio was no threat to her. The decision to release him, to give up this sudden advantage, was not easy.

She stared at him shrewdly. "And taking hostages doesn't fit into your plans. Isn't it about time you told me about them?"

Gabe hesitated briefly. If Laura found out about Vasquez's smuggling activities, she would refuse to go along with him. "I'm blackmailing him," he said softly. "He's involved in some shady business deals, here and in the States, that he would like to keep secret."

Laura looked at him with narrowed eyes. "What kind of deals? Drugs or smuggling arms to Central America?" When Gabe hesitated, she shook her head impatiently. "Dammit, I have a right to know."

"Drugs," Gabe said reluctantly, watching her reaction closely. He felt her body tremble and saw her eyes fill with fear. Ice-cold rage coursed through his body. The desire to finish Vasquez once and for all had never been as strong as now as he watched Laura try to absorb this latest blow.

"I've been gathering evidence for months." Gabe spoke close to her ear, his voice low-pitched and even, revealing the bare essentials of his plan.

"Is it going to work?" she asked.

"Trust me," Gabe said quietly. "I want Gino's freedom as much as you want Peter back."

"All right," Laura sighed. "We'll try it your way. I trust you with my life. What did you do with them?"

Gabe kissed her briefly before answering. "I left them on the bed trussed up like chickens. The maid should find them in a few hours."

Laughter briefly lit her eyes. "I'll bet this is the first time Julio has been found in bed with two men." Then the laughter vanished. "Will we have enough time to get out of Acapulco?"

"If we leave soon," Gabe said, admiration for her resilience and courage welling up in him. "Why don't you go down to the truck." He wanted her out of Vasquez's sight and reach. "I'll finish packing, return the key and join you."

"Thanks, guardian angel," she whispered.

In the bedroom, she avoided looking at the bed and its squirming occupants. She passed by three pair of shoes kicking against the rope linking their feet. With her dirty clothes bundled under her arm, she made for the door.

Julio cursed when she opened it. "Dammit, Laura, you can't leave me here."

She stopped. Looking over her shoulder, she held back a grin. The men lay facedown, arms and legs tied and strapped to the bed.

"If you cut me loose, we'll talk about Pedro."

"There's nothing to talk about," Laura said coldly. "Peter is mine. You kidnapped him." Fury broke through her restraint. "I'll make you pay for every lonely second." She walked through the door. Outside, she looked back at Gabe with a question in her eyes.

"I'll cut him loose, if that's what you want," he offered softly, handing her the key to the truck. Quietly he waited for her to decide Julio's fate.

Laura stared up at him. Perhaps Julio would agree to let her meet her son. Could she afford to toss the chance to the winds? This might be the only opportunity to convince Julio that Peter belonged with her. Then she remembered his lies and broken promises. She knew with bitter certainty that Julio would change his song once he was free. She would gain nothing.

With a sad smile, she shook her head. "I don't trust him." She looked with aching tenderness at the man who was willing to risk his own plans to help her.

She bolted down the hall. She wanted her son, but not if it meant endangering Gabe's mission. Premonitions welled up in her, dark, painful and frightening. What if there would come a day when she had to choose between Gabe's happiness and her son's? Blindly she pushed the elevator button, praying that she would never be forced to face a situation created in hell.

As she stepped out of the elevator and into the garage, the idea still haunted her. There was little she could do. She needed Gabe's help to get her son back, but if she stayed near him her hunger for him would grow, the small flame of love would brighten. Take one step at a time, she told herself firmly. Don't worry about tomorrow.

She found the camper parked near the exit. Unlocking the rear door, she slid into the vehicle. Her suitcases stood on one of the bunks. She opened one and chose a pair of jeans, a cotton shirt and a fresh pair of sneakers to change into. Then she checked her belongings, hoping that Gabe had found the purse she had hidden beneath the mattress yesterday, which contained her passport, traveler's checks and cosmetics. He had. Smiling at Gabe's thoroughness, she reached into her makeup case for sunscreen and covered her face.

Before Gabe left the room, he gagged the three men, listening to Julio's threats in stony silence before he shut him up. He would have preferred to take them out into the desert and have them walk back to the hacienda to give them a taste of their own cruelty. But getting them out of the hotel at this time of the morning would be dangerous. "Sleep well," he said pleasantly before drawing the door closed. The lock had been broken, so he wedged in a folded piece of paper to keep it from swinging open.

Laura sat on the bench of the cab. As she watched Gabe move through the maze of parked cars with his powerful animal grace, her fears faded into nothing. Seeing his strength and confidence, it seemed inconceivable that they might fail.

"You'll need boots," he said with a smile, his sharp senses noticing a difference in her, a certain withdrawal that had not been there earlier. Vasquez's doing, he thought grimly.

"We don't have time to wait around until the stores open," Laura said.

"Guess I'll have to carry you through tall grass." He said the words with teasing carelessness, watching closely for any sign of fear.

But her smile held no apprehension at the thought of being cradled in his arms. Instead, laughter bubbled in her voice. "Don't tempt me, Gabe."

He reached for her. Slowly he kissed her, alert to the slightest hesitation. But her lips were soft and eager. His arms tightened around her. He deepened the kiss with a roughness born out of relief and need. Savagely he wondered what he'd have done if she'd shied away from him. Gone back upstairs and beaten Vasquez within an inch of his life?

Laura arched into him, letting her hands slide into the opening of his shirt. He tasted good, he felt good. Everything about him was clean and strong. She answered his kiss with a wild longing that surprised her. Last night they had loved with gentleness and sweet desire, giving and taking pleasure. Now need roughened each of their movements, hunger driving them. Her fingers dug into the bunched muscles beneath her hands, testing the male power of his shoulders.

Gabe arched against her touch, savoring the uninhibited wildness of her response. He wanted to lie down next to her, to fit his body alongside hers, to feel her passion surround him.

Later, he promised himself. With a groan he raised his head, pressing her head into his shoulder, holding her until their breathing had returned to normal. "Let's get the supplies," he muttered into her hair. "I need to breathe fresh desert air."

An hour later, Laura stared at the *paneria*'s selection of breads and rolls, still warm from the oven. She had never seen so many twists and buns, sugarcoated or covered with crumbs, studded with raisins and slivers of almonds. Her mouth began to water and her stomach to grumble.

Gabe stood next to her, holding a flat basket already half filled with two big loaves of bread. "Which ones?" he asked, watching Laura's face, which was torn by indecision.

"You choose," she grinned up at him. "I'd take the whole lot."

Gabe chuckled. "You like crumbs?" When she nodded, he took two of the buns. "Almonds?" Again she nodded.

"Two raisins," she said when he pointed toward the twists, remembering that they were his favorites.

Laura looked at the six rolls, then back at the racks. "Is there room left in the refrigerator?" she asked.

Gabe shook his head, grinning. The small space was stuffed with butter, cold cuts, milk and other perishables she'd picked off the shelves at the supermarket. "Two more?" he asked, reaching for French pastries shaped like elephant ears and dipped in chocolate.

"I'll get fat," she sighed.

"Let's get out of here," he said, desire roughening his voice. "I'm hungry." He had not known that shopping could mean torture. But watching her move through the aisles, laughing and studying the foreign labels with curiosity, was testing his control. Every minute he spent with him his hunger for her grew.

"Yes," Laura agreed. Taking the basket from his hand, she went to the register. At the supermarket, Gabe had insisted on paying. She did not want to draw more attention to them than necessary, so she had not argued. Now she drew out her purse, staring at Gabe pointedly. "It's important to me," she said quietly. Gabe let her pay.

"I have no intention of letting you foot the bills for everything," she said when they left the bakery. She did not know how much money he had to spare. So many ranchers were land-rich but money-poor. Not that it made any difference. Even if Gabe was rolling in money, she had to pay her own way to keep her self-respect.

"A few groceries aren't going to break me," Gabe said in amusement, opening the cab door for her. He could not remember the last time someone had offered to share the bill.

"That's not the point," Laura said firmly. "We're partners. Even shares in everything."

"Sue me," Gabe growled, shifting the grocery bag to the seat of the cab. He then lifted her to the bench. "We can argue about it later." He saw the reservation in her frown and knew that she would not drop the subject. Gently he leaned forward and teased her lips. "I don't seem to get enough of you."

"You don't play fair," Laura protested breathlessly moments later, her hands resting on his broad shoulders to balance herself. Needs warred within her, passion against caution. She wanted to slide into his arms and live for the moment. But the voice of restraint checked the impulse.

Gabe stilled her protest. "Humor me. It gives me pleasure to spoil you a little."

They made one more stop for coffee, washing the rolls down with it. Then Gabe headed the truck up the steep, winding road. As they climbed higher, the glamour of Acapulco receded. The houses became smaller, uglier, crowded on patches of dirt. Acapulco's gold did not reach the many poor, though these people lived better than some.

Once they crossed the pass, the road descended sharply into Las Cruces. Gabe drove right through the small, sleepy town.

"Where are we going now?" she asked as they drove past stretches of brown, barren land.

"To a little village, not far from here. There's a woman, Oti, whose parents live on the hacienda. She has no love for the Vasquez family."

Laura's eyes narrowed with interest. "Is she one of Julio's castoffs?"

Gabe nodded grimly. "She's in her late twenties now, with a handful of kids. Don Emilio arranged her marriage to the local tavern owner before Vasquez went to New York."

"It doesn't matter, Gabe," Laura told him quietly. "Julio always had mistresses, even before we separated. *Casa chicas* they call them here. Women who live in little houses off the estate or in another part of town. I'm not embarrassed meeting one of them. Especially not someone who might help me get my son back."

"The last time I was here, she refused to talk to me," Gabe warned softly.

"Perhaps she was afraid. Her husband could be the jealous type," Laura said, hoping that she would have better luck.

The village was divided by a dirt road. Small houses leaned against each other for support, turquoise, white or pink paint peeling off adobe walls. In front of a cantina the men sat drinking while women swept their houses and hung up laundry. Barefoot children chased dogs or played hopscotch in the dirt. As Gabe drew up in front of the bar, all activities stopped.

Before they could climb out of the cab, children swarmed around them, huge black eyes staring at them from thin faces. Laura's heart contracted with pity and pain. With their tangled black hair and nut-brown skin, they reminded her of her son. Reaching into her purse, she took out a handful of coins, placing one in each outstretched hand. With a shriek of laughter the children ran off. Looking up, she found Gabe watching her with a smile.

The inside of the cantina was dim and clean. A small fan whirred noisily on a plastic table, dispelling liquor fumes and cigarette smoke. Behind the bar a woman wiped off the shelves, a young boy on her arm. She turned, her beautiful Indio features creasing into a frown when she recognized Gabe. "*Señor*, I told you not to come back. I can tell you nothing," she said firmly.

Calmly, Gabe slid onto one of the high stools. "A cola for the *señora* and a Dos Equis for me."

Tight-lipped, the woman opened the bottles, took freshly rinsed glasses from the sink and placed them in front of them with a thud. She held out her hand for the money, almost dropping the change, her dark eyes moving furtively to a door leading to the back of the house.

Each one of her movements spoke of fear. Laura wondered who had warned her not to talk to strangers. Julio, or the woman's husband? "Would you speak to me?" she asked gently. "The *señor* could wait outside."

Picking up the rag again, the woman pointedly turned her back. The boy peered over his mother's shoulder curiously with huge dark eyes, sucking his thumb.

"I have a boy. When he was small he looked like your son," Laura went on determinedly. "He has big blue eyes. Perhaps you know him. His name is Pedro."

For one instant the circular polishing movements stopped, then resumed with more speed.

"How many children do you have?" Laura persisted softly.

"Five," came the whispered reply. But the woman did not turn around.

"I have only Pedro. He was four years old when his father took him from me. I haven't embraced him in a year." Laura's voice trembled with the pain of her loss.

Gabe's hand closed reassuringly around the clenched fist in her lap, giving her support. The wiping motion slowly stopped. Oti hesitated for eternal seconds, then threw the rag aside and turned to face her. Laura sagged with relief.

"I have seen him. He has your eyes. He is well. More I cannot tell you. Now please leave." Again her eyes stared at the door. "My husband comes back soon. He does not like me talking to strangers."

"Can you meet me somewhere else?" Laura asked, excitement sparkling in her eyes. "During the siesta? Or tonight? I will pay you for your trouble."

"How much? One hundred American dollars?"

"Yes," Laura agreed swiftly, hearing the rear door open.

"We have no repair shop," Oti raised her voice. "Two o'clock, at the end of town. Not the *señor*," she muttered for Laura's ears alone.

A man in his fifties entered the room, his round face sweating profusely. *"Qué pasa?"* he asked, his small dark eyes moving suspiciously from one person to the other.

"They are looking for a mechanic," Oti said swiftly. "I told them that we do not have one. Old Pepe went to visit his son."

The husband nodded, wiping his face. "What kind of trouble?" he asked Gabe.

"A noise in the engine." Gabe finished his beer and rose to his feet. "I think we'll make it to Acapulco. *Muchas gracias.*"

Heading out of town, Laura grinned broadly. "That went rather smoothly. Do you think Oti will come?"

"Probably. But you may not get much information out of her," Gabe warned softly, hoping that the woman's greed was greater than her fears.

The thought of Laura facing Vasquez instead of Oti chilled his blood.

Chapter 7

At two o'clock Laura jumped from the truck. Gabe had parked at the top of the hill overlooking the village. Five new twenty-dollar bills crackled in the rear pocket of her jeans. Joining her, Gabe stared at the small town below, shimmering in the hottest part of the day.

Nothing stirred. No people. No dogs. Not even chickens. Looking through a pair of binoculars, he searched the village. The fluttering of curtains was the only movement to be seen.

Then, from the shadows behind the last building, Oti stepped into the sun. Twice she looked behind her before swiftly walking to the road. Tensing, Gabe waited, searching the houses again. "She's alone," he said finally, lowering the glasses.

Laura slumped with relief. Since they had left the village earlier, Gabe had warned her repeatedly not to hope for too much, to suspect every shadow and examine every word.

Laura shared Gabe's suspicions. Oti had agreed to the meeting perhaps too readily. Still, she preferred to believe in the bond of motherhood. "How could a mother of five children not feel sympathetic?" she had asked Gabe.

"Especially someone with firsthand knowledge of Julio's cruelty."

"Fear for her own children could overwhelm her sympathy," Gabe had countered roughly. "Vasquez can destroy their future with a snap of his fingers."

Whether it was hate, or greed, or the understanding of another woman's suffering that had brought Oti, Laura did not care. The only thing that mattered was that the Mexican woman was down there, waiting for her.

"I'll be back in a few minutes." She smiled at him with more confidence than she felt.

"At the first strange noise, you run." His voice was quiet and restrained. He did not want her out there. Alone. Again he scanned the land and the buildings. He did not trust the silence—nor the woman. Everything was too quiet for his taste. He reached out his hand to cup her chin. "Take care." He kissed her mouth. At her instant response his fingers slid around her neck, delaying the moment when he would have to watch her face danger alone.

"I will." With great effort, Laura left the security of his arms. Now that the moment had come to walk down the slope, she had second thoughts about meeting Oti without Gabe. Briefly she hesitated, then began walking. A few steps down the hill, she turned. "Call the 212 number in my billfold if—"

Gabe swore silently, his hands clenching at his side. He had been a fool to listen to her persuasions. Narrow-eyed, he measured the distance between the truck and the houses. Half a mile. One minute. Close—and too far away when split seconds counted. He went to the truck and started the engine. Then he watched and waited.

Drawing nearer, Laura observed Oti closely. She stood completely still, her black eyes never shifting. Only her hands moved continuously, wrinkling the edges of the clean white apron covering her flowery dress. Was her agitation caused by fear of detection or by a guilty conscience?

Laura's own hands were damp. "*Hola*, Oti," she said when she came within hearing distance.

"*Señora*, I cannot stay long. What is it you want from me?"

"Only a little information," Laura said soothingly, walking steadily closer. "No one will know that you gave it to me. Is there a way to get into the hacienda easily?"

"No." Oti shook her head emphatically. "It is very difficult. The *patron* doesn't like strangers on his property. My mother even has to ask the *patron* for permission when I want to visit them."

"Does all your family work for the *señor*?" Laura asked softly.

Oti nodded. "My father takes care of the horses. My mother works in the kitchen. And my sister—" She stopped, biting her lip.

"Your sister takes care of my son," Laura guessed, finishing the sentence for her. It was a long shot. Yesterday, from the height of the rocks, she had been unable to see the maid's features closely enough. Oti's sudden withdrawal, the startled widening of her eyes, confirmed her suspicion.

"She won't help you," Oti warned. "She has little ones of her own to take care of, and a husband."

"Why are you willing to help me?" Laura asked gently.

A look of hate flashed in those obsidian eyes. "I was engaged to Benito before the *señor* made me his mistress. He was young, handsome, and too proud to marry me after Julio was through with me. When my father complained to Don Emilio, the *patron* bought me a husband twice my age who beats me and gives me a child every year. I love my children, but five is enough. I want the money to see a doctor to...to get birth control," she said with a mixture of defiance and fear. She held out her hand. "You have it with you?"

Laura's eyes softened with pity as she looked at another of Julio's victims. "Yes, I do. But I want a few more answers before I pay you," she said gently. "Does my son ever leave the hacienda?"

"Only when he sees the *medico*."

A doctor? Laura tensed. "Does he get sick?" He had looked healthy when she had seen him yesterday.

"Pedro? No, not often. Last summer he fell off a horse and hurt his leg. But the *medico* said it was nothing serious," Oti reassured her swiftly. "He also complains of stomach pains at times."

Laura clenched her hands so tightly her nails bit into her palms. She should have been there when he was hurt. She should be there to take care of him now. "Is he going to visit the doctor soon?"

"I'm not certain. My sister did mention an appointment next week, because she promised to buy pills for me there."

"Can you find out if Pedro is going?" Laura asked, holding her breath.

Oti bit her lips, her hands wrinkling the white apron like tissue paper. "If my husband learns what I do, he will beat me."

Laura hesitated briefly. From Oti's frightened expression it was obvious that her husband punished her frequently. She did not want to add to the woman's burden, but the need for her son made her press on. Gently stilling the twisting hands, she said softly, "There's no need for your husband to find out. Can't you contact your sister and ask when she needs the money to buy the pills?"

Oti nodded reluctantly. "How much will you pay me if I get the information? Another one hundred dollars?"

Laura hesitated, though not because the asking price was too high. She was afraid that Oti would be tempted to spend some of her extra money on children's toys and clothing. What if her husband noticed the sudden influx of wealth and beat the source of it out of Oti? It was a risk she would have to take, Laura thought. "I need the date and time of Pedro's appointment, and the name of the *medico*," she said firmly.

When Oti nodded, she reached in her back pocket and withdrew the five bills. "If you give me the information tomorrow, I will pay you another hundred dollars. And find out who else will go with Pedro to Acapulco besides your sister."

Handing her the money, Laura cautioned, "Be careful how you spend this. Only buy a few things at a time, or your husband will get suspicious and will want to know from whom you got this. I'll meet you here tomorrow. Same time?''

Nodding, Oti folded the bills, hiding them inside the front of her dress. "I will buy only sweets. And perhaps a ball for the children—and a toy for the baby," she added, her eyes brightening as she thought of the ever-growing number of gifts she would shower her children with. Two hundred dollars! Nervously she looked over her shoulder. "I have to get back." Before Laura could reinforce her warning, Oti hurried toward the back of the house, her low-voiced *"Hasta mañana, señora,"* barely audible above the slapping sound of her sandals on the hard-baked ground.

Gabe's eyes had been glued to the scene below, carefully monitoring Oti's expression through his binoculars. The moment Oti left, he started toward the village, the deep lines of tension easing into a grin when he saw Laura almost skipping up the hill. "You look pleased with yourself," he drawled when she climbed into the cab.

Until she had reached the safety of Gabe's truck, Laura had tried to control the steadily growing excitement bubbling inside her. Now the words tumbled out of her mouth. "We may be in luck." Her eyes sparkled in her flushed face as she repeated what Oti had told her. "I promised to meet her again tomorrow."

Gabe's eyes narrowed suspiciously. What if Oti lost her nerve and confessed to her husband what she had done. "Do you trust her?" he asked sharply.

"I think so," Laura said, frowning. "I'm pretty sure that she's not going to tell her husband about the meeting, not unless she's pressured into it. What I'm concerned about is that she might spend the money too freely and cause suspicion. Her husband seems to be the type of man who would enjoy beating a confession out of her." Laying a hand on Gabe's arm, she continued with that mixture of courage and quiet determination he had come to know so well. "I've got to take the risk and meet her again tomorrow."

Pushing his hair off his forehead, Gabe searched her face. He agreed with Laura's assessment of the woman and the situation. But his thoughts went beyond the next meeting, examining the possibilities and recognizing the dangers involved. After this morning's humiliating defeat, Vasquez would be furious and extra-cautious. Gabe doubted that he would allow the child to leave the hacienda for any reason. "In Mexico doctors still make house calls," he said bluntly. "If you were Vasquez, would you let Peter leave your fortress?"

"No," Laura agreed, her excitement vanishing, leaving her face pale and her eyes shadowed. Slowly her hands balled into fists. "On the other hand, why should Julio be suspicious? I doubt that he's even aware of the appointment. Besides, there are a number of reasons why Peter might need to go to the office. X rays for one, or blood tests. They could use this trip to buy him new shoes or clothes." Her eyes were pleading with Gabe. "We may never get another chance like this."

Gabe tensed with the need to shake some sense into her and to kiss her until passion erased the meeting from her mind. But knowing her persistence, he tried reason instead. "To do what? Kidnap him in the doctor's office? Or do you plan to stop the car on the way to town?" Gabe shook his head, concern for Laura roughening his voice.

"Yes," Laura lashed out, hearing only mockery, not concern. "I have the means to hire as many men as it takes. I'm tired of wasting time. I waited a whole year while others tried to come up with a solution. Not any more."

In the face of her distress, Gabe did not tell her his suspicions that Vasquez might substitute the boy for another child, setting a trap himself. It was what he himself would do in Vasquez's place. He took his hand off the steering wheel, stilling her twisting fingers. "We'll meet Oti tomorrow," he said with quiet firmness. "Then we'll decide what to do."

Laura clung to his hand, close to tears. Desolation smothered her hope like a thick blanket, dark and suffocating. Would she ever find a way that wasn't too risky, too dangerous and too unlikely to succeed? Perhaps Al was right. Perhaps she should give him the go-ahead and contact the ex-marine with the survival camp. Perhaps Gabe's skills were outmatched by numbers. He was only one man against Julio's army. And he was a man with divided loyalties.

Indecision tore at her. She felt like a leaf, rising, falling and twirling with the ever-changing currents of her emotions: her love for her son, her need for this man. She wanted it all. Peter and Gabe. A family. She looked at the strong, silent man, and dreams softened her face. Each minute with Gabe, each touch, each word showed her the stark loneliness of a life divided between her son and her work.

Sensing her distress, Gabe took his hand off the steering wheel and caressed her face. "We'll find a way," he promised her, drawing her against him.

All afternoon, while Gabe circled Vasquez's land, the doctor's appointment nagged at him. He couldn't explain the unease he felt every time he thought of it. Was it gut instinct or fear for Laura's safety that let him imagine the worst?

He glanced at Laura, curled into his body with the trust of a small kitten, her breasts rising and falling in the gentle movements of sleep. He felt a yearning he had denied since his mother had returned to the city when he was thirteen— the yearning to share his life with the small woman with the courage of a lioness.

Silently cursing his thoughts, Gabe slowed down at the outskirts of a village. Three days ago, when he had stopped here for a meal, the place had looked like any other: dusty streets, paint chipping off houses, and the local taverna filled with the jobless and hopeless.

Today, it looked different, alive, festive. Bright paper flowers were draped over doors and windows. Young girls paraded down the street in beautifully embroidered lacy dresses while the boys showed off their long pants and hats.

As he drove up the main street, the faint strings of mariachi music became louder. At the plaza long tables had been erected, groaning with food. Balloons and paper snakes hung from bushes and trees. In front of the old

Spanish church a priest stood surrounded by the villagers, a bridal couple in their midst.

Laura stirred, sat up and rubbed the sleep from her eyes. "A wedding," she said with awe, almost blinded by the bright sea of colors swimming before her eyes. "Gabe, can we stop? I've never seen a real fiesta."

There was an odd wistfulness in her voice, and her eyes sparkled expectantly like a child's on Christmas morning. "If you want to," he said, smiling tenderly and slowing down to park the truck at the curb.

With a swift few strokes Laura brushed her tangled hair. When she would have tied it back with a rubber band, Gabe stayed her hand. "Leave it loose," he said huskily, touching the shiny midnight-black waves.

"It tangles so easily," she protested weakly, restoring the brush to her purse.

His thoughts filled with the memory of Laura wearing only the tangled mane of dark silk. Desire shuddered through him. He kissed her, searching the moist textures of her mouth with slow strokes of his tongue. A sound of startled surprise broke from her lips, changing to the deeper-throated sound of pleasure.

Gabe finally drew away. "You're driving me crazy." He watched her eyes slowly open. "I can't seem to keep my hands off you."

A slow, provocative smile curved her lips. "Words," she scoffed, "from the strong, silent man?"

"Repeat that tonight and see what happens."

Her smile deepened as she slid to the edge of the seat. "You will sleep under the stars and I in your camper." With a chuckle she opened the door and slid to the sidewalk, barely evading his lunge. Her breath caught in her throat as she watched that slow, dazzling smile creep over his face.

"Dreamer," he growled softly.

After locking up the truck, they crossed the street to the small park. Gabe's arm rested across her back, their sides rubbing against each other as they walked. If Gabe had suggested at that moment that they drive out into the desert, Laura would have followed him eagerly.

"I see you liked our little village so much you brought your wife." A small, rotund man stepped into their way, a bushy mustache almost hiding his teeth. He was dressed formally in a white shirt and black suit with a gold watch chain draped across his stomach. "I am Manuel Sanchez, the mayor." He presented himself proudly to Laura. "Your husband ate in my restaurant the other day. I never forget a face."

Laura shot Gabe an expectant look, waiting for him to correct the mayor's assumption that they were married. But Gabe merely introduced them by their first names. It was the easiest way to avoid questions.

"He enjoyed your food so much, that he wanted me to taste it too," Laura said. "It was chicken mole he ordered, wasn't it?" She looked up at Gabe and saw his lips twitch. "Too bad your restaurant is closed today," she went on blithely, then almost yelled at the sharp pinch Gabe punished her with.

"Oh, that's no problem." The Mexican smiled genially. "You are welcome to join the fiesta. My wife cooked plenty of chicken mole for my daughter's wedding day. Come with me, please."

When she looked up at Gabe, his eyes were glinting down at her, promising retribution at a later date. "Thank you, that's very kind of you." Gabe shook the manicured, pudgy hand.

During the next half hour they were introduced to the bride, Mariela, and to the groom, Luis, who was the son of the village's only policeman, and to an overwhelming number of relatives. The whole village seemed to be related in some way or another. Mariela proudly wore a modern wedding dress with lace ruffles and held orange blossoms. But some of the older women were dressed in white native shifts with beautiful bands of embroidery.

At the end of the introductions, Laura and Gabe were drawn into separate circles. During the long meal that followed, the women questioned Laura about her trip. What had she seen? Had she been to Acapulco? How did she like Mexico?

Laura would have shown enthusiasm about their country even had she hated it. As she answered their questions, though, she realized that she did not have to pretend. Mexico had cast a spell over her.

When she turned to the mole on her plate, her eyes searched the group of men with Gabe in their midst. The sauce tasted slightly bitter, yet was subtly flavored with a multitude of spices Laura couldn't identify. It was unusual, rich and delicious and not nearly as tangy as Gabe had described it—until she had swallowed the bite. Suddenly her mouth and throat began to burn as if scorched by flames. She began coughing, tears rushing to her eyes.

Gabe turned his head at the sound, his brows raised questioningly. She managed to form the word "mole" with her lips. He caught the message and grinned, then waved a tortilla in the air.

"Here, drink this." Manuel Sanchez's wife, Juanita, handed her a glass of wine. *"Es muy picante, verdad?"* She smiled, her kind face wreathed in concern.

Laura nodded. It was hot! She doused the fire with the wine and a tortilla. *"Si, muy picante,"* she said when she could talk again, wiping the tears off her face with a smile. "But it tasted delicious—before it burned. I'm not used to spicy foods," she added apologetically.

The women surrounding her laughed understandingly, then proceeded to offer her other dishes until Laura began to protest that she couldn't eat another bite.

Later the women proudly presented their children. In each dark-haired child Laura spotted some resemblance to her own son. With each hug her determination grew to snatch Peter away from Julio.

Gabe watched Laura hold a small child that might have been a small replica of her son, her face filled with tenderness. He felt hunger, hot passion and something more shoot through him. He experienced emotions more gentle and more complex than he had ever experienced before. He wanted to protect and ravish her at the same time. He wanted to give her Peter and whisk them away to the loneliness of his ranch to keep them forever out of Vasquez's reach.

Yet he had no right to take advantage of Laura's vulnerability and innocence, no matter what the motivations and temptations. She was too inexperienced to realize that what she felt for him was not love but a mixture of desire, need and gratitude, emotions not strong enough to withstand the heat and dust and loneliness of Texas.

With a taut smile he made his way toward her through the crowd, dismissing the fantasy. What he felt was adrenaline pumping through his body. The wine must be getting to him.

Laura watched Gabe's approach, noticing the almost angry expression on his face. Before she could find out the reason for it the mariachis, resplendent in their *Charro* suits, tailored waist-length double-breasted jackets and narrow pants studded with silver buttons, frilled shirts and wide sombreros, began to play.

Gabe's arms came around her, drawing her among the couples dancing a few feet away. "Enjoying yourself?" he asked softly, his eyes caressing her face.

"Yes. Everyone is so friendly and warm." With a small sigh she curved into him, feeling his arms tighten around her, pressing her against his powerful length.

"So are you," he drawled huskily, his eyes smoldering, his gaze scorching her skin. Bending his head, his lips brushed over her cheekbones.

The by-now-familiar shock of excitement shuddered through her body. With each breath she took she was falling in love with Gabe. She had always prided herself on her skills in making the right choices in her life. But Gabe uncovered feelings in her that she had been unaware of. Her own sensuality was so new to her that she did not know how to handle it. Sooner or later she would have to learn to control her steadily growing need of him. With an effort, she drew away from him.

"Do you know if there's a phone I might use?" she asked, looking around. "I have to call New York."

Gabe perceived her sudden withdrawal, remembering similar small incidences since their encounter with Vasquez. Had that meeting triggered nightmares that had haunted her for years? Swearing silently, he wished that they were alone so he could erase the incident from her mind.

"I saw one in Manuel's restaurant the other day," Gabe remembered, none of his thoughts showing. Looking for the mayor, he found him sprawled in his chair, raising an almost empty bottle of tequila to his lips. "But I don't think he's in any condition to help," he said with a grin. "Perhaps the priest knows of another phone." He drew her through the throng of dancers to a table where a group of older men sat discussing politics.

Padre Fernando was a slim man with graying hair, dry parchmentlike skin and humorous gray eyes. His lined forehead creased when Gabe introduced Laura and asked him for the nearest phone.

"You may use the one in my house," he offered.

"I hate to take you away from the party," Laura said hesitantly.

"Manuel Sanchez has the only other phone in the village." Smiling, he looked down the table to where the father of the bride was raising the bottle once again. "I doubt that he's able to find the restaurant tonight. I could do with a walk to clear my head." He rose to his feet with a rueful smile. "Too much wine."

The padre's small house stood right behind the church. "The service is a little slow," he apologized when he handed her the phone in his Spartan study.

Dialing the operator, Laura wondered how she could talk to Al with both the padre and Gabe listening to her conversation. She felt guilty that she had asked Al to probe into Gabe's life. When she heard the priest suggest that Gabe help him to make coffee, she flashed him a grateful look.

It took the operator five minutes to complete the collect call. Al's Spanish was practically nonexistent, but finally he understood that the woman was asking him if he would accept the charges.

"Run out of money already?" he asked when the line was clear.

"I'm calling from a private phone."

"Not Vasquez's, I hope."

"I doubt I'd be calling you if I were Julio's guest," Laura said dryly, shivering slightly when she remembered their encounter. Without Gabe...

"I got the information you asked for," Al went on with unusual briskness. "Gabriel Borga appears to be a highly respected citizen of a place called Little Water, Texas. Population two hundred and eighty-three. He's thirty-eight, is single and enjoys his freedom. So watch out that you don't fall for the cowboy. Seems he runs when the affairs get too hot—that's a direct quote from the local postmistress. Until May this year his nephew lived with him. The nephew is now in a Mexican prison serving time for the possession of drugs."

"I know that part. Julio framed him," Laura said quietly. Gabe's dealings with women came as no surprise. He had been painfully honest with her from the beginning.

Al whistled. "I wouldn't like to be in Julio's shoes. That cowboy was once the toughest and most successful man the Marines had. You could have done worse, kiddo."

"Yeah," Laura agreed. She debated whether to tell Al about Oti, then decided against it.

"Where are you, by the way?" Al asked.

"At a village wedding." Al's hiss of exasperation made Laura smile. "I told you not to worry about me," she chuckled. "Why don't you unpack your bag and relax."

"I will—after I pick you up at the airport," Al said smoothly. "Heard anything from Julio?"

"The last time I saw him he was roped facedown to a bed."

"Care to tell me about it?"

"When I get back," Laura promised firmly. "Try not to worry. I'll call you tomorrow."

"That's what I thought." Al sighed resignedly. "Take care of yourself. And don't get in too deep with the cowboy. I wouldn't want you to be left behind in a cloud of dust."

Hanging up the phone, Laura stared into space, Al's warning still ringing in her ears. Her lips tightened at the cruelty of fate—giving and taking in one smooth motion. The moment she held Peter again, she would have to part from Gabe.

With a dispirited shake of her head, she walked to the heavy oak door. Things could have been worse, she told herself sternly. She might have turned up empty-handed, without Peter or Gabe. Soon she would hold her son again, and his laughter would once again fill her life.

But never as completely as before. At night she would feel the aching loneliness a child can never fill.

When she entered the kitchen she found only the padre waiting for her. "Sit down and have a cup of coffee," he said, pointing at the tin coffeepot standing on the clean, scrubbed table. "Your friend will be back shortly." At her startled expression, he said kindly, "I know that you are not married, *señora.*"

Finding no condemnation or hidden threats in those sharp gray eyes, Laura smiled. "No, I'm not," she admitted.

"But you wish you were," he said shrewdly, pouring steaming coffee into an earthenware mug. "Sugar?" He looked at her questioningly. When she nodded, he put two spoonfuls into the mug. Stirring it, he continued, "I'm not sitting in judgment of you. Your sins are between yourself and God. But if you need someone to listen to your pain...." He shrugged his shoulders. "Sometime talking helps."

"Thank you, padre," Laura said softly. "I'll remember that." She sat down in the high-backed oak chair and reached for the cream. "Have you been here long?"

"For almost thirty years. I came here fresh from the seminary, full of ambition. Two years later I was offered a diocese in Cuernavaca and turned it down. I never regretted my decision—except during the hottest summer days," he added on a whimsical note.

Laura knew that Cuernavaca was the summer playground of wealthy Mexicans. If he had accepted the post he might have been bishop or even a cardinal now. Instead, the priest had chosen to help the poor rather than deal with the power struggles of church politics. The padre was telling her that power, ambition and wealth meant nothing to him, but the reason for his oblique revelations eluded her.

"I don't think I understand what you're trying to say," Laura said warily.

"Let me explain." The priest smiled faintly. "Once or twice a year I visit an old friend of mine near the Hacienda de los Leones. On my last trip I met Don Emilio's grandson when he came to church with his grandmother. When I first saw you this afternoon, you reminded me of him. But it was only when I watched you with the children that I realized who you were."

Laura's eyes shimmered with sudden tears. She said nothing, however, waiting for the priest to continue.

"Servants talk rather freely in front of priests," Padre Fernando went on. "They know they have nothing to fear from us. And neither do you, *señora*. I know your son was taken from you, and I think I know why. Yours is not the first child taken from its mother in anger." He shrugged his slim shoulders beneath the black robe. "I would like to help. Perhaps I could arrange a meeting for you with your son."

Laura's hands clenched around the mug in an effort to hold back the tears that threatened to fall. When she was in control of herself again, she said softly, "Thank you. I think it's only fair to warn you that I haven't come all this way for one meeting with my son."

"Well, steps follow one after the other—" Padre Fernando smiled his understanding "—but it's that first step that counts."

At that moment Gabe entered the kitchen and slid into the chair next to hers. Always attuned to her emotions, he noted Laura's tension instantly. "Everything all right in New York?" he asked.

Laura nodded, his concern wrapping around her like a warm blanket on a cold winter night. "Padre Fernando has offered to arrange a meeting with Peter," she explained, watching him pour coffee into a mug with the same fluid motion with which he did all things.

Thoughtfully Gabe set down the tin pot and reached for the sugar. "I doubt you can bring it off," he drawled, looking at the padre. "Julio Vasquez will never agree."

Padre Fernando agreed with a sad nod of his head. "Dona Elena might listen, though," he said.

"It won't hurt to try, but I don't hold out much hope."

Remembering her own futile attempts to contact Dona Elena, Laura tended to agree with Gabe. Besides, it might take weeks to set up a meeting. If Oti was to be believed, she would not have to wait that long to hold her son again.

With tenderness she watched Gabe count three heaping spoonfuls of sugar into the bitter coffee. His sweet tooth was endearing in a man so dominantly male. Just looking at him made her desire stir. "Where did you go?" she asked.

"To get our bags. Father Fernando has kindly offered us shelter for the night. I've accepted because I've had too much to drink to drive any further."

Laura cast him an odd smile. Beneath the heavy fringe of her lashes, her deep blue eyes contained an undefinable look.

Disappointment? Relief? Gabe could not tell which. Her voice held nothing but politeness when she thanked the priest.

Later, on her way up the narrow stone stairs, Laura wondered why Gabe had changed his plans. Not because he was drunk. Laura knew that he was as sober as she.

The kiss he gave her at the door to the Spartan single bedroom was hot and filled with desire. When he finally raised his head, she searched his eyes. "Why did you decide to stay here?"

"I'm going out again," Gabe explained gently. He had jumped at the padre's unexpected offer for two reasons. Laura's safety was the main one. The priest's house was as secure a place as he could find anywhere in the state of Guerrero. The second was a little more complex—he believed that they both needed breathing space. Separate bedrooms would give Laura a chance to forget the encounter with Vasquez this morning and himself the opportunity to cool his steadily growing desire.

"I have to monitor the pickup of the envelopes I leave for Vasquez every night."

Before Laura could protest that she did not want to be left behind, Gabe captured her mouth with a passion that made her tremble. "Be careful," she whispered against his lips, kissing him with sudden fierceness.

Later, when she heard Gabe walk past her door, she realized how he must have felt when he had watched her walk down the hill to meet Oti: cold with dread. If she had not known that his trip would be faster and less dangerous without her to worry about, Laura would have followed him.

An hour later, halfway between the village and Acapulco, Gabe reached the spot where he had left the second envelope. Moving silently in the pale moonlight, he circled the area where he had left the green fluorescent tube. Everything was quiet. No sign of Vasquez's men. He could almost smell their presence, though. They were hiding somewhere within shooting range, he guessed. How many were there? Two? Three?

Surefooted, he climbed the cliffs. Five minutes later he almost stumbled over the first man. The Mexican was stretched out on his stomach pointing a gun at the spot below where Gabe had left the envelope. Within seconds the man was disarmed, tied and gagged. The second man never knew what hit him from behind.

When Gabe looked for the tube, it was gone. In its place a note awaited him. *What do you want?* Gabe stared at the printed message with a grim smile. Vasquez would get his answer soon enough.

On his way back to Santa Ana, Gabe activated the radio. Pressing a button behind the ashtray, he heard the power drive of the antenna hum as it stretched toward the sky. He fitted a microphone into the socket hidden behind the knob of the radio, flicked a button and listened to the crackling static.

The equipment was the newest state-of-the-art electronics. With complete disregard for Mexican laws, Herb had fitted it in place of the old stereo system before Gabe had left for Acapulco. Its power supply consisted of two powerful batteries hidden beneath the bench seat of the cab, giving him a signal strong enough to span the necessary distance.

For a while Gabe switched the dials and listened to voices speaking Spanish. Finally he turned to the prearranged frequency.

"Cougar calling Lonely Hunter."

Within a short time Herb answered the call. "Don't you ever sleep?" he grumbled. "I tried to contact you earlier. You had the damn thing turned off."

"I went hunting. How's the Goat Herder?" Gabe asked tersely.

"Dreaming of his flock."

"Tell him to start counting instead of dreaming. The snakes are hissing," Gabe said, smiling when he heard Herb grunt in satisfaction at the news.

"More than hissing. Heard that someone caught three of them, bagged them and left them for a maid to find. Now they're out for blood. Make sure you don't get bitten."

"Not me, my friend. I'm wearing boots," Gabe said with a grin, not surprised that Herb had already heard about the morning's incident. His network of agents was widely spread. Gabe suspected that his friend had stationed several men in the area in case he needed help.

"What's that supposed to mean?" Herb asked, exasperation vibrating in the air.

"Just a little private joke," Gabe smiled.

Static silence crackled once again. Herb's voice when he spoke was sharp and clipped. "Word's out they're hunting for a rare bird with black feathers and blue eyes. Want it bad enough to pay fifty dollars for information. Five hundred for her capture. A fortune for a campesino."

The words wiped the smile off Gabe's face. His features settled into a hard mask, a muscle working in his jaw the only sign of his silent rage. "Don't worry," he said, his voice grim. "The bird is safe, at least for now."

Herb swore loudly. "I warned you not to become involved in that mess. By the way, the story checks out."

"I never doubted it, my friend," Gabe drawled. "That mess, by the way, is drawing the heat away from us. The snake doesn't have enough men to split them up. Couldn't have come at a better time, if you ask me."

"If you say so," Herb grumbled. "Anything else?"

"That's all for tonight. Give Edith my love."

Just before dawn, Gabe reached the padre's house. Silently he walked up the stairs. As he passed Laura's room, his steps slowed. The need to know that Laura was safely sleeping beyond the door was like a pulsing, driving force. Gently he turned the knob and looked inside.

She lay in a pool of moonlight, her black hair falling around her like a curtain of silk. Watching the gentle rise and fall of her breasts, he felt his body tense. Then, subtly, her breathing changed, and he knew she was awake. She opened her eyes and looked at him, her voice husky with sleep as she said, "I'm glad you're back."

Desire mingled with the rage that had churned inside him since Herb had mentioned the price on her head, making his blood boil. His need for her was so intense that he was afraid of losing control and frightening her with his passion. "Go back to sleep," he said with a soft groan. He fought temptation and turned away, gently closing the door behind him.

When the guards were found the following morning, both reported that they had been attacked by a group of heavily armed men. Grinding his teeth, Julio Vasquez ordered four men to keep watch the following night.

Dismissing the others from his study, he looked from Jorge to Juan and said, "Tell them to get plenty of sleep this afternoon. I want to know who's behind this." In a fit of fury and anger, he crumpled the note the men had brought and threw it across the room. "Any news of my wife and the gringo?" Oh, how he wanted those two. He had some nice little games planned for them. His dark eyes gleamed with hate and lust. He could almost feel his hands closing around Laura's white throat, pressing, choking her while she writhed beneath him with the gringo watching. He'd teach her once and for all that no one scorned and ridiculed a Vasquez.

"No, *señor*," Jorge muttered between clenched teeth. "We checked all the hotels. They're not in Acapulco."

"Search the villages," Julio ordered.

"We don't have enough men," Jorge pointed out, fingering his mustache nervously. Vasquez in this mood was unpredictable.

Muttering a curse that made even Juan and Jorge cringe, Julio walked to the window overlooking the center courtyard. The four men he planned to send out that evening would have to sleep if he wanted them alert. The other two were useless for now. "Raise the reward to one hundred dollars for any information, a thousand if we catch them," he ordered.

Chapter 8

Laura overslept because she'd rested very lightly the night before. By the time she had showered in the aged bathroom and dressed in tan cotton pants and a soft linen safari-style shirt, it was already past ten.

Downstairs in the kitchen, the padre's housekeeper, a small gray-haired woman with flat Indian features and a dark complexion, greeted her, explaining that Señor Borga and Padre Fernando were in the office. Crossing the flagstone foyer, Laura knocked on the door.

The moment she entered the small, Spartan room, she sensed the tension. Padre Fernando was sitting behind the heavy oak desk, talking on the phone, his forehead creased. At her entrance he looked up, the angry glitter in his eyes easing into a smile as he acknowledged her with a nod.

Her eyes flew to Gabe's powerful figure, silhouetted against the window, the sun gilding his tawny hair, brightening faded denims and blue linen shirt. Her gaze lingered on his broad back, noticing how the soft material stretched and molded across wide shoulders.

Laura's breath caught at his male beauty. The longing to touch him was a need so strong the intensity shook her. Last night, fearing for his safety and waiting for his return, she had told herself that her desire was a momentary madness. But in the bright morning sun she could not deceive herself any longer. She loved this man and wanted him. She wished she knew how much she meant to Gabe.

Gabe turned, the harsh lines of his face softening when he looked at her. "Sleep well?" he asked, studying her face. After her long rest she looked stunningly beautiful.

Nodding, Laura closed the door behind her and went to him. Her eyes settled on the fresh lines of weariness marking his face. "Did you get any sleep at all?" she asked, her voice pitched low so that she would not intrude on the priest's conversation.

"Some." Gabe thought of the hours of restless tossing and turning, wanting her. "I missed you," he said, watching her with a mixture of hunger and regret. Last night had shown him that he could control the passionate hunger of his body but not his equally passionate thoughts. Never before had he felt a loneliness so acute that it had kept him awake. The idea was deeply disturbing because it showed him how close Laura was getting to a part of him that had remained untouched. She threatened his peace.

His admission made her heart skip a beat. Had Gabe accepted the padre's invitation because she was getting too close to him? A smile curved her lips as she recognized the truth. Gabe wanted her but resented the fact. Before she could tell Gabe that she had missed him, too, Padre Fernando joined them.

"My friend, Father Raoul, has just confirmed your words," he said gravely, his gray eyes troubled as he looked at Gabe. "But the price has doubled since then."

Gabe drew in a sharp, angry breath, his hands clenching in silent rage. He knew why Vasquez had doubled the price on Laura's head. He was feeling the squeeze. The news that last night's events had had the desired effect gave him no satisfaction. He was furious with himself for endangering Laura even more.

Laura's puzzled gaze flitted between the two men. "Will someone please tell me what's going on?"

"I'm going to see if Rosita is making hotcakes for breakfast. Gabe will explain," the priest said, walking to the door.

Gabe looked at Laura's face broodingly, wishing he could keep this news from her. But in case of an emergency the knowledge might make the difference between capture and escape. "Last night I heard that Vasquez has offered a reward for information about you," Gabe said, his voice emotionless. He wished Vasquez was within his grasp so he could squeeze the life out of him. He thought of Laura's softness and grace and her surprising fire. He knew he could not have her, should not even want her. Last night had shown him that he seemed to be unable to control his own desire for her. But he could prevent Vasquez from laying his hands on her again. "Don't worry," he ground out, drawing her against him, "there's only one way Vasquez will get to you. Through me."

Despite the sunshine flooding the study and the warmth of Gabe's embrace, Laura shivered. The idea of being hunted like an animal was terrifying. The nightmare wouldn't end with each new day, it would continue every waking and sleeping moment as long as she stayed in Mexico.

She looked at Gabe's hard face and sighed with regret. Although Gabe had not mentioned it, she was certain that Julio was hunting for him, too. "I'm sorry I got you into this," she said, stepping out of his embrace. "When I asked you to help me, I didn't know how ugly things could get. I don't think it's fair to keep you to your promise any longer. Perhaps it is time to dissolve this—partnership, if you can call it that." A tremulous smile played on her lips. "I seem to have been the one who has reaped all the profits and you the losses."

Denial welled up in Gabe, swift and hot. "That's not true. Vasquez raised the reward because of me," he said, his voice harsh. "I roughed up his guards last night." This was just the beginning, he thought grimly. Things would get a lot uglier before this was over. His rage was directed as much at himself for using her and wanting to keep her with him as at Vasquez.

He looked at her pale face, her eyes shadowed with fear, and wanted to reassure her. But he dared not touch her. Wanting her as he did, he would find it impossible to send her away to safety.

"I have another suggestion to make," he drawled, his eyes cool and distant. "I have friends at the embassy in Mexico City that would take you in. You would be safer there than here in Guerrero." When Laura opened her mouth he cut through her protest. "I'll get Peter back for you."

Laura stared at him searchingly. "Are you sending me away because you no longer need me? Or is it because I'm getting too close to you?"

For a long time, silence reigned in the room. Then Gabe spoke. "Both. Laura, I've been honest with you from the beginning," he reminded her roughly. "There is no future for us together. When we leave Mexico, our ways must part." He hated himself for hurting her. But the words were necessary, as a warning to himself as much as for her.

Laura had known all along what his answer would be. She knew it had been stupid to try prying a confession of undying love out of him. He desired her, even cared for her, probably more than he admitted to himself. It was not love, but she was getting under his skin. And she had no intention of letting him ship her off to safety, putting distance between them. "I want to be with you for as long as possible. I want to share with you every moment left to us. One night of lovemaking simply wasn't enough."

Gabe searched her face for a long time. Her eyes were brilliant, huge pools of deep emotion, her lips parted, tempting him. "Are you sure?" he asked quietly, torn between the desire to accept her sweet offer and the knowledge that he was risking her safety if he did.

She nodded, swaying toward him.

With a groan he enclosed her in his strong arms. His mouth ravaged her in a kiss that showed her how much her answer meant to him.

She gave herself to him with unconcealed need. Her lips opened beneath his, meeting his tongue with the sweet changing pressure that she had learned from him.

Laura was not a gambler. But until now she had never been desperate. She only had a few more days for Gabe to fall in love with her, but refused to think about the outcome. The odds against winning scared her.

After a breakfast of fluffy pancakes, sweet papaya and strong, bitter coffee, Padre Fernando said, "Father Raoul and I are going to try to find a peaceful solution to your problem, Laura. For the child's sake, you understand."

Refilling Gabe's mug, Laura hesitated. "I am grateful. But I wouldn't want to cause any trouble for you and your village," she said quietly.

For an instant the priest's gray eyes hardened, showing a strength that would have sent him up the ladder of the church hierarchy had he desired it. "Healing family conflicts is one of my duties. Neither Don Emilio nor his son would dare violate church rights."

A cynical smile twisted Gabe's lips. Desperate men were unpredictable. Still, in Mexico the influence of the church was far-reaching, especially in rural areas, where it played a dominant role. In the daily lives of the villagers the priest was the authority, often even in matters unrelated to the church. "I wish I could share your confidence," Gabe said. "But I'll leave a number where you may reach us."

"God works in mysterious ways," Padre Fernando replied, his tone gently reproving. Looking at Laura, he added, "You are welcome to seek shelter here if you need it."

Laura thanked him, hoping it would never come to that. She knew that the only time she would need a refuge would be if Gabe was injured and she needed help.

Before they left Santa Ana, Laura called Al at his office, telling him not to expect any calls during the next few days.

There were no pay phones lining the back roads Gabe traveled. They would have to go into villages to make the calls. And sooner or later they would find Julio waiting in one for them. It was a risk Laura did not want to take.

They reached Oti's village with time to spare. Gabe circled the small town twice at a distance before stopping on top of the hill. Only after he had satisfied himself that the place was truly as quiet as it seemed did he help her from the truck.

With the same furtive behavior as before, Oti came to the meeting place. "I called my sister," she said, her eyes shifting constantly. "She goes into Acapulco tomorrow morning with Dona Elena and Pedro." Fumbling in the pocket of her apron, she withdrew a small scrap of paper. "This is the address of the *medico*. Their appointment is at ten."

Laura smoothed out the badly wrinkled note and studied it. The uneven scribble was barely readable. "Dr. Rodriguez, No. 9 Calle Sanchez."

Until now, Laura had not dared to believe that Oti would be able to get the information. But seeing it in black and white, hope soared. *"Muchas gracias,"* she whispered, her eyes slowly filling with tears. Reaching into her pocket, she withdrew the money and held it out to her.

To Laura's surprise, Oti hesitated, seemingly reluctant to take the bills. Laura tensed, searching her face, a shiver of fear feathering down her spine.

"Vaya con dios," Oti whispered. Then, in one swift motion, she grasped the money and turned away, running around the corner of the house as if pursued by the devil.

Startled, Laura looked from empty doorways to empty windows, searching for the cause of Oti's flight. Then she heard the roar of the pickup as it sped down the slope, coming to a screeching, dusty halt in front of her.

"Get in," Gabe ordered harshly, throwing the door open. Laura jumped inside. The truck picked up speed almost before she could close the door, hurtling over the rocky surface up the hill at an alarming speed.

Grim-faced, Gabe watched the village receding in the rearview mirror. At the crest of the rise, he slowed down and leaned out of the window. Dust was rising in their wake, making it difficult to see if anyone was following them. It was the silence more than the slowly clearing visibility that convinced Gabe that no one was pursuing them.

"I told you to run at the slightest unusual sign," he said curtly, driving on, wanting to shake her and kiss her until his fear receded.

"She took me by surprise," Laura protested. "I don't know what made her run off."

"Guilty conscience, maybe?" Gabe speculated, his face tough and hard. "Did you get the information?"

Laura felt her earlier excitement bubble up again. "Peter has an appointment with a Dr. Rodriguez tomorrow morning at ten. She said that Dona Elena is taking him. This is the address." Handing him the piece of paper, she said thoughtfully, "Oti was more afraid and more jumpy than yesterday. Perhaps she heard about the reward. But I don't believe she's told her husband anything." Yet. Laura didn't say the word out loud, but one look at the taut line of Gabe's mouth told her that he shared her thought.

"That's a risk we'll have to take," he said, smoothing out the paper across the steering wheel. While she watched Gabe read the address, another problem troubled her. Tomorrow was too soon. Where would they find men they could trust to help them in such a short time?

Returning the note, Gabe saw the nervous clenching of her fingers. He stilled them with a reassuring squeeze. "We're going to Acapulco on one condition," he said firmly. "If it's a trap, we run so fast he can't catch us."

Laura hesitated, reluctant to give a promise she might have to break. She knew that if this attempt failed, she would try again and again. "I'm not asking you to risk your neck."

Gabe shrugged his shoulders, a hard smile on his face as if he looked forward to action. "Let's assume that Oti has leaked the information—we have to be prepared for a trap.

If I were in Vasquez's shoes, I would not call off the appointment but use it to my advantage instead. What we need is one reliable man to watch the hacienda and report back to us who gets into the car.''

"Where can we hire someone at such short notice?" Laura asked. "And are you sure we don't need more than one?"

"Yes." More men meant possible leaks. Gabe had learned from bitter experience that even men who were immune to bribes or threats often caved in under the combined pressure. Therefore, Laura's suggestion that they hire a stranger was out of the question.

Suddenly a slow smile curved his firm lips. "And I know just the one I want." There was one more man, besides Herb, whom he trusted with his life. Larry Jenkins, the man who thought he owed him for carrying his brother through the jungle to safety. Gabe had never acknowledged that debt, in fact had forgotten about the incident until they met in Mexico.

Larry had not. He had moved heaven and earth until he had proven the connection between Gino's fight with Vasquez and his imprisonment.

Gabe glanced at his watch. Three o'clock. Too early to contact Herb and find out where Larry was. He met Laura's troubled gaze with that slow, dazzling smile. "Everything will be fine," he reassured her, drawing her against him. "Trust me."

Laura leaned against him. "I do," she said with a simplicity that made him catch his breath. "With my life and my son's happiness."

He looked down into her eyes, shimmering deep blue like the sea, tempting him. He stopped his truck and bent his head, kissing her like a man wandering the desert looking for water, always thirsty.

As the afternoon slid into dusk, Gabe turned off the narrow road he had followed through the hills and stopped the truck. Laura raised her head from Gabe's shoulder and looked around. To one side, wide pastures stretched with black, white and brown cattle grazing nearby. In the opposite direction, a small village surrounded by fields was barely visible as darkness descended. "Is this our campsite?" she asked, staring at the small houses, where here and there lights began to flicker.

"No," Gabe said, opening the ashtray. "I have to make arrangements for tomorrow. I can't wait until later." He leaned across her, opened the glove compartment and took out the microphone, removed the stereo button and plugged it into the hole. Listening to the power drive of the antenna, he turned to Laura and found her watching him with wide-eyed amazement. Briskly he explained, "The radio is set on the right frequency. You press the button on the microphone to talk and release it to listen."

Laura nodded. She knew the reason Gabe was telling her how to use the radio was so that she could call for help in the event that he was injured—or even worse. The thought was terrifying. She shook her head in silent pain. She wanted her son back, but feared she was endangering Gabe.

"Cougar calling Lonely Hunter," Gabe spoke into the microphone, listening to the crackling static before repeating the call.

"I hear you, Cougar. What's up?" Herb's voice was sharp with urgency, cutting through the static with unusual sharpness. "Aren't you a little early?"

"I want to get in touch with the College Boy," Gabe explained calmly. "Tonight."

"Trouble?" Herb asked.

"No. It's a matter of wanting to be in two spots at the same time."

Laura listened to Gabe explain his plan and the disembodied voice argue about the risks involved. She tensed when the man on the other end swore and said, "I told you not to become involved with that woman. What do you plan to do with them afterward? Every inch of coastline—and the airport—will be searched. You won't be able to move for days. That is if College Boy agrees to this lunatic plan."

A gasp escaped Laura's lips.

Hearing it, Gabe smiled at her. "Herb's been sitting too long behind a desk," he said before suggesting calmly into the microphone, "Why don't you ask the man if he's willing."

A sharp laugh crackled over the air. "Don't know of any man who wouldn't prefer a piece of action to shuffling papers." An exaggerated sigh followed, then, "I'll relay the message. Keep your ears on."

Laura listened with amazement as the two men joked for a few moments before getting off the air. Gabe's eyes glowed with the same excitement her uncle Sean showed when he talked about an upcoming race. Her own fears eased somewhat.

Gabe started the motor again and followed the track past large oak trees, rocks and occasional small houses. From time to time, spotting cattle on the lane, he slowed to a crawl.

An hour later, Gabe stopped at a small area protected by a semicircle of cliffs. He had found the place a few days earlier while searching for easily accessible open spaces to leave the envelopes. Its location suited him. The site was less than a mile off Vasquez's land, sheltered, with a small creek nearby. The closest house was about three miles away, too distant to alert the campesinos of his presence, yet close enough to monitor Vasquez's actions.

Climbing out of the truck, Laura stretched, tilting her head back to look at the sky. The stars seemed like bright specks of pale silver, almost close enough to touch. The big full moon was partially hidden by a cloud. Leaves of the oak trees dotting the cliffs rustled in the mild night breeze.

Laura watched Gabe gathering sticks and broken branches, finding pleasure in the gracefully fluid way with which he moved across the space. He piled the wood against the higher wall of the cliffs, then created a circle of small rocks a few feet away. "Ever made a fire?" he asked, looking at her over his shoulder.

"Yes," Laura said softly, walking towards him. She picked up twigs and began breaking them into small pieces as he did. "We should have brought marshmallows," she joked.

"Hungry?" he teased, piling the sticks into a small heap.

"Very. My stomach must be getting used to those three square meals a day," Laura said lightly. "What are you going to cook tonight?"

Gabe shot an amused glance over his shoulder. "Are marshmallows the only thing you can fix?"

"Over an open fire? Yes. Unless you like your meat charcoaled." Laura tossed her head, her black hair swinging over her shoulder.

Gabe's eyes narrowed as he looked at her laughing, sparkling face, desire leaping within him. He rose to his feet with the powerful fluid motion of a big cat and closed the space between them. "I'll teach you to cook," he said against her laughing lips, threading his fingers through the midnight-black waves. "Among other things."

Laura molded herself to his body, clinging to him with a fierce strength. "Yes," she whispered. "What other things?"

"Not to tease a man while he's driving," Gabe muttered between kisses. "All afternoon I've wanted to do this." His tongue traced the outline of her lips, its tip dipping into her mouth and retracting, now teasing her in return.

Laura drew back and looked at him, her eyes glazed, her lips trembling with the passion that only Gabe could stir. "I didn't," she protested, then stopped. She had sat nestled against him most of those hours, enjoying the closeness, the movements of their bodies rubbing against each other as the truck dipped and swayed over unpaved roads. She had enjoyed watching the play of muscles beneath his hair-roughened skin. Each movement, each breath he had taken had been stored in her memory. "I wasn't teasing," she denied huskily. "I wanted to be close to you."

Gabe deepened the kiss. He was not used to such simple trust and openness. She never ceased to surprise him. Always, when he thought he knew everything about her, she would reveal another facet of her complex personality. Each new discovery deepened his hunger and increased his thirst. Would he ever get enough of her?

Abruptly he released her and turned away. That too became harder with each kiss. "How about steaks for dinner?"

Laura recognized the self-control he was exercising over his emotions. With a small, secret smile she said, "Fine. I'll make the salad."

In an incredibly short time a small fire was burning, flames licking eagerly at the dry wood. Gabe placed an iron grid on top of the rocks and seasoned the steaks.

Laura peeled and sliced tomatoes and cucumbers, cut up lettuce, then topped the mixture with Italian dressing. When Gabe put the meat over the fire, the flames soon hissed with the splatters of fat, leaping high.

"This reminds me of my childhood," Laura said, staring into the flames. "My Irish cousins made bonfires whenever I visited them. We used to sit around the fire and sing Irish ditties until the flames died down. Then they'd fill my ears with stories of the little people. For years I slept with a light on in my room because I was afraid they'd get to me. But every summer I asked for more stories."

She smiled and her eyes were alight with memories. "Last year, they spun their yarns for Peter. As each tale was told, he stood up and told them that they were lying. Still, despite all his protests that he didn't believe their tales, he slept in my bed that night.

"What stories did you grow up with?" she asked, turning to Gabe, wondering what his childhood had been like.

He leaned back on his elbows and stretched his long, powerful legs. "At roundup time, we spent weeks out on the range. Around the camp fires at night, the cowboys would talk about their experiences, some real but exaggerated for effect, others outrageously false. They told of cougars that spooked the cattle, and wolves that carried off calves. They told of days so hot and dry you couldn't put two sticks together without them catching fire, and nights so cold only a big fire would stay lit. Year after year, Hank, one of the hands, would repeat the story of his chase of a wild black stallion. Sometimes Hank caught him and rode him as a bucking horse. At other times the mustang got away, stealing some of his mares. Later I would fall asleep to men talking to the herd.'' With a fork he reached for the steaks and turned them over.

"One year was different from the rest, though. We had a student from Germany working his way around the globe. He told us stories a famous German writer, Karl May, told about the West. Ever hear of Old Shatterhand and Winnetou? Old Shatterhand was a German adventurer who became blood brother to an Apache chief, Winnetou, whose tribe lived along the Rio Pecos, not far from the ranch. They were fascinating. The following year I took German in school because I wanted to read the books myself.''

"And did you read them?" Laura asked, staring at his sculpted face by the shadowy light of the flickering flames.

"I finished the first volume of the trilogy. It took almost a year to get through it. A great story. But reading it with a dictionary took a lot of the suspense away.''

Laura smiled in admiration. "That's quite an accomplishment.''

Gabe shrugged off the compliment. "It kept me distracted," he said offhandedly. He stared at the fire as he added in a voice so low Laura barely heard the words, "That was the year my mother left the ranch.''

Laura gasped, not knowing what to say. Words like "I'm sorry" seemed so inadequate. She had been nineteen when her father died, leaving a desolate feeling of loss. "How old were you?" she asked softly.

"Thirteen. Too old to cry and too young to understand why she left. She loved us, but she hated the loneliness more.''

She stared into the dancing flames, imagining a lonely teenager plowing through a German book because at thirteen he was more man than boy.

"Did she ever come back?"

"Only once. For my father's funeral. Dad loved her too much to divorce her. He never gave up hoping that one day she would realize that she needed him more than bright city lights. But she never did. He clung to that dream for five years until his accident."

"What happened after your father's death?" Laura asked softly, wanting to keep Gabe talking until she knew everything that had shaped this hard, yet gentle and lonely man.

"Each of us, the two kids and my mother, was given one-third of the ranch. My sister and my mother voted to let a manager run it while I went to college. It wasn't what I wanted, but I was outvoted. College wasn't as bad as I'd thought it would be." He grinned wickedly, his eyes teasing her. "The girls were pretty and the parties were fun."

Laura chuckled, wishing that she had known him as a carefree student. "Did you learn anything?"

"Yeah. To stay away from mixed drinks." He shook his head and added, serious now, "That's when I got interested in animal husbandry. It's a subject that still fascinates me."

"Do you see your mother from time to time?" She thought that he had forgiven his mother, because there was no bitterness in his voice when he spoke of her. But he still carried the scars she had inflicted. Was it during that first bitter year he had learned to walk alone?

"Two or three times a year."

The fire crackled, flames hissing and leaping. Gabe tried to lift the grid with the aid of two sticks. The steaks started to slip, and Laura swiftly reached out and held them in place while Gabe balanced the tray on two larger stones. Juice stained her fingers. She raised them to her lips.

"Let me taste," Gabe said huskily, catching her by the wrist and raising her fingers to his mouth. His tongue was like rough velvet, sliding over the sensitive palm, curling around the fingers with soft, long strokes. A quiver of pleasure went through her, and she swayed toward him.

"How do you want your steak?" Gabe asked, drawing her slender body against him. "Medium rare?"

"Hmm." Laura teased his bottom lip with her teeth. All thought of food had been swept from her mind, replaced by a different hunger.

Gabe laughed softly, heat rushing through him. "You've come a long way since we met." One arm tightened around her, molding her against him while his other hand ran up her back in a slow caress. "You've gotten used to my touch."

"Much more than that," Laura whispered, teasing his lips with the tip of her tongue. "I'm afraid you've created a monster, greedy and insatiable. Let's forget about the steaks." One arm unwound from around his neck, sliding down the strong column into the opening of his shirt.

Gabe shuddered when her nails scraped lightly across his chest. It took all of his control to stand passively while her fingers stirred his desire. He almost broke down when she tilted her head and stared at him with a knowing smile. "If this is a sample of what you've planned for tonight," he said, "I need food to survive."

Suddenly his hands clamped around her waist. He lifted her off her feet and carried her to the camper, where he released her. "Go get the plates." His hands lingered, brushing upwards to cup her breasts. Then he turned away to take the steaks from the fire.

Once they had filled their plates with salad, rolls and steaks, they sat down on the blanket Gabe had spread on the ground.

He watched Laura purse her lips and blow, then test the temperature of the meat with the tip of her tongue. The gesture was delicate and unconsciously sensuous. It seemed that every one of her movements stirred his desire.

Broodingly he watched her eat. Would loving her once, twice, three times free him of his hunger? Or would flames always recall the shimmering silk of her hair, and bluebonnets in spring remind him of the laughter and desire in her deep blue eyes? Quickly he ate, washing down his food with beer. He needed to get away from her. A brisk walk would help him regain control of his senses.

"I'll check the area beyond the trees while you finish," he said.

"I want to come with you." Laura stared up at him.

He lifted one tawny brow. "Are you afraid of the dark?" He knelt down at her side in one fluid movement and stroked the midnight-black hair from her face. "There are no little people here. No big scary ones either for that matter."

Shaking her head, Laura denied any fear. She was not uneasy about being left alone. She knew that Gabe would never move farther than a shout.

"For these few days I want to live in your world," Laura said with simple honesty. "I want to know what it's like to walk in the night with you. I want to be part of the silence, the moon and the mountains."

Gabe's hands curled in her hair. She had bewitched him. Knowing the dangers of opening his world to her, he still found he could not deny her. "Do you know what you're doing to me?" he said in a low voice.

"Same thing you're doing to me," Laura said shakily. "Filling my world, until I wish..." She stopped and sighed.

Balancing herself with her hands on his broad shoulders, she got to her feet. The more she knew about him, the deeper she was falling in love. She wanted to share his life forever. But these days were all they had. And when they were over she had to be strong enough to smile him on his way without regrets.

She turned away to hide the sudden sheen of tears. His arm came around her from behind, drawing her against him. "I wanted to give you pleasure, not pain," he said into her hair, his voice filled with regret.

"You do," she whispered, leaning against him, giving him one of her tender smiles.

He hesitated, torn between the desire to show her the beauty of the harsh land and the knowledge of what it might do to his peace of mind. Yet his need was greater than his caution. He put his arm around her shoulder and led her from the fire.

Chapter 9

They walked across the clearing and up the hill. Beyond the trees overlooking the campsite, darkness and silence spread over the land. But it was a different darkness than Laura had ever known. She felt none of the fears that had made her hurry past the shadowy and dimly lit spaces of city streets.

Here, the shades of gray and black held peace. Occasionally moonlight would appear between the covers of clouds, painting the rocks with the color of pale pearls.

After the first few hundred yards, Laura once again adapted to Gabe's stride. She was never as silent as the tall man by her side, but her steps didn't sound like those of a charging bull, either. She heard the splash of water before she saw the tall grass growing along the creek or heard the rustles in the undergrowth as they neared it.

"How deep is it?" Laura asked when they reached the narrow band of flowing silver.

"Two, maybe three feet," Gabe said. "Too shallow to swim in, but deep enough to sit in. Not at night, though," he added. "A few days ago, I saw a water moccasin cross to the other side."

"Thanks for scaring me," Laura said dryly. The thought of meeting a snake while she was bathing sent shivers down her spine.

"It's a warning, not a scare," Gabe said, his teeth flashing white in his shadowed face. "Animals don't attack with a lust to terrify you. They attack when threatened and kill when hungry. Some of the predators look like they toy with their prey as they teach their young to survive, or they may get caught in a killing frenzy, but only humans are capable of cruelty. More people get murdered every year in cities than get attacked by animals. And you can avoid most of those attacks by taking simple precautions."

"Like by not stepping into a viper's nest," Laura said, smiling.

"Wearing boots helps," Gabe teased.

Chuckling, Laura turned toward the creek. Suddenly she saw an armadillo running past them only a few feet away, looking for all the world like a toy tank steered by remote control.

"I wonder if Peter has been out at night. He loved the World of Darkness pavilion in the Bronx Zoo. Last summer, in Ireland, he learned to ride bareback. Once he could handle the pony we hardly ever saw him. He cried when we left for New York. My mother begged me to let him stay with her until Christmas. I've often wondered if he would still be with me if I'd agreed to leave him in my mother's charge."

"Probably not," Gabe said quietly, circling her small waist and drawing her against his side. He understood her self-recriminations. He, too, had lived with them for months. If he had not agreed to that trip, Gino would now be a carefree student at Texas Tech.

"It's almost over," he added soothingly.

Laura shook her head. "Nothing will ever be as it was before. Peter has changed since I last saw him. I can't help worrying about the adjustments both of us will have to make. It won't be easy to be firm with him when all I want to do is to hug and kiss him."

She turned within the circle of his arms, tilting her head back to look into his hard face. "Peter is young, however. New experiences, like school, will soon replace the old ones. But how is your nephew going to cope?"

Gabe's face tightened into harshness, his hands clenching at her back. "It won't be easy," he agreed in a low bitter voice. He knew what captivity and cruelty could do to men. He had seen the personality changes in some of his friends. He knew of the nightmares that haunted their sleep and the suspicions that were too deeply ingrained for them to trust completely ever again. "It's going to be a long hard winter," he said quietly. "But also a happy one."

Laura nodded. "And a lonely one," she added, hoping that Gabe would offer to keep in contact to share their joys and difficulties.

Gabe only nodded, stifling the desire to prolong their relationship.

His arm tightened around her at the bittersweet thought. "Let's go back to the camp," he said, hunger and need roughening his voice, kissing her as if this was their last night, their last kiss.

Laura melted against him, her arms clinging to his neck. She refused to think about tomorrow. She would take one day at a time.

When they returned to the campsite, the fire had burned down to a glow. Gabe went to the camper and drew a sleeping bag from it. Rolling it out close to the fire, he asked, "Made up your mind about where you're going to sleep?"

"That depends on whether you take your boots off," she countered.

Gabe straightened, staring at her as if weighing the pros and cons. One hand reached up to stroke the hair out of his face. "I don't know, ma'am," he drawled broadly. "A cowboy and his boots sort of stick together." He flashed her his slow dazzling smile and held out his hand.

Laura noticed that his hand was slightly unsteady, trembling. A great wave of longing swamped her, leaving her breathless. "Gabe," she whispered, unable to say more.

With swift movements he came to her. His fingers curled around her neck and drew her closer. He kissed the corners of her mouth with restrained violence. "I never wanted another woman in my sleeping bag. I never wanted to share the beauty of the bright stars, the silent desert nights or the first kiss of the sun with anyone. Until now." He drew her to the quilted bag, his arms closing around her, hard, strong and warm.

Slowly his words sank into her, their meaning bringing tears of aching happiness to her eyes. This was as close to loving as he would ever come. With the shadow of a smile, she touched the moonlight and warmth caught in his face. "Love me," she murmured, asking for more than his touch, his hunger or his strength.

"Yes," he said, his hands moving over her with strong sureness. "I want to see you bathed only in moonbeams," he whispered against the hollow of her throat. Gently he shifted her, lowering her to the down-filled bag. Powerfully he kissed her, the slow movements of his tongue stirring her to passion. Linking her arms behind his head, she drew him closer. She felt his body lower and roll partially on top of her.

His kiss hardened with passionate restraint, his hands gentle as they slid through the midnight-black silk of her hair. Finally he lifted his head and breathed against her skin, "I half expected you to shrink from me. I was afraid that yesterday's events had stirred your old fears."

A smile curved Laura's lips. She slid her hands over his broad shoulders and down his back, enjoying the subtle shifting of strong muscles beneath her touch. "No," she said. "You set me free. Your touch is like a steel armor, shielding me from Julio's barbs."

Hunger ripped through him, changing his touch. Laura felt his rough urgency and his hard need. Her hands went to the buttons of his shirt, opening it until she could scrape her nails gently over the golden curls. Noticing the tremor of desire that shook him, she murmured huskily, "You like that." Following the trail of her finger with the tip of her tongue, she asked, "Do you like this, too?"

His answer was a powerful groan that broke from lips taut with desire. She laughed softly and continued her explorations, following the trail of hair down to his waist.

"You tease," Gabe said hoarsely, framing her face, his teeth white in his dark, bronzed face. "The last time you undressed me. Now it's my turn."

His hands devoured her, removing her clothes, his hard palms sliding smoothly over her soft feminine curves. When she was finally naked, he pushed up on his elbow and looked at her. For long moments he did not touch, just gazed admiringly at her perfect form, at her skin glowing in the moonlight with the luster of the most precious of pearls.

Hunger hammered in his blood with driving need. He knew then without a doubt that he had never known a woman like this. And he knew too that he would never want another woman again. Not with such tenderness and desire and all-consuming need.

"Gabe?" Laura whispered.

"You're more beautiful than the desert stars and the pale light of dawn. I never knew I could want a woman as much as I want you." With his eyes never leaving her, he took off his own clothes and lay down beside her.

When he touched her, it was with the lightness of a desert breeze, a caress that went from her hair down her body to the tip of her toes. The stroking reverence made her arch her body, asking silently for more. He answered her request with the weight of his hot, hard body and a kiss that scorched all thoughts from her mind. He touched her slowly, his hand running down her curves, cupping one breast as if cherishing its weight.

A vision flashed through his mind of his child suckling there, and he felt a piercing pain of regret for what could never be. Abruptly he raised his head and stared at her. "I should've thought of this before. You weren't protected last time. Can you get pregnant?"

Slowly Laura opened her heavy-lidded eyes. It took a moment for the meaning of his words to penetrate the cloud of pleasure she was floating on. It took another few seconds to count back fourteen days. Then she smiled. A glow lit her face, hauntingly beautiful and utterly mysterious.

"Don't worry about it," she said, hoping, wishing, praying as she had never prayed before, for a son with Gabe's golden eyes and tawny hair, with his strength and gentleness. For a part of him that no one could take from her. A part of the man she wanted so much and could not have.

"Are you sure?" Gabe stared into the mysterious glow of her eyes, unable to read her thoughts.

"I'm sure," Laura said firmly, reaching for him. "I've never been more certain of anything in my life." If God granted her this one wish she would learn to live without Gabe, she promised herself.

With a hoarse sound he lowered himself, sliding his hand over the silky skin of her breasts. Slowly, with infinite patience, he caressed and savored, teasing her until she tossed her head restlessly, sighing and shifting, inviting greater intimacy.

He shaped the curves of her hips with the palms of his hands. Finally his fingers sought her midnight-black triangle of curls. When he felt her liquid fire and heat, he knew that she wanted him as much as he wanted her.

With a powerful movement, he shifted, covering her body with all of his. He enveloped her in a sensual cloud of pulsing desire and ever-spiraling need, claiming her more deeply with each wave of pleasure, until she came apart in his arms.

Sobbing his name, she gave herself to him, her hands stroking his heated flesh with frantic urgency until he, too, let go of all restraint, succumbing to the lure of her siren's call.

He held her tightly pressed against him until their fervid breathing slowed to an even rhythm. Then he rolled on his back and pillowed her head on his chest. Gently he stroked the damp curls from her face.

Her breath sighed out in contentment and happiness. "I didn't know that each time would be more wonderful than the last."

Gabe groaned softly, the sound muffled by her hair. If he had needed a confirmation of her feelings, she had just given it to him. "That's the difference between just having sex and making love," he told her evenly. At this moment he could not deny his feelings for her, but he found no joy in the admission.

His words checked her breath. Startled, Laura raised her head, searching his face with wondering hope in her eyes. But when she saw the taut line of his jaw, hope froze, leaving her face oddly pale.

"Damn you, Gabe Borga," she whispered, trying to roll away from him. When his arms tightened around her, she struggled, trying to escape the hold of the man who within one breath had teased her with a glimpse of heaven and consigned them both to hell. "Not all women need neon lights and disco music."

"True," he said quietly, restraining her until she stopped fighting him. "Those born in sandstorms and growing up chasing tumbleweed love the land as much as their men."

Gently he cupped her face, stroking the petal softness of her skin. "My mother loved roses. She spent hours each day pruning, spraying and fertilizing them. For two years she kept them alive. Then we had a dry winter and no spring rains. By August two wells had run dry and the third pumped more sand than water. Within a month only brittle sticks remained in her rose garden.

"How long would you last, my Irish rose? How long before dust storms chafed your lovely skin to hard, tanned leather? And how long before tumbleweed choked the dreams from your eyes, leaving nothing but shriveled love and bitter regret?"

The hard finality of his voice made her shiver. But her chin tilted with the same stubborn determination that had brought her to Mexico. "I'm not one of your hothouse roses. I come from good peasant stock. It was women like me who followed their men from the old country and settled this land from Boston to California."

Shaking his head, Gabe kissed the words from her lips. "Let's enjoy what we have."

"You make it sound as if you live at the end of the earth," Laura protested. "I had Al Wilkins check you out." At the sudden alertness tightening his body, she added dryly, "I'm sure you did the same."

"Yes," he agreed with a slight smile. "Not that I needed the confirmation."

"And neither did I," Laura reminded him. She had spent the night in Gabe's arms before Al had confirmed what she had known all along—that this was the one man she could trust. "Anyway, he said that you only lived a few miles from town."

"A post office, a grocery and hardware store. A church and an elementary school. No restaurants, no department stores," Gabe said with quiet emphasis. "It's an hour's drive into Roswell, New Mexico and a little further into Lubbock. When the roads are clear." Gently he touched the tip of her nose. "Your skin is already peeling."

Laura traced the sculptured curve of his lips and fought the tears threatening to fall. When she could trust her voice, she said, "I forgot to put sunscreen lotion on this morning." Then she scrambled to her feet, turning her back to him while she slipped into her clothes. Her fingers fumbled with the buttons and zipper and the laces of her shoes. Behind her she heard Gabe get to his feet, dressing with much more speed. When she stood up she found him watching her, a smile tugging at the corners of his mouth.

"Going somewhere?" he drawled, staring at her feet. "Or do you plan to sleep with your shoes on?"

The temptation to put as much distance between Gabe and herself as possible was great. As if reading her thoughts, he reached for her.

"Laura—"

"I'm all right," she said, covering his lips with her fingers. Gabe was too strong a man to give in under pressure. Nothing she said would sway his mind. And running away would only deprive her of the short time of loving they had together.

Gabe released her and knelt in front of her, taking her sneakers off again. Then he went to the camper and took out another sleeping bag, zipping the two together. While Laura slid between the down-filled layers, Gabe locked up the camper. When he joined her, she caught the dull blue-black gleam of a gun.

It was a potent reminder that, however pleasant this camping trip, danger lurked in the shadows.

"Are you going out again tonight?" Laura asked, nestling her head on Gabe's shoulder.

"After Larry calls," Gabe said evenly. "I won't be gone long. An hour and a half at the most. There's nothing to worry about," he went on, feeling the tension of her body tightly wrapped against him. "Don't stay up and wait for me. I want you rested and alert tomorrow morning."

"How far is it to Acapulco from here?" she asked, giving him no promises.

"An hour, more or less," Gabe said, raising his head and kissing her until she forgot about questions and danger. For some time he watched her struggle to stay awake. But eventually lack of sleep and the unusual exertions of the last few days caught up with her.

Gabe slept too, until the low buzz of the radio reached his ear. With the sudden alertness of a man who is used to snatching rest amid danger, he crept from the sleeping bag.

Closing the window of the truck's cab, he picked up the microphone and turned up the sound.

"College Boy calling Cougar."

"Took your sweet time, College Boy," Gabe grumbled.

"Your fault, Cougar. You've kept me busy. I've been following the snakes everywhere."

"Anything interesting?" Gabe asked, grinning. He should have known that Herb had chosen Larry to report Vasquez's movements.

"The place has been like an anthill all day. Workers crawling in and out."

Gabe's grin deepened. The only way Larry could know about the activities on the hacienda was if he had been watching the comings and goings. "Well, I'll be damned," he said, chuckling. "It's a wonder we haven't bumped into each other."

Larry's laugh was as boyish as his looks. "Once or twice you almost did. You're still as good as my brother always said you were."

"Not quite," Gabe said ruefully. "Did Herb talk to you?"

"He sure did. He told me bluntly that the department would deny all knowledge and responsibility. Heck, what else is new? What do you want me to do?"

"Watch who gets into the car. How long does it take you to get from that point to town?"

"Guess about fifteen minutes less than the long way round." Barely suppressed excitement crackled through the air.

"I'll leave the radio on."

"I call you the moment the snakes stir," Larry promised.

Gabe slid from the truck and drew on his boots, pocketed the gun and fastened the knife to his belt. He crossed to the fire and dispersed the last of the glowing embers. Before he merged with the shadows, he looked back, hesitating.

Even from this distance, Laura's huddled form was barely noticeable. The dusty camper seemed to merge with the cliffs. He knew that Laura was in no danger. He disliked leaving her, but the only other choice was waking her and taking her with him. She was safer staying behind.

Abruptly he turned and moved through the night. Twenty minutes later, he neared the area where he had left the second fluorescent tube partially hidden in the hollow of an ancient oak.

The huge tree stood alone. Gabe had chosen this particular spot because there was no place to hide except in the branches. He waited and watched until he was sure that the foliage harbored nothing more dangerous than birds. Still, he made no move to cross the open space.

Where were Vasquez's men?

His eyes narrowed, searching the brush beyond the free circle. How many of them were waiting tonight? His guess was that Vasquez had at least doubled the guards. Crouching low, his head barely skimming the brush, he moved farther away from the oak.

He heard the first two before he saw them. Their low whispers rustled like dry leaves in the silence. Gabe slid forward until he was close behind them.

Tonight they did not take any chances. Their rifles lay across their folded legs. Even while they talked, their eyes were scanning the area. Gabe knew that he was more than a match for them. In a surprise attack he could silence the first one with one swift blow. But the second man would have an instant to cry out and warn the others before Gabe could knock him out.

Like a dark shadow, he moved on, passing an outcrop of limestone. He found the next two a few minutes later, facing the oak from the opposite side.

Cautiously he completed the circle, adrenaline pumping. The part inside him that was man, uncle and lover screamed for action and revenge. The soldier had no personal feelings. To him, the success of the mission was what counted.

Long seconds passed. The soldier won. Quietly Gabe retreated. If Vasquez had left a note in the oak, he could pick it up tomorrow or not at all. The little satisfaction he would gain from Vasquez's response was not worth the risks.

He took a different route back to the camp, just in case someone had been following him. But no matter how often he stopped and listened he heard nothing, saw nothing and felt no threat.

The camp was as he had left it, silent. Laura still slept in the same position as before. Quietly, he crossed to the sleeping bag, placing the gun within easy reach. The knife he hid under the pillow where he could grab it and throw it in one movement.

Laura barely stirred when he slipped between the down-filled layers. Gently he drew her against him, stroking the silky hair, smiling when she curled into him and threw one leg over his. Warm contentment made him tighten his hold.

His last thought before he fell asleep was that a man might easily get used to sharing his sleeping bag.

* * *

Pale dawn tugged at the edges of darkness when Laura opened her eyes. The first thing she became aware of was the warmth of Gabe's body, his hand moving over her in long caressing strokes. She stretched with feline contentment, her voice a husky purr. "Good morning."

She turned to look at him. His hair fell in tousled disorder onto his forehead and a stubble covered his chin once again. She raised her hand to touch his face. His skin felt cool and crisp, like the morning air.

He smiled lazily. "You sleep like a kitten curled into a ball. You even make the same funny little noises. What did you dream about?"

Laughter wiped the sleep from her eyes. "I don't remember. Do you like kittens?"

"Hmmm." He nuzzled her face. "But they don't fill my arms and hands as you do." He opened some buttons, his hand slipping beneath her shirt to cup her breast.

Laura turned onto her back, reaching for him. Slowly, without urgency, they undressed each other, their hands moving, clinging, stroking with languid pleasure. When he finally came to her, she was moaning his name softly, crying out in sweet agony that only he could end. He moved powerfully yet slowly, claiming her as surely as dawn called on day.

Laura had never started a day with such utter contentment, fulfillment and shining hope. Today she would hold Peter in her arms again. But they had hours before they could drive into Acapulco.

She made a small sound of protest when Gabe moved away from her. Dressed only in his briefs, he emerged from the sleeping bag. Laura caught her breath at the powerful beauty of his rippling muscles. She admired him as he gathered up his clothes and walked to the camper. Moments later he returned, dropping a towel near her head.

"Coming?"

Laura viewed the soap container in his hand with distaste, shivering at the thought of bathing in cold water. Checking her watch, she snuggled deeper into the bag. "It's only five. I'll wait until the sun heats up the water."

Gabe flashed her a white grin. "Want to share the warmth with snakes?"

Grabbing her clothes, Laura shot to her feet, sliding into her panties. As she shrugged into her shirt, she heard Gabe chuckling. She cast him a baleful look, then smiled. "That was a mean trick," she said accusingly, tossing her hair over her shoulders.

"It worked." Unrepentant, he knelt down to help her slide into her sneakers.

Laura grabbed hold of his thick hair in a threatening gesture. Gabe looked up from tying her laces, his eyes daring her to pull. She did, not hard enough to hurt but with playful firmness. Her laughter ended in a gasp as she felt her feet leave firm ground. Her hands slid to his shoulders and down his back as Gabe hoisted her in a fireman's lift.

"Put me down," she protested, struggling against his hold.

"Soon," Gabe said, sliding into his boots. He picked up the towels and soap and walked up the hill. At the edge of the creek, he hesitated suggestively.

"Don't you dare," Laura protested, laughter bubbling in her voice.

"I've never refused a dare in my life," Gabe drawled softly, balancing on one foot to slide the other one out of his boot. He turned his head and kissed the satiny skin where her shirt had ridden up above her waist.

"There's always a first time." Laura gasped at the touch of his mouth, retaliating by lightly running her nails up his flanks.

Gabe drew in a sharp breath. He lowered her, enjoying the sensation of her soft curves sliding over his skin. When their faces were level, he caught her mouth. Laughter stilled as hunger ripped through them. Their lips clung, pressed together in rough need until both broke apart, gasping for breath.

With slow, deliberate strokes Gabe peeled off her shirt, his lips sliding from her neck down her body as he knelt in front of her. Her fingers dug into his shoulders as she tried to control the shuddering desire racing through her while Gabe took off her shoes.

She became aware of excitement building relentlessly in her. She knew she was in danger of losing herself to him completely. With a sob she tore away from him, stepping backward—into cold water.

She stumbled, flailing her arms to keep her balance. But instead she sank, sitting down with a splash and a shriek.

Gabe stared at her, his eyes still darkened with passion. He started to laugh, the rumbling deep in his powerful chest. With arms akimbo, he stood above her like a Viking conqueror.

Laura stared at him, a wicked grin slowly spreading over her face. With two swift strokes she skimmed the water's surface, spraying him.

His laughter stilled abruptly, replaced by a yelp. His eyes narrowed. Hastily Laura got to her feet and hurried upstream. A look over her shoulder confirmed that Gabe was following her. Soon she could sense him gaining, the steady splashing of his longer and more powerful legs bringing him closer with each step. Suddenly rough hands grasped her waist, spinning her around and pulling her off balance.

Struggling to hold her slippery body, Gabe lost his foothold on the uneven creek bed. With a twist of his body he cushioned her fall before they sank beneath the surface. Gasping, they emerged with water streaming down their faces. Her smoldering gaze looked into his glistening face. His eyes blazed, but his fingers were gentle as they brushed strands of hair away from her face.

She made no protest when his hand continued downward to cup one breast. He bent his head and teased the nipple with soft strokes. Circling her waist with his arm, he drew her closer until she straddled his legs.

Laura could feel his hard desire entering her. A gasp of surprise broke from her lips. He moved his hands to her waist, lifting her and pushing with his legs until his back rested against the bank of the creek.

Slowly they rolled over. She felt his rhythmic, strong strokes as he possessed her more deeply than ever before.

When he shuddered against her she caught a look of stunned surprise on his face, as if his strong passion for her startled him.

With a sob of triumph she drew his head down. Gabe might never love her the way she loved him, but what they had just shared was more than he had ever given to anyone else. Laura hugged that knowledge to her with fierce satisfaction. For now it had to be enough.

Later, while Laura dried her hair with a towel, Gabe fried thick slices of ham in a pan placed over the open fire. Sitting in the open camper door, she watched him cook their breakfast with an efficiency that spoke of long experience.

"Who takes care of you at the ranch?" she asked idly, rubbing wet strands of hair between the fluffy cotton layers.

Placing the ham slices on a metal plate, he broke six eggs into the frying pan. "The wife of one of the hands cleans and washes for us. Gino and I share the cooking. I make breakfast and he fixes dinner."

"And what about holidays?" During those days of family gatherings, Laura always regretted that she had no relatives living nearby.

"Thanksgiving we usually spend with Irene. Christmas and New Year's they visit us. What about you?"

"My mother always comes for Christmas. As for the other holidays, Ireland is too far away for numerous visits."

Lifting the eggs out of the pan, Gabe's hand stilled in midair. Laura's life seemed to be more lonely than his own. Then he realized how dangerous it was to compare their lots. Placing the eggs on a paper plate, he divided them, two for Laura and four for himself, then filled the frying pan with two rolls.

"Is your hair dry?" he asked, walking toward her. Taking the towel, he rubbed her hair vigorously.

"That's about as dry as it'll get," he said a few moments later. Picking up the brush from Laura's lap, he drew it through the tangles with infinite care. "The sun is warm enough now to finish the job." Tilting her head back, he looked at her fresh face and felt desire stirring all over again.

It seemed that with each time they made love his hunger for her increased.

"Breakfast is getting cold." He turned away, denying himself the pleasure of kissing her.

With a knowing smile, Laura slowly followed him.

When Gabe handed her a filled plate, Laura realized how hungry she was. Sitting on the rolled-up sleeping bags, they ate in silence. When Laura wiped her plate clean with a piece of her roll, a smile tugged at Gabe's lips. "Next time I'll give you more."

Laura emphatically shook her head. "I'm stuffed, but it tastes too good to waste." She ate the last piece of bread, then reached for the coffee. "Tell me about Gino. What does he look like? Do you have a picture of him?"

Gabe reached into the rear pocket of his jeans and withdrew his billfold. He handed her a photo of a young man in his graduation gown. His hair was a shade lighter than Gabe's, his brows darker, his eyes a clear, steady gray. There the differences ended. The similarity of facial features was striking. Laura felt as if she was looking at Gabe twenty years ago, the harshness of his expression softened by youth. "He looks proud," she said, eyeing the rakish angle of Gino's head.

"He had reason to be. He graduated fifth in his class and had a successful business going on the side." Gabe's hands curled into fists when he thought of the defeated, painfully thin face behind bars. Five more days, he thought, and I'll have him out of there. He held out his hand for the photo and stood.

While Laura washed the dishes, Gabe cleaned the truck windows and checked the fluid levels. She was inside the camper storing away the pots and plates when a buzzing sound rent the silence. Swiftly she closed the cupboards and jumped to the ground. In the distance she saw a small dark spot dotting the clear blue sky. Was it Julio's helicopter searching for them? She didn't wait to find out.

Dousing the fire with dishwater, Laura dried the bowl and ran to the camper. She locked the back door and climbed into the cab.

Before joining her, Gabe checked the site. The only sign of their stay was the small circle of rocks he had built the fire in. Small wisps of smoke still rose into the air. He knew that by the time the helicopter flew over the site they, too, would have faded.

One look at the helicopter told him that he would have enough time to move the truck up the cliff and hide it beneath the trees. As the roar increased, Gabe drove slowly up the steep hill, careful to stir as little dust as possible.

To Laura, the trees seemed to offer little protection. From above the leaves might shield them, but from a lateral view the trunks were too thin and too widely spaced to hide the truck.

Recognizing her apprehensions, Gabe said with quiet confidence, "They won't spot us and will fly right over us unless they know what they're looking for." He stopped the truck, leaned across her and reached for the binoculars stored in the glove compartment.

Laura nodded, but her face remained tense, her eyes glued to the dark spot growing swiftly larger and more threatening. The helicopter was losing altitude, and the chopping sound became more distinct. Then, to her relief, it changed course and dipped out of sight.

The continuous drone of the engine was a muffled warning that the search was not yet over. A short time later it rose once again, climbing higher in a graceful arc and then turning around. Laura followed its flight with bated breath.

Color flooding back into her pale face, Laura turned to Gabe, who still followed the path of retreat through the binoculars. When he lowered them, his face was set and firm. "Until now things have gone smoothly. I don't anticipate any real trouble, but it's always better to be prepared. Should something happen to me, I want you to take the truck and get the hell out."

Laura's eyes widened with shock. "No," she protested fiercely, shaking her head.

Gabe ignored the angry pain in her eyes. He would deal with it later. He had to impress on her that leaving might mean the difference between success and failure for both their missions.

"Should something happen to me, Gino's freedom may depend on your actions. Your best bet will be to return to Father Fernando's house. Then contact the American embassy and ask for Herb Miller. He's a friend and will advise you further. If you can't find your way back to the village, drive north. Sooner or later you will hit a road that will lead you to one of the bigger towns. You can make that call from there. But don't try to drive the truck across the state line. There are military checkpoints all along the borders of Guerrero."

The ruthlessness in his voice told Laura that he would refuse to listen to arguments. Reluctantly she nodded, praying that she would never be forced to choose between following Gabe's order or trying to help him.

Gabe smiled at her grudging agreement, drawing her into his arms. "Sometimes it takes more courage to run than to stay and fight," he said soberly. Gently he tilted her head back and stopped her protests with his mouth.

Laura arched into him. She opened her lips to his tongue and became pliant in his arms. When a soft moan of pleasure escaped from her lips, he eased her back onto the bench. He was so hungry for her.

He opened her shirt and freed her breasts from the lacy cups and buried his head between them, drinking in the fragrance of the soap and his own scent, which still lingered on her skin. His mouth sought and found one dusky nipple, sucking, caressing and tugging at it until she moaned.

His hand followed her slender curves down to the waistband of her pants, unsnapping the button and opening the zipper. His rough fingers slid beneath the lacy fabric, seeking and finding her woman's warmth, feeling the evidence of her need for him.

Laura curved into his hands, her head tossing from side to side at the exquisite agony shooting through her. Beneath her lashes she watched him push down his jeans. Her eyes glazing with desire, she reached for him, welcoming the pressure of his powerful sleek body.

Chapter 10

After the bare hills, stony desert and dusty villages they had traveled through during the last two days, Acapulco seemed like a decadent paradise with its lush vegetation, luxury hotels and gleaming chrome. On the beach, cleaning crews armed with rakes and plastic bags met all-night revelers in their creased satin gowns and limp tuxedo shirts.

On the sandy beach near the harbor, Laura and Gabe sat drinking coffee as they watched tired fishermen unload their nightly haul and brightly garbed youngsters stock pleasure yachts with cases of beer and soda for a day of deep-sea fishing. Like bees around a honey pot, small powerboats buzzed around a big cruise liner anchored in the deeper waters of the basin, supplying it with fresh fruit and fish.

Atop the sheer cliffs of the western peninsula sprawled the retreats of the rich and the famous, large villas with red tiled roofs, pristine white walls and open elevators descending to private docks. Hidden from view on the opposite side lay La Quebrada, where young mèn risked their lives daily diving from the tops of the cliffs into the churning, shallow waters beneath.

Laura felt like one of those divers, nervous and edgy. She envied Gabe the calm interest with which he watched the activities around them. She let her eyes slide over his long, powerful legs. His light blue checked shirt was open at the neck, revealing glimpses of his strong, broad chest. His tawny hair was tousled by the slight breeze, giving him a rakish appearance. The only signs that he was vulnerable were the lines, more pronounced than the morning before, fanning from his eyes and mouth.

Fear tightened her stomach as she thought of the dangers ahead. What if Gabe got hurt or was caught in one of Julio's traps? He had become so very important to her. She knew now that all these years, until three days ago when he had jumped from the ledge into her life, she had simply been marking time.

Gabe turned his head and caught her intent stare. She had braided her hair into a single thick rope that brushed provocatively across her hips when she walked. Now it lay like a shining black coil across her shoulder, moving the silky fabric of her white blouse over her breast with each breath.

He felt his body tighten in instant response. He just had to look at her and his desire leaped to life. Every kiss, every touch, seemed to increase his passion. Abruptly he tore his gaze away. He had damned well better slake his thirst for her in the few days they still had left.

"More coffee?" he asked, holding the thermos out to her.

Shaking her head, Laura got to her feet and brushed the sand from her red flowered cotton skirt and pale bare legs. "Shouldn't Larry have called by now?" The waiting was grating on her already tightly strung nerves. She did not need the additional stimulus of caffeine.

On their drive to Acapulco, College Boy had contacted them briefly to inform Gabe that he was at his observation post and had just watched Vasquez return in the helicopter with four of his men. Since then there had been silence, and now it was close to nine. If Peter did have a doctor's appointment, he should be on his way by now.

As if on cue, the radio began buzzing in their truck, parked a few yards away. Gabe poured out the coffee and got to his feet with seemingly unhurried grace, crushing the paper cup in his hand. Laura followed him, her fingers clenching in the crisp cotton of her skirt, holding her breath as Gabe reached for the microphone. With rising impatience Laura listened to the preliminary exchange.

"They're on their way. The old lady, a boy about five years old and a maid," Larry reported.

"Are you sure it's the right child?" Gabe asked, his voice crisp.

"Couldn't get a look at his face," Larry said. "But he threw a fit when he wasn't allowed to take his dog with him and yelled at the old lady."

"That's the one," Gabe agreed. He doubted that one of the ranch hands' children would dare to yell at Dona Elena. "Who's driving?"

"An older man. He's at least sixty. This is going to be a picnic."

"I hope you're right. Where are you?" he asked briskly.

"Right on schedule. Should make it with fifteen minutes to spare. I need directions."

In a few precise words Gabe told him where Dr. Rodriguez's office was. "Don't get stopped for speeding."

"Don't worry," Larry said. "I have diplomatic plates. Cops rarely pick on us. See you soon."

"Now what do we do?" Laura asked Gabe as soon as Larry had gone off the air. Face flushed, she shifted from one foot to the other to relieve the excitement coursing through her.

"The best time to strike is when Peter gets out of the car." Raking his hand through his hair again, he muttered, "It all seems too damn easy."

"If Oti kept quiet, why should they be suspicious?" Laura objected tightly, the light fading from her eyes.

Gabe shook his head impatiently. "At this point it doesn't make a hell of a lot of sense. If positions were reversed, would you let Peter out of your sight with only one elderly woman and a maid for protection? Vasquez knows that you have the funds to hire men, cars, helicopters or whatever else it takes to get your son back."

"You forgot the chauffeur," Laura pointed out lamely.

"An old man?" Gabe shook his head decisively. "That's another thing that bothers me. Their regular driver is a man in his forties. What happened to him?"

"People do get sick." But the longer Laura thought about it, the more she agreed with Gabe. She guessed that it was this hard core of suspicion that had made him so successful as a marine and had kept him alive. Silently she picked up the thermos and slid into the cab.

Gabe parked the truck on a side road near the Zocalo. Dr. Rodriguez's office was just around the corner in an old Spanish house with black wrought-iron balconies and grill-work over the first-floor windows. The street was narrow. Except for a space reserved outside the house, cars were parked bumper to bumper on either side, leaving barely enough room for two cars to pass each other.

That fact would work to their advantage, Gabe thought. If Larry parked his car at the opposite intersection from the pickup, it would not matter from which direction Vasquez came. Either way, they would be gone long before the black limousine could circle the block.

Larry arrived five minutes earlier than expected in a tan Ford Mustang, a car as common in Acapulco as American tourists. Lanky and of medium height, with brown wavy hair, freckles and a cheeky smile, he looked like a college sophomore on vacation in Mexico.

"Hey, good-looking, I'm Larry," he said to Laura, his brown eyes running appreciatively over her.

His smile was so engaging that Laura grinned despite her tension. For a moment she wondered how much use this young kid could be to them. Then his gaze shifted to Gabe, suddenly alert and keen. "Where do you want me to park the car?"

Pointing toward the opposite intersection, Gabe took Laura's arm and followed the Mustang to the next side street. As in Manhattan, there was no parking space on either side of the road. "Double-park it," Gabe said.

On their way back to the doctor's office, Gabe and Larry discussed what seemed to Laura more a sketch than a plan. But, watching Larry, she realized that he did not need detailed explanations. For all his youthful looks and easygoing charm, the man was a professional.

Gabe checked his watch, then grabbed Laura's arm. Drawing her inside the building, he stationed her behind a solid oak door. The wood was well-seasoned, and thick enough to protect her from bullets if necessary. He would have preferred to have her wait in the car, but Gabe doubted that she would have stayed safely out of firing range.

"Don't move from here until I call for you," he warned. He held up two keys. "This one is for the truck. Use it only in an emergency, because I don't think Vasquez has a description of it as yet, and we want to keep it that way. This other one is for the Mustang. If things go wrong, I want you to get the hell out of here. Larry and I can take care of ourselves." Laura nodded, her face taut with anxiety. "Don't worry about me," she said firmly, her chin set and determined.

Gabe searched her tense face. She was pale, but as calm as could be expected. He kissed her lips. "Peter may scream when I grab him," he warned. "Don't rush out in a panic if he does."

Laura nodded once again. She knew her role in the rescue. She was to stop Dona Elena or her maid from running up to the doctor's office for help. Once Gabe had Peter she would follow him to Larry's car. Larry would drive the pickup truck to the meeting point at the airport road. There they would exchange vehicles, and Larry would then draw the pursuers into the airport. While they'd be searched for in the parking lot and the airport building, Gabe would drive south, losing their pursuers in the mountains.

At this point, Laura did not dare consider failure. "Be careful," she whispered, clinging for an instant to Gabe's strength. "I couldn't bear it if something happened to you."

Gabe stopped her words with another hard kiss before smoothly jumping down the two stone steps. She watched him scan the street up and down before vanishing from her view.

Laura looked at her watch. Ten minutes to go—if Dona Elena was on time. Ten minutes before she held Peter again. Nine minutes and thirty seconds.

She felt adrenaline pumping through her, sharpening her sense of danger. The palms of her hands became slippery, and perspiration trickled down her neck.

Would Peter recognize her? Would he run into her arms? Or would he start screaming for his grandmother? And then another thought occurred to her. She had only one set of clothes for him, and she didn't even know if they would fit.

How long would they have to hide in the mountains? Perhaps it would be better if Gabe took her to Padre Fernando. From there she could make arrangements with Al. She would not have to stay there long, a day at the most. Without her, Gabe could concentrate on getting Gino out of prison. The thought of leaving him brought tears to her eyes.

Seven minutes forty seconds to go.

A whistled tune, "The Yellow Rose of Texas," Gabe's signal, made her stiffen. Stepping back into the darkness of the hall, she stared through the open door.

A dusty black limousine slowly drew to a stop in front of the building, its dark reflective glass hiding its occupants. Laura wiped her wet hands on her skirt, willing the doors to open.

The chauffeur was old, his movements slow and careful as he climbed out of the car. The peaked cap hid most of his face, only showing glimpses of silvery hair. Slowly he walked around the front of the car, pausing at the curb before stepping up.

Laura frowned at the sight of the stooped figure. How could a man so feeble steer the big car over the uneven track, which had taxed all her strength? Her gaze sharpened, and suspicion grew when he opened the rear passenger door with seemingly great difficulty, then helped a woman to her feet with the strength of a much younger man.

Laura recognized Dona Elena immediately. She was dressed in an exquisitely styled white linen suit with black lapels, cuffs and buttons. She stood by the door as if undecided whether to enter the building or sink back into the seat of the car. Laura saw her face tighten at a word from the chauffeur, then answer back angrily. That, too, was unusual. From what Laura had seen and heard, servants did not bicker with their employers. Not in Mexico.

Then the chauffeur turned his face to look at the house, giving Laura a glimpse of his features. She saw features that had haunted her nightmares for five long years. Even without their last confrontation they would have been clearly etched in her mind.

Julio.

A cold shaft of fear shot through her. Gabe was hidden behind a van several feet away. Had he noticed the trap? As she opened her mouth to shout a warning, a small dark head appeared next to Dona Elena. Was it Peter? Eagerly Laura moved forward to get a better look.

Suddenly Larry jumped Julio from behind. At the same time, Gabe dashed past Dona Elena toward the child.

"Gabe, it's a trap," Laura cried, running for the door.

"Laura, get back!" Gabe shouted.

From the other side of the limousine two men rolled into the street, getting to their feet with guns in their hands. Then Laura saw a silver flash as Gabe's knife sliced through the air, hitting one man in the arm. With a howl the Mexican fell back, dropping his pistol. The other ran to hide behind the next car.

Gabe's warning to her barely registered. All Laura's attention was focused on her son. She jumped down the steps, her only thought to fold Peter into her arms and protect him from the fighting.

As she reached the sidewalk she saw, out of the corner of her eye, Larry struggling with Julio, keeping the brute's body between himself and the gunman. When Dona Elena stepped into her way she pushed her aside, but Dona Elena caught and tugged sharply at her hair, pulling her off balance. As her eyes filled with tears, she saw the face of the child Gabe lifted for her to see, kicking and screaming. Then Gabe drew back, crouching behind the car.

"Peter!" Laura was unaware that she had screamed his name. At the sound of her vaguely familiar voice, Peter abruptly stopped screaming and kicking and looked around. "Mama!" he cried when he saw her.

Hearing Peter calling for her gave her new strength. She twisted and faced the woman who had been part of this deception, yelling at her, "Let me go." She tugged at the rope of her hair, sobbing as much with anger as with pain. Suddenly she turned on the older woman, taking hold of the thin shoulders, pushing her backwards.

The unexpected change of tactic took Dona Elena by surprise. Instinctively she reached for Laura to steady herself, releasing her hold on the braid. Laura jumped back, turned and ran toward Peter and Gabe. A bullet whistled past her head.

Swearing, Gabe surged forward with Peter in his arms. He raised his gun and fired just as Peter kicked him. The shot missed as the target withdrew behind the car. Taking advantage of the respite, Gabe thrust Peter at Laura, shielding them with his body. "Run," he shouted. "Don't wait for us."

Laura closed her arms around her son and ran toward Larry's car. As she hurried past Julio, he twisted, freeing his

mouth. "Shoot her," he shouted before Larry could sub-
due him.

Laura heard a crack and a whistle as the bullet flew past
her, barely missing her, ricocheting off the stone facade of
the house. Peter began to cry, clinging to her. In his terror
his arms tightened around her neck, almost choking her.
"Hush, Peter, it's all right," she panted. He felt heavier with
each step she took. She thought she would never make it to
the corner. But she did. Laura's last glimpse of the scene was
of Gabe uncoiling with lethal power as he hurled himself
over the black limousine.

The moment she reached the Mustang, she bundled Peter into the back seat. "Lie down, love," she told him, sliding behind the wheel. Quickly Peter obeyed. She put the
wrong key into the ignition first. Her hands were shaking so
badly she wasted several seconds finding the right one, but
finally she heard the roar of the motor. Putting the car into
drive, she floored the gas pedal and shot forward, crossing
the Calle Sanchez where the men still struggled.

She did not stop, but she wanted to. Had it not been for
Peter, she would not have left. A small hand curled around
her arm, stilling her thoughts. Peter's face appeared at her
shoulder, tugging at her shoulder to get her attention.

"Are you all right?" she asked him, her eyes firmly glued
to the crowded street as she dodged cars pulling out of
parking lots and people crossing the road.

"Como no." Peter scrambled into the seat next to her. A
swift glance at his face told Laura he was fine. His eyes were
huge and sparkling, but with excitement now, not fear.
Jumping up and down, he grinned—a gap-toothed smile.
Tears blurred her eyes. When had he lost his first baby
tooth? How many other big events had she missed? Blinking, she reached for him and kissed him.

"Where have you been?" Peter asked when she released
him, as if they had been separated for a week instead of a
year. "Did you go to see Nana?" Although expected, it was
strange to hear him talk in fluent Spanish. She guessed that

it would take him some time before he would feel comfortable using English again.

"Of course not," she told him in English, and gave him a swift hug and kiss.

"I told *Abuela* that you wouldn't go without me. Where did you go?" he asked, then rushed on, "I have a dog. His name is Diego. And a horse. A big one, not a pony. And *Abuela* promised me that if I was good at the *medico* she would buy me new boots."

"That's nice," Laura said, turning into another narrow street, checking the rearview mirror again to see if someone followed her around the corner. No one did. But it was too soon to feel safe. Within minutes the police would be alerted. Would Gabe and Larry get away before they arrived? Of course they would, she told herself firmly. They both must have been in worse situations.

Moments later she drove past the Zocalo, the large square in front of the cathedral, and knew that she was nearing the Costera Aleman, the four-lane boulevard that led past the luxury hotels to the airport. It was a very busy street, crowded with shoppers, tourists, taxis and delivery vans. She glanced at her son, kneeling in his seat, enjoying the unaccustomed sights flashing past him. "Peter, put your seat belt on."

"I can't see if I put the belt on," Peter objected.

"Then sit in the back," Laura said firmly, afraid for his safety. Cars weaved from lane to lane, speeding one moment and braking the next. When Peter ignored her, Laura moved behind a bus, stopping when it came to a halt. Reaching past Peter, she snapped the seat belt into place. She could not resist placing a swift kiss on his upturned mutinous face.

"*Abuela* never makes me put on a belt," he complained.

"Her car is bigger," Laura forced herself to explain patiently. Her hands were shaking, and her palms were wet with perspiration. The bus moved slowly, too slowly for Laura. When a space opened up in the bumper-to-bumper traffic of the left lane, she shot into it, tires screeching, drawing the attention of two policemen standing on the center strip. Silently Laura swore. The last thing she wanted to do was make herself conspicuous.

Despite her growing sense of urgency, she forced herself not to switch lanes again, moving with the flow of traffic past the Condesa Hotel and the Holiday Inn.

Just before the road narrowed into a two-lane highway, Laura saw a police motorcycle race up behind her, lights flashing and siren screaming. Was the hunt for them on? Her stomach turned, and her hands tightened on the wheel. Maybe not, she told herself firmly. Keep driving. Don't draw attention to yourself.

She felt rather than saw Peter fumble with the seat belt.

"Leave it on," she ordered, one shaking hand reaching to stop him from releasing it.

"I want to see the police car," Peter protested, twisting in his seat and craning his neck to catch sight of the flashing lights.

"You will when it passes us," Laura promised him.

But the motorcycle stayed behind her.

Had the driver recognized the car? Was he waiting for an opportune moment to pull her over without causing an accident? But, although he stayed right behind her, he gave no signal.

Ahead, the traffic slowed, merging into a single lane. The highway wound its way past the naval station, following the shoreline. On one side of the road were high cliffs, and on the other lay the sea. It was no place to pass cars safely—or to turn around.

She saw two cruisers leave the docks of the naval station, sliding side by side through the water toward the mouth of the harbor.

Peter moved restlessly, trying unobtrusively to slip out of the belt without opening it. Laying a hand on his shoulder, she held him down. "You'll see it in a moment," she promised.

To Laura, the passing seconds seemed like hours. Then the policeman flashed past her, barely giving her a glance, racing ahead on the center line.

By the time Laura finally reached the airport road, two more cycles had sped past her, followed by a beige Ford Galaxie with an antenna swaying on top. The color and make of the car, as well as the antenna, told Laura that they belonged to the secret police. As Gabe had predicted, they were closing off the airport.

Instead of following the police, Laura drove past the intersection and pulled to the side of the road, letting the motor idle. Peter opened the belt and knelt in the seat, his nose pressed against the window, watching yet another beige car turn toward the airport.

Laura did not protest. For now, the search for them was concentrated on the sea and the air. But within the hour roadblocks would pop up like sprinkler heads.

Where were Gabe and Larry?

They should have been here by now. Fear dried her mouth, panic shaking her. What should she do? If she waited for them too long, she would never get past the roadblocks. And yet she could not leave. Not yet.

Another five minutes passed. Peter was occupied counting the sirens and flashing lights. Laura reached for him, pressing him against her until he protested.

Then she saw the camper. It drew up in front of the Mustang in a cloud of dust.

With a hoarse cry, Laura saw the truck door open and Gabe race toward her. Only when his strong arms closed around her did Laura truly believe that he was real. Waves of fear crushed over her.

After a swift but thorough glance at her face, Gabe said, "Get Peter and let's get out of here."

Never again did he want to repeat the experiences of the last half hour. Not since Gino had been imprisoned had he felt such stark, soul-chilling fear. When he had heard Vasquez's order to shoot Laura, he had slipped the leash of his stringent self-control. He had lunged at the bodyguard in red-hot fury, knocking him out before the man could fire another round. And then he'd turned on Vasquez. If Larry had not intervened, he might have killed him.

The endless minutes he had spent wondering what was happening to her had taken years off his life. Now, holding her safely in his arms, he realized just how much she had come to mean to him. Setting her down on the bench in the cab, he stroked her hair with a soothing rhythm, his hand shaking.

To lose his cool in a moment of savage fury had been dangerous—and detrimental to his plans. Herb was right—he was becoming too involved in Laura's affairs. Perhaps he should ask Larry to hide Laura and Peter until arrangements could be made to slip them out of Mexico. But he doubted that Laura would agree.

It was his desire for her, however, that decided him against that plan.

"Is he asleep?" Gabe asked, watching Laura close the camper door.

Nodding, Laura crossed over to the fire. "He went out like a light the moment his head touched the pillow," she said, smiling ruefully. "I'd forgotten how worn out I used to be at the end of a day." She looked tired yet happy. There was a deep warm glow in her eyes that Gabe had never seen before.

Laura knelt on the blanket beside him. "Thank you for my son," she said, kissing his lips.

"You're not safe yet," he pointed out quietly. He reached for the gun he had taken from its hiding place before Laura had put Peter to bed. "Know how to use it?" he asked, holding it out to her.

The sight of the blue-black metal recalled memories of the morning's shooting. Laura shuddered and moved toward the fire in search of warmth.

They were surrounded by mountains. Laura had lost her sense of direction long ago, especially since they had avoided the small towns and villages which might have given her a clue. From the familiarity of her surroundings, though, she guessed that they had come full circle and that somewhere nearby lay the hacienda.

"Let me show you how it works," Gabe said quietly, following her. He raised her hand and curled her fingers around the cold handle.

"I don't need it. You do." Laura tried to remove her hand, but Gabe's hold merely tightened in response.

"I won't leave you without a means of protection," he insisted.

Laura sighed, leaning against him. "I wish it was all over and we both could get the hell out of here. Will you be gone long?"

"Three hours," Gabe said.

"That long?" The protest escaped her lips before Laura could check it.

"It's quite a climb over the rocks," Gabe said lightly. "But no more dangerous than a subway ride."

Gabe guessed that after last night's quiet vigil the men would be less alert tonight. Also, the place where he had hidden the envelope was more accessible. There were plenty of rocks and shadows to conceal himself in. Except for the last two or three yards.

"I'll feel a lot better if I don't have to worry about you," he insisted.

"I wish I had something to do to distract me while you're gone."

"Learn to handle the gun," Gabe said firmly. He released her hand and held up the pistol. Ignoring her muttered objections, he showed her how to load and unload the magazine. He had her aim and dry-fire until he was satisfied that Laura knew the mechanics of it.

Unfortunately, in the silence of night, so close to their enemies, target practice was impossible. But Gabe doubted that she would shoot even in an emergency. His main objective had been to familiarize her with the weapon. Even handling a gun expertly was often a successful deterrent to opponents.

At the end of the session, Laura dropped the gun into his lap as if the cold metal was burning her skin. But Gabe wasn't finished with her yet. "If I'm not back within three hours, I want you to get out of here."

"No." Laura almost shouted the word. She stared at the grim, ruthless set of his chin, her eyes huge dark pools of distress.

Gabe hesitated. The need to secure her safe escape was a hard, driving force that would not let him rest. He took her arm in a firm hold and led her to the wide track winding down between the rocks.

He delivered his instructions in a low, hard voice. "Stay on this road for about two miles until you reach a fork. Then take the right track. After about five miles you reach a paved road. Turn left onto it. Twenty miles further you reach the highway to Mexico City."

He paused, giving Laura the chance to absorb those facts. Then he went on, "There's a military roadblock close to Iguala on the state line. Pull off the road before you reach it and wait for Larry or Herb to contact you. I've left the radio on the right frequency."

Laura nodded. She didn't protest or argue or even agree. She couldn't. She was frozen with fear.

"It's only a precaution." Gabe took her in his arms, drawing her close. Tilting her head, he whispered against her mouth, "I'm afraid you got the worse part of the deal." He kissed her tenderly. "I'll give you a taste of this to look forward to."

Tenderness flared into passion the moment he touched her. He lowered her on the blanket. "A taste of you never seems enough," he growled. "I can't touch you without wanting all of you."

Laura slid her hands around his back, holding him as if she never wanted to let him go. "Being wanted by you is all I need."

"Is it?" he asked softly, searching her face.

"Yes," she whispered, her hands sliding up the strong column of his neck, framing his face. "Yes." She raised her head and caught his lips with a need as great as his.

She unbuttoned the top button of his shirt, then the second and the third. Her fingers moved beneath the soft linen material, searching and finding the mat of golden curls.

With a twist of his body, Gabe opened the rest of the buttons, rolling aside to shed his shirt. Standing up, he took off his clothes. His tanned skin gleamed. Moonlight flowed over ridges and sinews in an ever-changing play of shadows and highlights.

Laura caught her breath at the almost unearthly beauty of him. Tender and loving, strong and powerful. Hers for this one last time.

A shaft of piercing pain ripped through her. Her lips opened in a silent scream. They still had days to love and dream. Hadn't they?

The fierceness of her embrace startled Gabe. But the feverish intensity of her kiss drove all thought from his mind. His passion swelled to match hers. With swift, sure movements he helped her out of her clothes. Lifting her, he carried her to the blanket.

Their kisses and caresses were not gentle. Their need was too intense, seething, coiling and finally erupting into a blaze that scorched and branded.

Gabe's body glistened in the pale moonlight when he finally rose above her, sliding down her silken skin. The taut look on his face told Laura what he was about to do. "Gabe, no—" She gasped her protest.

"I want to possess all of you," he growled. And then his tongue created a fire that stripped her totally of modesty and control.

Her hips undulated with pleasure as he alternately stroked, sucked and soothed her vulnerable flesh. Little explosions shook her body. At last, when she felt consciousness fade, he called her back to him. With a strangled groan he filled her with his hard, driving need.

Together they reached their climax, creating the magic of love.

Afterward, Gabe drew her into his arms, wrapping the blanket around their damp bodies. He held her until her breathing grew shallow and even. Then he carried her to the camper and laid her on the bunk near her deeply sleeping son.

Laura was not asleep. The moment he closed the door, her eyes flew open. Through the small window she looked into the bright, star-studded night.

The silence suddenly became oppressive, and the bright night seemed to dim. The moment he walked from the campsite, Laura scrambled to her feet and followed him with her eyes until the night had swallowed him. Then she left the camper and picked up her clothes. She felt a heavy object wrapped in her jeans. Even before she saw it she knew what it was. Moments later she stared grimly at the pistol, shivering with fear.

It took Gabe forty minutes to reach the small valley where he had hidden the envelope. Sheer cliffs rose on either side from its bottom, split apart aeons ago by the earthquakes that forever reshape the mountains. The moonlight glinted on silvery veins running through the rocks. One straight wall lay in deep shadow.

As they had the night before, the guards had divided into two groups. Tonight, however, they were less alert. When Gabe spotted the first, one man was sleeping soundly while the other dozed over the rifle lying across his knees.

On a ledge on the opposite side of the gash splitting the mountain, Gabe saw the others playing cards by the beam of a flashlight.

His tension eased. If these men tried to use their weapons, they were likely to shoot each other. The fools had not considered the rocks behind them. Shots fired from one side would cause a hailstorm of ricochets on the other unless aimed directly into the canyon.

Silently he retreated until he reached a spot where the wall was rough enough to offer firm foot and handholds. Climbing down an almost vertical drop of twenty feet, he retraced his steps at the bottom of the gorge, hugging the shadows.

At an outcrop of boulders he stopped. The fluorescent green tube containing his envelope was gone. Crouching, he searched for the response he felt sure Vasquez had left. He found nothing on the moonlit side of the rocks. Silently he crouched in the shadow and ran his fingers over the rough dark surface, systematically searching each inch of the dips and sharp points. As his hand finally touched and closed over stiff paper, the back of it suddenly rubbed against smooth firm scales. At the same moment, he heard a sound like the rattling of dry corn husks.

With the note clasped between his fingers, he jumped back. At the same instant, white-hot metal seemed to sear the skin of his right hand. He muffled a cry of pain.

The noise, slight thought it was, alerted the guards. Suddenly a powerful beam of light turned the dark wall of the canyon into day.

For one startled second Gabe stood paralyzed in the brightness. Then he turned and ran, throwing himself behind some rubble, waiting until the spotlight had passed over him. Then bullets flew, creating showers of rocks. Gabe ran in a zigzag course, perspiration forming on his skin.

With grim satisfaction, he heard one of the men cry out in pain. Obscenities flew with the bullets across the gorge. When the spotlight picked out the group, Gabe reached for a rock and threw it at one of the men. A sharp cry told him that he had hit his target. A second rock at the two men behind the searchlight turned the two groups toward each other.

The few seconds of distraction were all Gabe needed. He reached the place of his descent and swiftly climbed out of the trap.

Gabe knew all about snake bites. His father had taught him about first aid the moment he was old enough to understand the instructions. Later, the army had broadened his knowledge.

Running would pump the poison through his system faster. But he dared not stop, not with those men in hot pursuit. He reached in his pocket for a handkerchief, wrapping the material tightly around his wrist, not so tight as to cut off circulation but tight enough to slow it down. As he stopped for precious seconds to tie the knot, he heard the men behind him closing in.

Briefly he wished that he still had his gun. He could shoot with his left hand. Not accurately enough to kill with the first bullet every time, but well enough to injure.

Laura might need the weapon now. By the time he reached the camper...if he reached it.

Abruptly he blanked his mind. He had been in tighter spots and escaped. He knew this land as well as his enemies did, and he had an advantage because he knew where he was heading. He was an expert on guerrilla warfare. They were amateurs.

In daylight that wouldn't have made much difference. But in the darkness the advantage was still his, because the men would have to split up in their search, wasting time examining each shadow.

A few minutes later, he stopped. Probing the bite revealed none of the dangerous numbness that was an early sign of a lethal dose of venom. Perhaps he had been lucky. Few people realized that snakes could control the amount of venom they injected. Some snakes frequently used small doses as a warning when threatened by animals too large to digest.

He reached for his knife and flicked it open. Cutting just beneath the two punctures, he began to suck. Experts were divided in their opinions about whether the sucking was beneficial. Some of the latest studies indicated, however, that even hours after a bite more than half the venom could be extracted this way.

Chapter 11

The silence was oppressive and threatening. With each passing second, the temperature seemed to drop. Shivering, Laura drew the blanket around her. Gabe had left a lifetime ago. "Dammit, where are you?" she whispered.

Into the silence following her words came the low buzzing sound of the radio. Swiftly Laura ran to the truck, afraid the sound might awaken her son. She reached for the microphone and pushed the button as Gabe had shown her last night.

"This is—" She stopped. How should she identify herself? "Who is this?" she asked instead, hoping it was friendly Larry and not the disapproving Lonely Hunter.

"This is Lonely Hunter." There was a pause. "I know you, so you don't have to identify yourself. I guess Cougar is not around."

"No." How long had Gabe been gone? Laura glanced at her watch. The three-hour limit he had given her had passed.

Fear momentarily froze her voice. He should have returned by now.

Men like Gabe did not make simple mistakes. They did not estimate crudely how long a trip would take. They knew within a few minutes the time necessary to cover a distance and complete a job. Which left only the other alarming possibility. Something had happened.

"—can't hear you. Push the button and answer me." The voice on the other end sounded impatient, even harsh. "How long has he been gone?"

"Too long," Laura whispered, visions of Gabe bleeding flashing across her mind. "Listen, I'm going to look for him. Call back later. Say in half an hour?"

There was a pause. "It's safer to stay put," the voice said firmly. "I'm standing by. Call me if you need me."

"Thanks," Laura said, sliding from the truck. The thought of heeding that voice never entered her mind. All her thoughts were directed toward one purpose. She had to find Gabe.

She jumped from the cab and slipped into the camper, checking to see if the conversation had disturbed Peter. He had moved around restlessly and thrown off the light blanket. Gently Laura covered him, placing a kiss on his head. He did not stir at her touch.

Laura knew she could not stray too far from the camper. If Peter awoke and found her gone, he could be frightened. Or worse, she thought with a tender smile, he might decide to look for her. But she had to do something. All her senses told her that Gabe needed her. She could not sit any longer and watch the second hand on her watch crawl while the vision of him injured became more vivid.

Lightly she ran past the cold fire to follow his trail. Halfway across the campsite, she remembered the gun. She snatched it from the cab, its cool weight suddenly more reassuring than threatening. Holding it in her hand, she went in the direction Gabe had.

Her progress was slow. Though her fears urged her to run, she forced herself to stop frequently, to listen and memorize landmarks. If she found Gabe, he might be in no condition to give her instructions on how to return.

Ten minutes later, she thought she heard a faint noise. Laura held her breath and listened. Low-voiced, she called, "Gabe?" Her whisper sounded like thunder in the silence.

Cautiously she moved forward, listened, took another few steps and listened again.

Then she heard the noise again. A faint sound, like a pebble crunching beneath a shoe. Not hers, because she had stopped to listen. Prickles of fear covered her skin. Instinctively her fingers tightened around the gun. Flattening herself against a boulder, she whispered again. "Gabe?"

Suddenly a huge shadow rose before her. Biting back a scream, Laura lifted the pistol.

"Don't shoot." Gabe's voice sounded low and breathless, a crackling of dry leaves.

Dropping the gun, Laura threw herself at him. "Thank God," she breathed, hugging him. "You scared the hell out of me."

In her relief, she failed to notice that Gabe's arms didn't close around her. Only when she pressed her face against his chest did she realize that something was wrong. His shirt was soaked with perspiration, his skin was clammy and cold and his labored breathing rattled in her ear.

Terror stilled her pulse. For weak seconds she clung to him, listening to the irregular pounding of his heart and his rasping breath.

"You're hurt." She raised her head and searched his face, cool reason replacing paralyzing fear. The night shadows hid the pasty gray color beneath his tan. Her exploring hands found only tension and cold sweat. The great strong body beneath her fingers trembled with exhaustion and weakness. Throwing one arm around his waist, Laura tried to draw him toward the boulder to make him rest.

Gabe resisted. "Pick up the gun," he whispered hoarsely.

Laura stooped, lifted the pistol and handed it to him. When he made no motion to relieve her of the weapon, she noticed the handkerchief tied around his wrist. Raising the hand into the moonlight, she bit back a scream. It was swollen and cold below the makeshift bandage, and blood oozed from small cuts.

"Rattler." Gabe closed his eyes to stop the dizziness. "How far?" Each word he whispered seemed to drain him of strength.

"Ten minutes." Laura swallowed a protest when he took his first slow steps. Although downhill, the distance seemed too far. But there was no other way to get him down the hill. He was too big for her to carry, or even drag, and the pickup was too wide for the narrow trail. Lifting his left arm across her shoulder, she encircled his waist, supporting him as best as she could.

The short trip was a nightmare. Each few steps they had to rest. After the first five minutes, Gabe seemed to slump more and more, dragging his feet and stumbling, while sweat poured from his body, drenching her.

Laura's greatest fear was that he would pass out before they reached the truck. She knew little about the effects of snakebite and even less about its treatment. She prayed that Gabe carried antivenin. How did one use it? she wondered wildly. Would Gabe be conscious enough to give her instructions?

She did not ask any of those questions aloud. Gabe needed every ounce of his strength to reach the campsite. Weaker men would have dropped to the ground long before. Gabe's powerful determination pushed him forward even when his body seemed to weaken.

Laura led him straight to the camper, but Gabe refused to enter it. "Motor. Open the hood," he gasped.

His words seemed to make no sense. Terrified, Laura wondered if Gabe was delirious. In the bright moonlight, his face looked like a death mask. His eyes, however, were clear.

They stumbled around the truck. Once they reached the hood, Gabe slid his arm from Laura's shoulder and slumped over it. "Water."

Within seconds Laura returned with a paper cup in her hand to find Gabe trying to raise the hood. "Do you have antivenin?" she asked, fear sharpening her voice.

"No," was his heart-stopping answer. Hands shaking, he reached for the water. Laura had to steady him to prevent him from spilling most of it. The cool water seemed to give him back some strength.

"I'm as weak as a newborn foal," he growled. "Help me raise the hood."

When Laura hesitated, thinking his words made no sense at all, he attempted a grin. "I'm not mad."

Together they raised the hood. When it was secured, Gabe asked for a flashlight, tape and a piece of wood. It took Laura long, anxious seconds to find the items. Not wanting to turn on the light in the camper and possibly scare Peter, she had to grope for them in the dark. When she returned, she found Gabe with wires in his hand.

"Put the wood between the wires and tape them in place."

Laura did not question him. She was past wondering. The scene was taking on a nightmarish quality.

"Kick over the engine." Leaning against the truck, Gabe held two wire ends in his left hand. Numbly Laura climbed into the cab. Briefly she hesitated, reluctant to turn the key. What was Gabe trying to do?

"Laura."

She responded to the firmness in his voice in the same way she had when the helicopter had tried to run her down. Blindly. With shaking hands, she briefly twisted the key in the ignition, then turned it back again.

"Again."

Laura responded again with a quick flick of her wrist. And again, four more times. Each time, Gabe's voice sounded weaker, more breathless. The silence following her last attempt made Laura cling to the steering wheel, quietly sobbing his name.

"Laura."

The whispered sound made her jump from the cab and race to his side. Gabe had slid to the ground, leaning against the truck with his eyes closed. He sat so quietly that Laura thought that he finally had passed out. Kneeling, she called his name.

He opened his eyes and smiled weakly at her. "It's all right."

The low, reassuring words stopped her spinning world. As terror receded, she noticed that he was shivering. Quickly she retrieved the blanket she had tossed aside before. Drawing him against her, she wrapped it around them both, holding him, warming him. After a while the shivering slowed, then stopped altogether. Finally his big body relaxed, and his breathing seemed to become easier.

Suddenly the buzzing began again. Gabe's eyes flew open, and his big body tensed. "That's your friend Herb," Laura said, getting to her feet. "He called a while ago. I guess he's as worried about you as I was." And still am, she thought. Bending, she brushed her lips across his forehead in a gentle caress. "I'm going to answer it," she said, turning away.

"I'll take it." Gabe shrugged off the blanket. He gathered his strength, held on to the truck, and drew himself to his feet. Dragging himself to the cab, he climbed into it.

Helping him up the step, Laura felt the muscles beneath her hand quiver with weakness. Vividly she remembered his smooth, powerful movements, the easy grace with which he normally did everything, and her eyes filled with tears. Blinking them away, she listened to the disembodied voice saying, "Lonely Hunter calling Cougar."

"I hear you," Gabe said, his voice a little breathless. Releasing the button, he said to Laura, "Come up here. It's cold without you." She did not need to be asked twice. Swiftly she climbed into the cab and nestled next to Gabe.

"I tried to contact you earlier."

Even through the crackling static, Gabe heard Herb's agitation. He tensed, asking sharply, "What's up?"

"The Goat Herder got caught in a knife fight this evening. He's cut up pretty bad. A slash in the face and another on his right arm. He's been asking for you."

Laura flinched at Gabe's fluent curses. The Goat Herder must be Gino. Gabe knew the shock of hearing about Gino's misfortune was coming too soon after his injury. He felt darkness reaching for him. Taking deep breaths, he exhaled slowly, willing the black shadows to recede. If he passed out, they all would be lost. Not now. They were so close.

Nightmares danced before his eyes. Laura beaten and bruised. Gino crying for him. Gino never cried. Then he felt warm hands reaching for him, holding him, pulling him back from the edge of the black void. He opened his eyes and saw Laura, her eyes wide with terror, her face tight with determination. "Dammit, don't pass out on me, Gabe."

She so rarely swore that the sound made him smile weakly. "I won't." His voice grew stronger as he spoke. He raised the microphone and asked, "Where is Gino now?"

"In the hospital. They're going to keep him there for the next few days."

Gabe's hands clenched in silent protest. If the hospital was in the same run-down condition as the prison, there was no telling what germs Gino might pick up. Already he was only a shadow of his former self. Constant diarrhea and lingering colds had destroyed his body's resistance. Gabe knew that Gino had little strength left to fight infection. "How is he?" he asked tersely.

"Shocked. Depressed. Angry. Edith agrees with me that you should come back as soon as possible. College Boy is on his way to Iguala now to meet you and help you in any way."

Gabe looked at his right hand, still swollen and numb. It would take at least an hour or two before he was able to drive the truck. In daylight it was a six-hour drive to Mexico City, but in darkness it might take him eight or nine. And then there was the military checkpoint at Iguala.

"Couldn't have come at a worse time," he muttered. "Can you send a chopper?" he asked, knowing before Herb spoke what his answer would be.

"After that damned stunt this morning, it's too risky to fly into Guerrero," Herb growled. "But in case of an emergency—"

"Forget it," Gabe said wearily. It would not be the first time he had driven with only his left hand. He could manage the two-hour drive to Iguala. "Tell College Boy to wait for me." Slowly he unplugged the microphone and hid it behind the partition of the glove compartment.

Laura had listened to the conversation, her eyes wide with a mixture of shock, pity and growing determination. Though Gabe seemed to be improving rapidly, the thought of him driving three hundred miles in his condition over dirt tracks and winding roads was out of the question. Gently squeezing his hand, she said firmly, "I'm going to drive."

Gabe smiled grimly. Not since his mother had walked out on him had he felt so dependent. It made him feel vulnerable at a time when he needed to be tough. Besides, driving a truck this size was outside Laura's experience. "Give me an hour and I'll be able to drive," he said, clenching his teeth to fight the sudden wave of dizziness. In an hour he would have regained enough of his strength.

"We don't have an hour," Laura protested. "I don't know how far we are from Iguala, but I guess it's at least two hours. We have to get to the state line before dawn. It's easier to avoid roadblocks at night than during daylight."

"Yes," Gabe agreed with grim weariness. "Except that I doubt we'll be safe even if we manage to slip out of Guerrero. I'm afraid that Vasquez's men caught a good look at me. If that's true, he knows who is behind the blackmail. Which means that from now on all his force will be directed toward finding us. If we split up, both of us stand a better chance. I'm going to take you to Father Fernando's house."

A great wave of anger surged through Laura. She moved away from him, climbing to the ground before facing him. "Damn you, Gabe," she said, her low voice vibrating with fury. "Always the strong man. Too proud to accept help, and too scared to let anyone near you. I won't let you drop me off. We're going to make it. Together."

The pale moonlight shining on her angry face emphasized her strength and determination. Looking down at her, Gabe thought that she had never been more beautiful.

He slowly smiled. Laura saw past that smile, sensing the first crack in the strong wall he had erected around himself.

"It's going to be a hell of a drive," Gabe said quietly, reluctantly placing his fate and that of his nephew on her slim shoulders.

His easy acceptance told her how weak Gabe still was. If he had been stronger, he would have dropped her at the village of Santa Ana against all her protests. Climbing up on the step, she melted against him. "We'll make it," she said, kissing him.

With his good arm Gabe pressed her slender body against him. Even weak as he was, passion flared to life. He drank of her sweet lips, losing himself in her warmth.

"Mama, what are you doing?"

At the sound of Peter's voice, Laura raised her head. Slowly she slipped from Gabe's arms and reached for her son. Lifting him, she hugged him to her. "Gabe and I were talking."

"You were kissing him," Peter said, resentment in his voice.

"Gabe hurt himself, and I was kissing it better," Laura explained swiftly. "Let's get some clothes on. We're going on a long trip."

"Are we going to see Nana?" Peter asked, his jealousy forgotten. In the past, all his long trips had been to Ireland. "Is my pony still there?" In his excitement he jumped and squirmed, making it difficult for Laura to pull his pants on.

"Of course your pony is still waiting for you. You'll see it soon," Laura promised. She managed to slip on his white pants and the blue shirt he had worn before.

"Can I take Diego with me?" he asked, his eyes pleading. "He's a good dog. Even *Abuela* says so, and she doesn't like dogs in the house."

"I'm sure he is. But I don't think he would like to ride in the truck for a long time," Laura said gently, pulling on his socks. "Dogs get restless."

"That's what *Abuela* says." Peter slipped into the shoes and stood up.

"And she is right," Laura said firmly, lifting him out of the camper. The way Peter spoke of his grandmother told her how much he loved her and had depended on her.

Peter forgot about his dog the moment Gabe asked for his help. Proudly he held the flashlight while Gabe replaced the ignition wires. Smiling, Laura heated water on the stove to make a thermos of coffee for the long trip ahead. Gabe was good with Peter and knew just how to handle him. For her son she took two bottles of lemonade and some crackers into the cab. Within minutes they left the campsite behind.

Driving a truck with power steering was easier than Laura had thought. Once she became used to its shape and weight, she handled it with the same efficiency as she had the Jeep. During the first few miles Peter had jumped up and down next to her, pounding Gabe with questions about his horses. Did he have dogs and cats? Gabe answered him patiently, even telling him the story of Hank's mustang stallion. Eventually Peter settled down and fell asleep in Gabe's arms.

The sight of them together made Laura smile. "How do you feel?" she whispered.

"Better every moment," he assured her softly. The pain and numbness had left his system, leaving only tiredness.

Laura thought that his voice certainly sounded stronger. Glancing at him, she saw him exercising his right hand.

"Care to explain what you were doing with those wires?" she asked curiously.

"Neutralizing the venom. The shocks hurt like hell. But the treatment is effective, and it doesn't have the complications antivenin can cause."

Laura knew that small electric currents were sometimes used to speed the healing process of fractures and open wounds. But the application of jolts of electricity in the treatment of snakebites was new to her. "I never heard of it before."

"Why should you? No need to worry about snakes in New York." He was quiet for a moment, and then said softly, "Thank you, darlin'. I know of few other women who would have kept a cool head."

"Cool?" Remembering her panic, Laura smiled weakly. "I was shaking like a leaf." She swallowed, then asked hoarsely, "How did you get bitten?"

"A rattler shared the hole with Vasquez's reply." Shifting Peter gently, he reached inside his shirt. With a shudder, Laura watched him take out the envelope that had almost cost him his life. Opening it, he read the brief note out loud: "One thousand dollars for each negative." Like the last note, it had been typed and was therefore useless as evidence. Gabe crumpled it in his hand. Grimly he wondered what Vasquez's next offer would be.

Leaning forward, he turned on the radio, trying to catch the police channel. Listening to the barely audible voices, he smiled with satisfaction. "They are not anywhere near here yet."

The highway to Mexico City was a narrow black ribbon winding its way into dark hills. In the next few hours they would climb from sea level to seven thousand feet. Several times Laura had to slow down to allow cattle across the road, and once she had to swerve sharply to avoid the carcass of a donkey. The worst hazards, however, were oncoming trucks with their often missing bright lights, which made them look like floating, blinking Christmas trees. Laura found it almost impossible to guess at their size or speed or the direction in which they were moving. Still, she refused to slow down and kept to the fifty-mile-per-hour pace she had set herself. Speed was vital.

"Want me to drive?" Gabe saw h   movements become more rigid. In the light from the dashboard, her face looked tense and weary. Silently he cursed the carelessness that had made him reach for the envelope without checking the spot first. This nightmare would haunt him for the rest of his life. He would never forget it—nor the woman whose courage and strength had seen him through it. He looked down at the small boy sleeping in his arms and smiled tightly. At least he had returned her son to her. The smile vanished as he thought of Gino.

"No. I can manage." Briefly she took her eyes off the road and looked at him. She knew he was trying to hide the weakness and pain that still lingered. She was determined to give him the hours of rest he needed to deal with the dangers ahead.

Besides, she liked the picture of Peter snuggled trustingly against Gabe's chest, his hair tousled, his fresh innocent face relaxed in sleep. God, how she loved them both. She could have driven forever. But soon they would reach Iguala and the military checkpoint. The thought made her shiver.

"Slow down," Gabe said a few miles later, near the outskirts of Iguala. "At the next intersection, make a right turn. Larry should be waiting for us about a hundred feet down that road."

Laura eased her foot off the gas pedal and flicked on the blinker. "How are we going to smuggle Peter past the checkpoint?" she asked, making the turn. "Can't we go around it? There must be other crossings."

"Any number of them," Gabe agreed gently. "But I suspect that every one of them is blocked by local police. Given the choices, I prefer to deal with the military. Soldiers are less exposed to corruption than the police." Sensing her fear, he reached across Peter and covered one of her hands. "Larry will have all the information we need. We'll decide what to do when we see him."

A few minutes later, standing outside the truck, drinking coffee that Laura had poured from the thermos, Larry confirmed Gabe's suspicions. All roads were covered. "There are cops everywhere, Gabe. I checked out three crossings, all barricaded. I guess you could crash through them with the truck. But in your condition I'd say that the military checkpoint would be safer."

Gabe flexed his hand and smiled. "I'm all right. Not strong enough to wrestle a cow to the ground, but certainly well enough not to lose control of the truck."

Larry looked at the freshly bandaged hand and shook his head. "I still can't believe those shocks did the trick. Okay, if you want to risk it, I'm game."

Laura could not hide the shudder going through her at the thought of crashing through barricades. "What makes you think that we might have a chance getting through the military checkpoint?" she asked Larry.

"I know the officer on duty. Lieutenant Alvarez would never stoop to doing police work. He considers that beneath his dignity. As long as you don't have Peter with you, I don't think he will detain you."

Laura's eyes flew to Peter's small figure curled up on the seat where they had left him. "Can't I carry him around the checkpoint?" she asked.

"He's too heavy for you," Gabe objected. "And you'd never keep him quiet long enough." He turned to Larry, explaining with a grin, "He talks a mile a minute when he's awake."

Larry frowned. "Would he stay quiet for a minute or two? I thought I'd hide him in the back seat of the Mustang. Alvarez rarely searches my car. It's one of the perks of having diplomatic plates."

Tears shimmered in Laura's eyes. "I can't ask you to risk your neck again," she said.

Larry shrugged his shoulders. "Gabe once risked his life to save my brother's. You're his woman." He raised the coffee to his lips. "Besides, I like to see justice done."

The tears brimmed over, running down her face. Gabe drew her against him. She was tired and worn out and scared. Her strength was fraying at the edges. The sooner they got past the checkpoint, the better for all of them. "Peter has a vivid imagination," he said thoughtfully. "He's also quite competitive. If we turn this into a game, I believe he won't move or make a sound until he's won."

Laura was surprised at Gabe's astute assessment and grateful that she did not have to frighten Peter to keep him quiet. She pulled away from Gabe and went to wake up her son.

As Gabe had predicted, Peter responded to the game eagerly. "You mean you will buy me new boots if I can stay quiet longer than you?" When Gabe nodded, he jumped up and down. "I can do it, can't I, Mama?"

Kneeling in front of him, Laura held him tight, desperately trying to control her tears. "Of course you can. Remember, people don't talk or move when they sleep," she lied.

He tolerated her hug for a moment, then slipped from her arms. "Let's go," he said to Larry. "Can I have boots like yours?" He looked up at Gabe.

Gabe nodded. "If we can find them. But first you have to win the game."

"That's easy," Peter said, tugging at Larry's hand.

Laura watched him climb into the back seat of the Mustang with a prayer on her lips. "Larry's not going to let anything happen to him," Gabe said firmly, helping her into the truck cab. Joining her, he drew her against him and kissed her. For once, Laura was slow to respond. She felt cold, frozen to her soul.

Five minutes, Larry had said. They were to give him a head start of five minutes. Laura watched the lights of the Mustang disappear and counted second after second. When Gabe started the engine, she wished she was still driving to keep herself distracted.

Dawn was creeping over the mountains as they reached the checkpoint. Larry's car was still there, and the barrier was still lowered across the road. Laura saw him leaning against the guardhouse, talking to a man in uniform. At their approach, he shook hands with the man and returned to his car. A soldier raised the beam and the car drove through.

"They made it." Laura hugged and kissed Gabe. In her relief she forgot about their own, more threatening danger, until the truck slowed down.

"Pretend not to understand Spanish," Gabe said softly. As the soldier walked up to them, he bent and brushed his lips across her mouth. "Another few minutes and we'll be safe."

Laura curled up on the bench, her face partially hidden in the crook of her arm. Her hair fell in wild disorder around her. She did not look up when she heard a Mexican voice demand to see Gabe's identification and car papers. The voice softened, asking if the *señora* was asleep.

Gabe grunted noncommittally, handing him photocopies of his papers.

"Where are you going?" the Spanish-speaking voice questioned.

"No entiendo," Gabe said, deliberately mangling his Spanish.

"Mexico? Cuernavaca?"

"Mexico," Gabe said in a low voice.

A second voice joined the first one, this one speaking heavily accented English. "Where you stay in Mexico?"

"With a friend. He works at the university."

"The *señora* is sick?"

"Stomach problems," Gabe explained easily. "She took some medicine which made her sleepy."

Tensing, Laura heard footsteps walking around the front of the truck. Then her door was flung open. The beam of a flashlight brushed over her face. "Open here," the second voice ordered.

Laura almost flinched when the glove compartment snapped open with a sharp click. Her muscles cramped with the effort to stay immobile and keep her breathing light and even. She could feel the Mexican brush against her as he rifled through the contents—maps and insurance forms. Then came the snap of the latch closing.

"Open the back." The staccato command cracked like a whip near her ear.

Startled, Laura opened her eyes—and stared into a narrow, impassive face shadowed by a military cap.

"I am sorry, *señora*," the officer apologized with smooth insincerity. Tipping his cap, his dark eyes studied her closely as if matching her features to an image held in his mind. "I do not wish to disturb your sleep, *si?*"

He knows who I am, Laura realized with ice-cold certainty. But none of the fear she felt showed in her face. She forced a polite smile to her lips and nodded. "That's all right," she said, wondering what his next move would be.

Then, to her amazed relief, he turned away. Walking toward the camper, he stopped just within her sight and threw over his shoulder, "You have beautiful blue eyes."

During the next five minutes she listened with ever-increasing anxiety to the sound of the thorough search coming from the camper. Laura guessed that the soldiers were looking for a reason to delay their departure from the state of Guerrero and Vasquez's influence. But they found nothing. No drugs. No gun.

By the time the camper door closed, Laura was bathed in perspiration. Briefly she heard someone climb up to search the rooftop. Then, miraculously, they were allowed to leave.

Laura waited until she could no longer see the guardhouse in the rearview mirror. Then she flung her arms around Gabe's neck. "Oh God, I never thought they'd let us go," she cried laughingly.

Gabe braked sharply. With a groan, he gathered her against him, laughing with her. He looked into her eyes, brilliant with laughter. She was dusty and disheveled—and he had never wanted her more. He bent and kissed her with endless hunger, drinking her life and her beauty. He felt her melt and dissolve in his arms.

Her eyes glazed over, and her lips trembled with a passion that only Gabe could stir. She wanted to tell him how much she loved him, but she could not. Not that it really mattered, she thought. They had fought danger side by side. They had shared the beauty of total surrender in bright morning light and under the stars. She had shown him in so many different ways how much he meant to her.

"We better stop this and drive on before Larry comes to the rescue," he groaned. He drank from her mouth one more time, then determinedly put her away from him.

"What did you do with the gun?" Laura asked as they reached the four-lane toll road.

"You're sitting on it." Gabe grinned, then turned into the rest area where Larry was waiting for them. When Laura rushed from the truck, Peter cried, "I did it." Running toward Gabe, he cried, "Larry said I won."

"We all did," Gabe said, shaking Larry's hand.

Lieutenant Alvarez stared after the receding lights of the camper. Thoughtfully he walked to the guardhouse, debating whether to call Vasquez now or in the morning before he went off duty.

He despised Vasquez and others of the same ilk who used their power and wealth for personal gain and not for the good of the country. He was a realist, however, and he knew that without patronage his career would stagnate. But men like Vasquez gave the republic a bad name. In time he planned to curb their power and stop their corruption and greed. But first he needed their help to climb the ladder to their lofty position.

He reached for the phone, then hesitated. What difference would a few hours make? He sat down at the desk and lit a cigarette. Since he had found nothing to hold the gringos for, he saw no reason why he should disturb the *señor*'s sleep and his own peace.

Ten minutes before eight, he picked up the phone and called the hacienda.

"What do you mean you couldn't hold them?" Julio barked, rubbing his red-rimmed eyes. "What about my son?"

"There was no child," Alvarez explained patiently. He doubted that a child had been involved at all. Most likely it had been one of Vasquez's devious tricks to get the support of the military.

Julio hissed with fury. Ever since his men had contacted him with a description of the gringo, he had combed the mountains for him and his wife. Hearing that they had slipped through his fingers once again made him grind his teeth. "Was the gringo well?"

"Yes, *señor*, except for a bandage on his hand. It is the *señora* who is sick. Stomach problems."

"When did they pass the checkpoint?" Julio asked sharply, a hint of panic in his voice. The days of chasing shadows were wearing him down. For the first time he was afraid that things were slipping beyond his control. How could the gringo have escaped with poison in his blood? The power, resourcefulness and resilience of that devil scared the hell out of him.

"A few minutes ago," Alvarez lied. "They were in a white Ford pickup with a camper top and Texas license plates."

It never occurred to Julio Vasquez that a mere lieutenant might be lying to him. Slamming the phone down, he swore viciously.

"Is Pedro all right?"

Julio spun around at the sound of his mother's voice. "That damned gringo has him. But not for long. I'm going to kill him and teach my wife a lesson she will never forget."

Dona Elena paled at his words, leaning against the doorframe for support. "I want to know if my grandson is safe," she said, staring at the hard, cruel face as if she had never seen him before. The bright morning sun clearly revealed her son's weakness, his cruelty and selfishness, confirming the rumors about him she had tried to ignore.

"I'll get him back," Julio snapped impatiently.

"No." She straightened her slim shoulders, facing her son with dignity. "I love the boy and I won't let you hurt him again. He's not a pawn, Julio." She stepped closer, a pleading look in her dark eyes. "Call off your men. Pedro belongs with his mother."

"It's too late for that." Julio pushed past her. Storming out of the house, he called for Juan and Jorge and took the helicopter into the air. This time, he vowed, they were not going to escape.

Dona Elena looked after her son with tears in her eyes. When she heard the helicopter start, she walked to the phone and called Father Raoul. She knew of no better source to find out what was going on behind her back. It might not be easy to face the truth. But if she wanted to save her son and keep in contact with Pedro, she could not afford to ignore reality any longer.

Shortly after eight, the truck and the Mustang climbed the four-lane highway cresting the mountains surrounding the capital. The view into the valley was obscured by a gray blanket of smog. Since Iguala, Gabe and Laura had shared the driving, relieving each other every hour. Now it was Gabe's turn at the wheel, and Laura's chance to hold her son. The stiffness and swelling in Gabe's hand had gone. Only the bandage reminded Laura of the snakebite.

The air was crisp at this altitude. For the last few miles, the heater had warmed the inside of the cab. Tall dark fir trees lined the road, their branches covered with night frost.

Descending into the valley below, Laura got her first glimpse of the sprawling metropolis of Mexico City, the largest and most congested in the world, outranking even New York and Tokyo. Blanketed in a dark haze, it stretched as far as the eye could see, an endless spread of rooftops, roads and trees.

The traffic was a nightmare. Cars zoomed past them with less than an inch to spare. At times Gabe seemed to be the only driver observing the speed limits and traffic lights. The Anilio Periferico, the four-lane highway circling the centrum, became a six-lane death trap as cars, trucks and buses drove so close to each other that even the slightest steering to the right or left would have caused a pileup of enormous proportions. Laura vowed that if she survived this ride, she would never again complain about New York City drivers.

As they neared the boulevard bisecting the center of town, the Paseo de la Reforma, the signs of last year's massive earthquake became noticeable. But the rubble and repairs, still visible everywhere else, vanished once they turned into the plush residential district of Polanco, where the wealthy and the diplomats lived. Honking and waving, Larry drove off.

The seasonal changes, which had been missing in Acapulco, had stripped trees of foliage. Leaves blew across the roads. Maids, wrapped in their colorful serapes, hurried along the sidewalks. Servants washed cars, warm water steaming in their pails, and smoke rose from chimneys into the gray sky.

Gabe parked before a two-story house with a tall white gridiron fence. "We made good time." The lines of his weary face eased into a satisfied smile. He stretched and smoothed his hair back, watching Laura run a brush through her long, silky mane of midnight black until it crackled with life.

"Yes." With a rueful grin, Laura looked from the stubble of gold covering his chin to Peter's dirty face. "We're a scruffy-looking lot."

Her grin slowly faded when she glanced at the house. Gabe had assured her over and over again that his friends would welcome her and Peter with open arms. Despite his words, Laura was apprehensive. Would his friends resent the danger she was placing them in?

There was another reason for her to be worried. She doubted that she could hide the easy familiarity between herself and Gabe, the subtle closeness that came only with intimacy. She had not been in a similar position before. Would his friends resent putting up Gabe's mistress and her son?

"Perhaps I should move into a hotel," she suggested slowly.

Gabe's smile vanished, a closed, hard look replacing it. He searched her face, feeling the morning chill seep into his bones. He knew he should not fight her decision. Putting some distance between them would make the final parting easier. "Is this what you want?" he drawled, his voice steady and cool.

"No." She gave him a sad half smile. "But your friends may object to my presence."

Gabe smiled sadly, sure that once she returned to her old life and the adrenaline wore off her perspective would change. Given time, she would realize that what she felt was nothing but the heightened emotions of shared danger and a feeling of gratitude. Perhaps it would be kinder to settle her in a hotel with Larry to guard her. But his desire for her was a weakness he seemed unable to control. He had to keep her close, where he could see and touch her.

The admission made him churn with quiet rage. The urge to make love with her was like a cancer spreading swiftly, eating at his conviction that his ranch was no place for her. How long before he found the words to let her go?

"Edith will be delighted. She's been trying to marry me off for years."

Grimly he promised himself that when the time came he would cut the strings with clean swiftness.

Chapter 12

Herb Miller was a tall man with a wiry frame, leathery skin, piercing blue eyes and ash-blond hair. His wife Edith was almost his opposite, petite and cuddly, a doe-eyed brunette with a dimpled smile. Both welcomed them warmly.

"We have plenty of room," Edith assured Laura, leading the way into the house. "Since the twins went off to college, the place is really too big for us. They're only sixteen, and I miss them terribly. But since I've two maids to take care of the house, I refuse to move to a smaller place." She looked at Peter clinging to Laura's hand, rubbing the sleep from his eyes. "Sometimes I wish I had a little one still in the house."

Laura nodded understandingly, knowing how lonely a house could get without children. Looking around the huge living room with its big windows and skylights, plants and comfortable furniture, she exclaimed, "This is stunning. The architecture of the house is fabulous."

"Mexicans are master builders," Edith agreed, adding ruefully, "except when it comes to heating systems. Not many of the houses have central heating, and with masonry construction it's badly needed. We have two fireplaces, but they hardly warm this place. During the day, when the sun shines, it's comfortable enough. But in the evenings it gets quite cold. And the wiring is so limited that more than one space heater will blow a fuse."

Looking at Laura's blouse and jeans, she added, "I hope you've brought warmer clothes with you. I can loan you a jacket or coat, but I'm afraid my clothes would fall right off you. And I have nothing for your son to wear."

Before Laura could assure her that she had a woolen suit she had worn on her flight from New York, Herb exclaimed, "Well, I'll be darned. I always had my doubts if it would work. Edith, I want you to look at this."

Turning, Laura watched Edith examine Gabe's hand, probing the small cuts with professional expertise. "It looks great," Edith said, running her hand up his arm to test it for tenderness, adding for Laura's sake, "I am a nurse."

Laura grimaced at the look of Gabe's hand. Only a professional, used to worse sights, would not have shuddered at the cuts and bloodstains. But it was a relief to have someone knowledgeable look at the wounds.

"Let's get this cleaned up," Edith said. Looking at Laura's anxious face, she smiled reassuringly. "Stop worrying. I'm sure you would like to get rid of some of the dust before we eat." She held her hand out to Peter. "Come, let me show you where you'll sleep."

"But I just got up," Peter protested. "I want to play. And Gabe is buying me a pair of boots. He promised."

Edith shook her head at the flow of Spanish. "Does he speak any English?" she asked Laura.

"He understands it perfectly. But it's been a year since he's spoken it. I'm certain it won't take long before he picks it up again."

"Children learn so fast," Edith agreed. She turned to Peter and said, "If Gabe promised you boots, you'll get them. He always keeps his word." Taking his hand, she said, "I think I still have some toys for you to play with." Walking to the stairs, she turned back to Laura. "Do you have any clothes for him? My next-door neighbor has a boy slightly taller than Peter. Perhaps she still has some sweaters and a jacket that will fit him. If you don't mind castoffs.''

"I don't. I brought one change with me. I'm not sure they will fit him, though. He's grown so much during the last year. But I hope that I will be able to buy a few items when we get his boots.'' Troubled, she looked at Edith. "I don't want to cause you any problems. If you want me to move to a hotel, I'll understand.''

"Of course not.'' Edith rejected Laura's offer firmly. "You're welcome to stay as long as you like. And don't worry about any trouble. We have diplomatic status. Even Vas—'' Looking down at Peter, she caught herself. "Even he will think twice before threatening us.''

Walking across the upstairs landing, she pointed out the bathroom before ushering Laura into her daughter's room. "Peter is next door.'' For a moment she hesitated, then went on, "Unless you prefer to have him sleep in here?''

"This is fine,'' Laura assured her swiftly. She did not like the thought of being parted from Peter for one minute. But she knew that smothering her son would not be good for him.

"If you change your mind, let me know,'' Edith said gently. "The maid will bring your suitcases up in a minute. I'd better see about Gabe's hand. Breakfast is in an hour,'' she added before leaving the room.

For a moment Laura just stood, staring at the pop-star posters pinned to the wall, but not really seeing them. She was tired. Now that they were safe, weariness seeped into her bones, dragging her down with lead weights. She looked at the bed, tempted to rest for a few minutes. But she was afraid that once she closed her eyes she would sleep for hours.

The thought that Gabe's problems were not over yet would not let her rest. She wanted to be with him when he visited Gino. Briskly she took Peter's hand and went into the bathroom. "Let's get you cleaned up, darling.''

The jeans and blue Shetland sweater Laura had bought were a little tight on Peter's sturdy frame, but at least they were clean. When Laura had bathed and dressed him, the maid took him with her to the kitchen. Clutching a model car in his hand, Peter followed her without protest. He was more comfortable eating in the kitchen than with the adults, Laura guessed.

During breakfast, which was served in a small open gallery overlooking the garden, Herb told Gabe, "I've cleared your visit with the warden. Gino's not a pretty sight," he warned. "He's got a slash in his face, another on his arm, and a deep cut in his shoulder."

Gabe looked grim. Laura longed to reach out and touch the clenched hand, the cuts now bandaged, to give him some comfort.

"Is there any way to have a plastic surgeon look at him?" she asked.

Herb shook his head. "I tried to have our physician examine him, but they refused." With a sigh he added, "The worst problem is not stitches, but infection. Their facilities are infested with streptococcus." He looked at Gabe with hard determination. "We will have him out of there soon."

Abruptly Gabe pushed back the chair and got to his feet, reaching for the brown tweed jacket he had hung over the chair. "Tomorrow, if I can arrange it." His face was hard and resolute, and deeply engraved with lines of exhaustion. "Sorry, Edith, I'm not hungry. Herb and I have to discuss a few things, and then I'm off."

Pointedly he looked at Laura's plate, where her eggs were congealing, still untouched. "Three square meals a day," he said quietly. "That was the deal."

Laura glanced at her food, then back at Gabe. "I'm coming with you," she said, her chin firming stubbornly. Peter was well taken care of. At present he did not need her, but Gabe did. Ignoring the startled speculative glances that passed between Herb and Edith, she continued quietly, "Don't shut me out."

Gabe stared at her, noticing that tiredness had painted dark smudges beneath her huge eyes and drawn taut lines into her pale face, heightening the air of fragility. Yet her eyes blazed with the blue fire of her indomitable courage, and her quiet determination kept her shoulders from drooping. Gabe found it impossible to refuse her.

Tenderness eased the harsh lines of his mouth. "Eat your breakfast," he said, a reluctant smile in his voice. "You have ten minutes." He left the gallery in Herb's company.

Edith's chuckle filled the silence that followed the men's departure. "I can't believe I saw what I think I just saw." Her eyes sharpened on the woman who had wrought such a startling change in Gabe. "Herb and I expected some beautiful but pathetic creature. You're certainly not that. I mean you're beautiful, but . . ."

"Thank you," Laura said, a smile tugging at her lips. "I know what you mean." She nibbled on some of the bacon, swallowed, then added, "Don't place too much significance in Gabe's actions." The admission darkened her eyes with pain. "We share a similar loss and fight the same enemy. In another day or two we'll go our separate ways."

Edith shook her head impatiently. "I've known Gabe for years. He was best man at our wedding. I've met quite a few of his friends. With you he is different. Softer, more approachable and more protective." She grinned, saying with forthright honesty, "I never thought I'd see Gabe share anything but a bed with a woman. Yet he's taking you to see Gino."

"Only because he knows that I refuse to be left behind." Laura wished she could read the same significance into Gabe's action as Edith did, but she had stopped deceiving herself. Gabe desired and cared, but not enough to make room for her in his life. She picked at the piece of toast, which was no longer crisp. "As soon as Gino is safe, I will return to New York."

Edith swallowed the words of protest hovering on her lips. She would save those for Gabe at some future date. Gently she said, "Herb told me what happened. The last year must have been a terrible ordeal for you."

Laura nodded, finishing her food. "It hasn't been easy. But at least I knew that Peter was well cared for, not suffering in some hole like Gino."

Edith's eyes darkened with pain. "I worry about that poor boy. I didn't mention it to Gabe, but I'm sure he realizes too that Gino can't endure much more." She sighed. "At least while he's in the hospital he's safe from some of the guards' cruelties. For one reason or another they've treated him more harshly than other prisoners. He is such a nice kid. My twins think the world of him. Gabe did a terrific job raising him."

"Gabe blames himself for what happened to Gino."

"So does Herb," Edith said. "Gino was staying with us when it happened. My son Fred saw the fight that started it all. Herb wanted Gino to fly back to Texas the following morning, but Gino didn't want to leave his truck behind. He'd just bought the pickup and was so proud of it."

Tears dampened her eyes and clung to her lashes. With trembling hands she wiped them away. "When you enter Mexico by car your visa is stamped accordingly," she explained. "In case of an emergency, if you need to take a plane out of here, Mexican authorities will take custody of the car. Gino didn't want to risk losing his prized possession, so he persuaded Herb to let him drive to Laredo the next morning."

Sighing, she went on, "I wish we'd never agreed to it. He was stopped by police outside the city limits. When they searched his truck they found two pounds of marijuana. We all know that Gino never touched the stuff." She blinked back the fresh tears rushing into her eyes. "Well, it should be over soon."

"Thank you for telling me about Gino. Gabe only explained the bare minimum." Laura rose to her feet, smoothing the heather-blue wool skirt down. "I'd better get my purse. If I'm not ready, Gabe will go without me."

In the upstairs bedroom, the two men talked about the events of the past two days.

"Laura is a lovely woman," Herb said. "How did she ever get mixed up with Vasquez?"

"Same way you almost got hitched to that nightclub dancer in Saigon. Loneliness," Gabe said, briefly explaining the death of Laura's father and her mother's subsequent return to Ireland.

"Don't remind me," Herb groaned. He was eternally grateful to Gabe for rescuing him and introducing him to Edith, who had been a nurse at the base. Laura had not been fortunate enough to have a friend like Gabe.

Gabe paced the room. "I was recognized last night," he said grimly. "By this evening Vasquez will know where I'm staying and draw the obvious conclusions. I'm afraid he's going to have Gino transferred to another facility if I don't move fast."

"I don't think you have to worry about that for a day or two," Herb assured him. "I promised the warden a case of my finest Scotch if he keeps Gino in the hospital ward until he's better. But we can discuss this later. Take my car while you're here. Your truck is too conspicuous. I'll have the gardener drive it into the garage."

When Gabe and Laura left the house to visit Gino, Edith handed them a basket with fresh fruit, candy and books, and a big plastic bag containing a quilted blanket, two pillows and a change of linen.

Everything was searched before they were allowed to enter the prison. The hospital ward was a nightmare. Everywhere they looked was chipped plaster, missing tiles and bare, dusty light bulbs. Last year's earthquake had added a crisscross pattern of fresh cracks in the high ceilings. The biggest gaps had been patched, but smaller fissures still showed crumbling plaster.

The thick walls and narrow windows prevented the sun from heating the cold building. Laura shivered in her woolen suit. At least the frigid temperature controlled the odors assaulting her nose. In summertime, she thought, this place must stink like New York during a garbage strike.

They had been met at the entrance by a middle-aged male nurse dressed in a snow-white uniform that, Laura guessed, had been worn especially for their benefit. On their way past crowded wards he assured them that Gino was doing as well as could be expected. Their main concern was not the stab wounds but dehydration from amoebic dysentery.

Outside Gino's door, Gabe thanked the man for the care he had given his nephew. He slipped some money into the nurse's hand and asked him to give them a few minutes' privacy. Gabe's eyes were dark and expressionless as he ushered Laura into the room. She squeezed his arm comfortingly. It was all she could do.

Gino's room had been cleaned very recently. The damaged floor was still damp where tiles were missing. The window was covered with a gray film of dirt that almost hid the bars over the outside. A narrow metal bed stood against one wall, an IV pole attached to its frame. Gray blankets were piled upon a body so thin that its still outline was barely noticeable beneath them.

Laura held out her hand for the packages. Handing them to her, Gabe strode toward the bed. The blond head, half-buried in the covers, refused to turn at the sound of his approach. "Gino?" Gabe bent over the huddled form, his voice soft and gentle, tenderly stroking the lanky hair. "Turn around and look at me."

For a long moment Gino did not respond. Then he slowly turned his head. Laura saw Gabe's shoulder muscles contract at the sight of the injured face. But his voice never faltered. "It must hurt like hell. Worse than being butted by a goat."

With a wrenching noise from deep in his throat, Gino rolled onto his back, giving Laura a glimpse of the thick bandage covering the right side of his face. A gauze-wrapped arm was flung around Gabe's strong neck. "You promised to get me out of here," he cried in a hoarse whisper.

With damp eyes, Laura watched Gabe gather the thin body into his strong arms. In this room filled with raw despair, love and tenderness, she had no place. Quietly placing the presents on the floor, she fled into the hall. Stifling a sob, she leaned against the wall, closing her ears to the ragged sounds drifting through the half-open door. Tears shimmered in her eyes, running unchecked down her face.

At the sight of Gino's suffering, her own problems faded into insignificance. She ached for Gabe, feeling his frustrated rage and helpless pain at seeing the person he loved most fading away.

The tiny flame of hope, which had flickered inside her with tenacious persistence, died in that dingy hall. No matter what the outcome, how could either Gabe or Gino ever forget that it was a Vasquez who had wrought such misery?

When Gabe finally joined her, his eyes were glittering. The hand that reached for her was like ice. Laura curled her fingers around it and clung to it all the way back to the car.

Hurrying through the halls and past the guards, she wondered if Gabe was even aware of her presence. Lost in his private hell of pain, he was shutting her out. It was as if the closeness of the last few days had never existed.

Over lunch Gabe discussed with Herb the merits of flying Gino to the Houston Medical Center for treatment. Neither man seemed to have any doubts that Gino would be released soon. Edith promised to take care of all the arrangements right after lunch. Then she looked at Laura. "What are your plans for this afternoon? If you want, I can ask my neighbor's son to come over. David will be good company for Peter."

"Laura and I are taking Peter to buy some boots." Gabe's eyes sharpened on her pale face, for the first time noticing the haunting darkness in her eyes. He covered her hand, frowning at its coldness. "I should have never let you come with me."

"I wanted to come," Laura reminded him.

"It meant a lot to me," Gabe admitted huskily. The sight of Gino, suffering in that cold, damp, stinking place, had shocked him, freezing him to his soul. He had been unable to respond to Laura's warm support. But he had treasured it.

Curling her fingers around his hand, she said, "Then I'm glad I came."

Withdrawing his hand, Gabe turned to Edith. "After our shopping spree, Herb and I will meet at the embassy. So if you want to make arrangements for Peter then, go right ahead."

"Peter would enjoy having someone to play with," Laura agreed, a lump in her throat. Despite his worry about Gino, Gabe still made time to honor his promise to Peter, and Edith was so very thoughtful. "Thank you," she said quietly.

They went to the Palacio de Hiero, one of Mexico's most luxurious department stores, to buy Peter's clothes. "Don't let Peter stray," he said quietly after he had parked the car. "I'm almost certain that no one followed us. In fact, so far I haven't seen any sign of Vasquez or his men. But let's not take any chances."

Laura's grasp on Peter's hand tightened instantly. But it wasn't easy keeping an active child under control in the crowded store. He reached out and touched, pulled away and examined, curiosity constantly drawing him away from them. Laura marveled at the selection of wares ranging from European imports to hand-knit sweaters made by *indiginos* in the outlying villages. She was tempted to buy Peter a whole wardrobe. But she did not dare linger too long, and bought only enough for his immediate needs.

"Boots," Peter said firmly when Laura had paid for the underwear, shirts, sweaters and jeans.

"Please," Laura prompted him.

Peter tilted his face up to her, showing his gap-toothed grin. "Please," he said in English before reverting to Spanish again. "Now can we go?"

"A man always keeps his promise," Gabe told him, chuckling. "Let's see what they have."

They found a pair of brown leather boots with a lizard-skin design, not exactly like Gabe's but close enough to satisfy Peter. To an outside observer, the discussion must have seemed strange. The child stating his wishes in Spanish, the blond Texan gravely considering his points and answering in English. Sitting back, Laura enjoyed their interaction, wishing, dreaming and storing those precious minutes with all the other memories.

Looking up, Gabe caught the look in her eyes, the joy and the pain. He wanted to reassure her, but he could not. He wanted to kiss her. That, too, had to wait. Abruptly he turned to the salesclerk and handed him the boots Peter had chosen, and paid for them.

As they neared the house, Laura turned to him with a smile. "Thank you for taking the time for Peter."

"Thank you," Peter echoed his mother, holding the box containing his boots tightly pressed against him.

"I enjoyed it," Gabe said, getting out of the car. Cautiously he looked up and down the street. Only when he was certain that no strange cars were parked anywhere near did he open the door on Laura's side. Peter dashed into the house to show off his boots. Carrying the shopping bags, Gabe and Laura followed at a slower pace.

"Don't go out again," Gabe advised, putting the bags down in the foyer. He drew her against him and brushed his lips across her cheek. He felt his body tense. Even bone-weary and tired as he was, she had that effect on him. His gut twisted at the thought of never seeing, holding or tasting her again once they left Mexico. Life would be lonely without her, more lonely than ever before.

But perhaps there was no need to let her go. He shook his head at the thought. He was too damn tired to make such decisions now. "I don't know how long I'll be." He hesitated briefly, then explained, "Time's running out. I have to get Gino out of prison before he can be transferred to another institution." He brushed back his hair, wearily massaging his neck. "If Vasquez is in town—which is very likely—I'll phone him to arrange the deal."

"You make it sound like a simple business transaction." She clenched her hands at her sides to keep them from clinging to Gabe and preventing him from leaving. "I didn't believe that the first time you suggested it, and I know you much better now. Even then I knew it would be dangerous. Don't take any risks." Julio was so unpredictable and totally blind in his rages. With his world crumbling around him, he could try to destroy the person responsible for his downfall no matter the cost to himself. Gabe was strong and resolute. In an open confrontation she would not have feared for his safety. It was treachery she feared, a shot in the back Gabe could not guard against.

"There has to be an alternative to confronting Julio. We need to find someone who has some influence over him. Someone he listens to." Frowning, Laura considered the options. "His father?"

Gabe shook his head. "I can't prove that he's also involved in the drug deals, but I'm almost certain of it."

"Dona Elena?" The moment she spoke her name, Laura shook her head, dismissing the woman as ineffectual. Then she reconsidered. "She seemed absolutely furious with Julio outside the doctor's office yesterday morning." Had it been only yesterday? So much had happened since then. She frowned. "I'm trying to remember what Julio used to say about her. She's very proud, very haughty, but she loves her family. And she stood up to Julio yesterday morning."

"You may have something," Gabe agreed thoughtfully. "We can discuss it later," he promised her. He walked to the door and opened it, then looked at her before stepping outside. "Try to get some sleep," he told her gently.

"What about you?" Laura said huskily. "You have slept less than I have during the last few days."

His face softened, the tired lines easing. "I've never dreamed so much in my life." Then, as Laura started to ask what he meant, he closed the door behind him.

Before Laura lay down, she called Al in New York. He was ecstatic about the news that she had Peter and wanted her to hop on the first plane to New York.

"I can't do that," Laura told him firmly. "Not before Gino is released. Don't worry about me. For the moment I'm perfectly safe. I'll call you tomorrow," she assured him before hanging up. Then she checked on Peter and found him playing in the kitchen, cars spread all around him on the floor. Thanking the maid for watching him, she went upstairs.

It seemed like only minutes later that Edith shook her awake.

"There's a phone call for you," she said, smiling apologetically. "I think it's important. A Father Fernando wants to talk to you."

Laura jumped up, excitement rushing through her. She ran downstairs, grabbing the phone before Edith could join her.

"Yes, Father Fernando, this is Laura speaking." Her voice was breathless.

"I promised I would call if I had any news for you. This afternoon Dona Elena came to me with my friend Raoul. She is greatly disturbed and wants to talk to you."

Laura frowned. "I am not going back to Guerrero."

"She realizes that. That is why she has come to Mexico City. She asked me to come with her because she was afraid you would refuse to see her otherwise."

Laura's hand trembled with excitement, and her eyes glowed with hope. This was the break she had been hoping for. "Where are you now?" she asked.

"In Colonia San Angel. We arrived at the airport less than an hour ago by private plane. We can meet you anytime."

Laura looked at Edith, standing so close that she could follow the conversation. Now she whispered, "Let her come here. But we have to contact Herb and Gabe first."

Nodding, Laura spoke into the phone. "Can I call you back in a few minutes?"

"Of course. That will give us time to have a bite to eat."

Edith picked up a pencil and wrote down the number Laura repeated out loud. "I'll call back within the half hour," Laura promised, and hung up.

"What do you think? Can you trust the priest?" Edith asked with a mixture of excitement and caution.

"Gabe does." The simple statement reassured Edith. "Where is Colonia San Angel?" Laura asked.

"It's a plush old neighborhood south of here," Edith explained, picking up the phone to dial Herb's number. "I know that Julio does not live there. Gabe once mentioned that he has an apartment in Polanco in the center of town."

"Then Julio may not know that his mother is here."

"That's probably true," Edith agreed. Impatiently tapping her foot, she listened to the phone ring several times before it was picked up by Herb's secretary, only to find that

Herb had left his office a while ago and was not expected back that day.

"Damn," Edith swore, bringing a smile to Laura's lips. "I don't know where they have gone or when they plan to come back. Do you want to go ahead without them?"

"Yes," Laura said firmly. "Gabe's afraid that Julio may have Gino transferred someplace else, so time is important."

Dona Elena and Padre Fernando arrived ninety minutes later by taxi. Both Laura and Edith had dressed formally for the meeting. Laura still wore the heather-blue wool skirt, but she had changed her blouse to a green-and-blue patterned silk one. She had put up her hair in a heavy chignon. Edith wore a brown silk dress enhanced by a heavy gold chain.

When they saw Dona Elena step from the taxi, both were glad that they had taken the trouble. Dressed in a smart flannel suit with pearls gleaming at her throat, ears and hands, the woman looked both elegant and self-assured.

But there was a haunting sadness in her eyes as she greeted Edith and Laura. "Is Pedro well?" she asked anxiously.

"Yes," Laura said softly. Peter and his new friend David were playing in the family room in the basement under the supervision of the maid. She turned to Padre Fernando. "I don't know how to thank you."

"I'm glad I could be of help." Looking around, he added, "I was hoping that Gabe would be here."

"He's been very busy," Laura said evasively. "I could not contact him on such short notice."

"I understand." The priest nodded, his gray eyes thoughtful.

Sitting down, Dona Elena came right to the point. "I've come here for two reasons," she said, smoothing the slim gray skirt over her knees. "One is my grandson." She looked at Laura pleadingly. "I would like to see him from time to time. But we can discuss this later. There are more pressing matters to consider first."

She took a deep breath, then continued. "Even as a child, Julio was wild. But to me he has always been a loving son.

So I closed my eyes to what I did not want to see. When my husband sent him to New York, I hoped that he would accept responsibility. But instead he resented our interference and married you, despite the fact, or because of it, that he had a fiancée waiting for him, the daughter of an old and valued friend.''

Laura's eyes widened. "I never knew."

With a faint smile Dona Elena said, "I realize that now, but at the time both my husband and I were very angry. Still, when we found out that you were pregnant, we were prepared to accept you. The hacienda has been passed down from father to son for the last hundred years, and my husband wanted an heir.''

"When Julio told us that you had left him and refused to let him see the child, we were angry. I'm afraid we inadvertently pushed Julio into abducting the child. We wanted our grandson, but we did not want you. I deeply regret our attitude now. You would have been a daughter to be proud of.''

Laura smiled ironically. There had been a time when she would have welcomed those words. Now she did not care whether Dona Elena approved of her or not. "I appreciate your openness," she said. "But that's all in the past. Why are you here now, Dona Elena?''

For one moment the dark eyes flashed with angry pride. Then they dimmed again, and her hands anxiously twisted the heavy gold rings on her fingers. "I did not believe until yesterday that my son was capable of cold-blooded murder. But when I heard him order his man to shoot you, I could not deceive myself any longer. I began to ask questions. What I found out made me turn to Father Fernando for help." She looked at the padre.

"Dona Elena is very concerned about your safety and that of her grandson," Padre Fernando said in his calm, direct way. "But she was afraid that you would not trust her."

"That is one of the reasons," Dona Elena said crisply. "I have already talked to the police and assured them that you took the child with my consent. If you agree, I will also make the necessary arrangements for your departure. You need not fear that my son will interfere."

She hesitated, fixed Laura with a direct stare and asked, "Are you going to marry Señor Borga?"

Laura's face became expressionless, a porcelain mask sliding over her face to hide the raw pain. She was certain that Gabe could never love her. Want and desire her, yes. But every time he looked at Gino's face he would be reminded of the past. Marrying her would keep the wound open, never closing because of the constant tearing. In time he would come to resent that she kept memories alive that were best forgotten. She could change Gabe's conviction that his ranch was no place for her. But she could not change the fact that she had been Vasquez's wife.

"No."

The single word had an odd effect. Laura had expected censure, resentment, distaste, but not the sudden despair that drew all color from her face, leaving a sickly olive tinge.

"But you have some influence with him? Enough to convince him to stop ruining my family name?" The dark eyes were pleading now.

Pity softened Laura's eyes. In some ways, Dona Elena was just another of Julio's victims. Then she thought of Gino and the horror of that prison, and of the many unknown lives Julio had destroyed with his drugs. "Your son has caused a lot of pain and misery," she said, her voice hardening with purpose. "Do you know that he sent an innocent boy to prison on trumped-up drug charges? That boy is dying, and you talk about besmirching a name."

Dona Elena's eyes darkened with horror. She turned to Padre Fernando and asked, "Why did you not tell me?"

"I didn't know." He looked at Laura with troubled eyes. "Is the boy Gabe's son?"

"His nephew." Edith spoke for the first time. "It happened while he was staying at this house." Briefly she explained to Padre Fernando the events leading up to Gino's imprisonment, her voice bitter and filled with pain. Finally she turned to Dona Elena, her usually gentle face hard. "If

Gino dies, there won't be a place on this earth your son will be safe.''

Dona Elena sat slumped in her chair, aging before their eyes while the words echoed around the room. Padre Fernando's parchmentlike skin stretched tautly across his cheekbones.

Laura met Edith's eyes somberly. She could not have presented Gino's plight more poignantly. In the silence settling over the room, Laura could almost hear again the hoarse, racking cries, see that thin body shake with despair. And feel Gabe's hand, frozen.

Abruptly she got to her feet, her face tight with determination. Facing Dona Elena, she said, ''You wanted me to intervene with Gabe Borga. I can't do it. We all have paid too high a price already. Now it's up to you, Dona Elena. Gino's life is in your hands. You know the people who could release him tonight.''

''Not tonight,'' Dona Elena protested, some color returning to her face. ''Tomorrow perhaps. I cannot promise you anything. But if you give me the boy's name, I will talk to the president. We have been friends for a long time.'' She looked at Padre Fernando. ''Do you have some influence with your cousin?''

Laura's eyes widened. ''Your cousin?'' she whispered. ''If I had known—''

Padre Fernando smiled at her. ''He is a third cousin. I told you God worked in mysterious ways.'' He rose to his feet, smoothing out his long black gown. ''We will contact you later. Perhaps by that time Gabe will have returned.'' He turned to Edith. ''If you would give me the name of the prison and the full name of the boy, we will go immediately.''

After Dona Elena and the padre had left, Edith and Laura looked at each other. Slowly their eyes brightened with hope.

''Do you think—?''

''Perhaps—''

''Probably—''

''Yes!''

Oh, yes, Laura thought, it had to work. Briefly she closed her eyes and tried to imagine what it would be like to live without fear. What it would be like to cross the street and not glance over her shoulder. How it would feel to look forward to each morning because Peter was there.

She couldn't imagine it yet.

But she knew what the nights would be like. Long, dark and lonely. "I wish the men would come back."

"I can't wait to see their faces," Edith sniffed, wiping the tears away with the back of her hand.

"Let's have a drink," Laura said huskily, dislodging the lump in her throat. She longed to watch the worry lines on Gabe's face ease into smiles. She wanted to see those eyes slowly light up with happiness.

They did light up, but more with the pleasure of seeing her than with joy at the sudden turn of events. Both Herb and Gabe were skeptical. "I always look a gift horse in the mouth. What does she want in return?" Gabe asked suspiciously.

"To stop harassing Julio, I imagine."

"Once Gino walks through those doors, I'll get the hell out of here," Gabe said. "And I don't plan to come back anytime soon. So it would be an easy promise to keep."

The call came at nine twenty-seven. They all crowded around Herb as he answered it. When he silently handed the phone to Gabe, Laura knew something had changed. Dona Elena would have asked for her instead of Gabe.

"It's Father Fernando," Herb explained, trying not to look anxious, but failing.

They listened to Gabe's monosyllabic answers, trying to make sense out of no's and yes's. When he concluded, "I understand. You tried your best," their hopes shattered.

Perhaps because she was so perfectly attuned to him, Laura was the first one to notice that Gabe looked worried, furious, even suspicious, but not filled with despair. He stared at his scuffed boots and said, "They're going to release Gino tomorrow at noon—if certain conditions are met. Apparently Don Emilio found out about his wife's activities. He's willing to go along with her plan in exchange for the negatives.''

He raised his head and looked at Laura with eyes that showed no emotions. ''And Dona Elena wants you there with the negatives.'' Damn. He wished that there was some way he could keep Laura out of this. But Padre Fernando had been quite emphatic. No Laura—no exchange. Only the two of them would be allowed inside the gate. Dona Elena did not want gossip to spread.

''Of course I'll go,'' Laura said firmly. She knew Gabe did not want her there because too many things could go wrong. A small smile lit her lips. ''Actually, I'm quite grateful to Dona Elena. If it wasn't for her, you'd leave me behind.''

''Damn straight,'' Gabe groaned. He drew her against him, holding her tight.

''We have a partnership,'' Laura reminded him softly.

''To hell with it,'' Gabe said roughly.

The house had been quiet for hours. When Gabe opened the door to Laura's room, she was sound asleep. Broodingly he stared down at her sleeping form, his conscience telling him to leave her alone. But his bed was cold and lonely, and his sleep disturbed by Gino's cries for help. Tonight he wanted the comfort of her clean, soft flesh and a few hours of forgetfulness. He shrugged out of his robe and reached for her.

In the pale moonlight shining through the window, her skin shone with the luminescence of precious pearls, her thick sooty lashes hiding the smudges of exhaustion.

With a small contented murmur she turned to him. ''You're late,'' she muttered, her voice slurred with sleep.

Pillowing her head on his shoulder, Gabe smiled. ''Go back to sleep,'' he whispered softly into the midnight-black hair sliding over his skin like ebony silk.

For a while he was content to hold her and listen to her breathing. Weary as he was, though, he could not fall asleep. In his mind he went over the arrangements he had made for Laura's safety. Were they adequate? Was he placing too much trust in the padre's ability to shield her should Vasquez turn up?

His arms tightened around her slight form, his body responding to the slim curves pressed against him. His hands stroked over her lace-covered breasts, sliding down the straps of the satin nightgown she wore.

Drowsily Laura opened her eyes, arching into Gabe's caresses with sensuous lassitude. What had driven him from his bed into her arms? If she had any pride, she thought, she would send him away. But her love for him made her weak. This might be the last night they had together. "Love me," she breathed, raising her face for his kiss.

"Yes." His hands gently cupped her face. He kissed her, and his hands slid down her throat, stroking her bare breasts until they swelled. Turning her over on her back, he rose above her on his knees and slid the white nightgown down her body.

Laura shivered as the cool night air touched her skin. But when her arms would have drawn him on top of her, he slid down her body, his lips tasting, stirring, consuming her. She squirmed when his tongue sought the warmth of her womanhood. "Gabe, no," she protested, trying to hold him off.

But Gabe would not be denied. He held her with his strong hands, loving her until the night exploded into shimmering stars. At last, when she thought she would lose consciousness, Gabe joined her with powerful strokes and driving need. Wrapping her arms around his neck, Laura held him as if she would never let him go.

Morning came all too soon.

Chapter 13

Laura and Gabe arrived at the small rear exit of the prison twenty minutes early. Both were dressed once again in jeans, their shirts topped with sweaters to keep out the cold. Gabe, his gaze shifting around the broken doorways and shattered windows of the deserted buildings facing the prison, carried the negatives in a big canvas bag.

"It's creepy," Laura said with a shiver. Dona Elena had apparently chosen this particular gate because of its deserted surroundings. There would be no unwanted witnesses to the exchange. The dingy walls were topped with razor wire and shards of glass. High above the walls stood a watchtower with armed guards.

Gabe threw one arm around her and drew her with him until their backs were against the wall, and repeated what he had told her once on their way over. "Herb and Larry are three streets down. After Dona Elena gets here, they'll move closer. This time, you won't take any risks." He tilted her head back and kissed her. "If I'm not back within ten minutes, you take the negatives and run."

Laura nodded. Last night she had not realized the extent of the danger Gabe would be in. Once behind those high, dark walls, he would be as much a prisoner as Gino—unless Dona Elena kept her word. Her hand curled around Gabe's. "Everything will work out fine," she said with more confidence than she felt. All that stood between failure and success was Padre Fernando. Despite the taut suspicion on Gabe's face, there was a new spring to his step, that extra surge of vitality that comes from expecting your hopes to become reality.

At five minutes before twelve a taxi raced over the cobblestone pavement and came to a noisy stop. Padre Fernando stepped from the car, waving a good morning at Laura and Gabe before helping Dona Elena alight.

"Do you have the negatives?" Dona Elena asked briskly. In the wine-red coat with its black accessories, she looked as cool and elegant as always.

"Yes." Gabe shook hands with Padre Fernando, but waited until the taxi had left before unzipping the bag and showing the many strips of negatives wrapped in clear plastic. Apparently the mere sight of them satisfied Dona Elena. Nodding, she said, "Let's get this over with. Laura, you stay here with Father Fernando."

Handing her the bag, Gabe cupped her chin and brushed his lips across her cheek. "Don't take any chances," he whispered before turning away. Cupping Dona Elena's arm, he helped her over the cobblestone pavement to the gate in the wall.

Laura's hands clenched over the straps as she watched the small gate open, then close behind them.

"Everything will be fine," Padre Fernando said soothingly. "Tell me about your son. Is he adjusting well to the changes?"

Laura managed a weak smile. "He's doing fine. His English is very rusty, but that will change with time."

While they talked, her eyes were firmly glued to the door. Minutes passed like hours. And then, suddenly, Gabe appeared. With one strong arm wrapped around the thin waist, he more carried than supported Gino. Her face bright with happiness and relief, Laura ran toward them.

Suddenly a black car raced around the corner. As Laura jumped back to avoid getting hit, the car came to a screeching halt next to her. The door opened and, before she could run, Juan and Jorge jumped into the street, pistols drawn. Grabbing her, Jorge forced her into the back seat before Padre Fernando could come to her aid.

At that moment Dona Elena stepped into the street. "No, Julio," she cried out in protest. "Everything is arranged. I have the negatives. Let Laura go."

Gabe thrust Gino behind him, preparing to jump Vasquez the moment Juan lowered his gun.

Julio's face twisted. The moment he had spotted his mother and Gabe coming from the warden's office, he had known the game was over. He had rushed to his car, rage blinding him, desire for revenge filling him until all he could think of was how to hurt the Texan. "No, I have them," he corrected her, his eyes gleaming with triumph. "And Laura, too." As he stared at Gabe, the triumph changed to hate. "You have your nephew, gringo," he snarled. "Go home. Forget about my wife and son."

Jorge slipped into the car, crawling across Laura to the opposite side. Through the rolled-down window he kept his pistol aimed at Gabe, while Juan climbed in on the other side.

As the car leaped forward, Laura caught a glimpse of Gabe running, pistol in hand.

As it raced through the deserted street, shots rang out after the car. Jorge and Juan fired back through the open windows. Before they turned the corner, Laura saw Larry's Mustang stop and pick up Gabe. From the next side street, Herb's blue sedan shot across the road, trying to block it. Julio steered into the gap between the car and the house. Metal was crushed against wall, then the powerful car shot forward along the narrow street.

None of the three men paid any attention to Laura now. Julio steered the speeding car into the heavy traffic, hopping from lane to lane. Jorge and Juan knelt next to her, watching their rear.

They flashed through stoplights, swerved around corners and weaved their way through traffic circles, but the Mustang stayed right behind them. Laura fumbled for the seat belt, buckled herself in and clung to the back of the front seat. "Julio, slow down," she pleaded. "You're going to kill us all."

"Shut up," he ground out between clenched teeth, sending the car at high speed around another sharp curve. As they shot blindly out of the last corner, a truck was turning into the narrow street.

Laura screamed, her world darkening, seeing the scene before her in slow motion. The truck was trying to evade the oncoming car, but there was no place for it to go. Brakes screeching, Julio tore the steering wheel to the left, hitting the concrete wall of a house. Spinning away from it, the car catapulted into the truck, its tons of metal racing toward them. In the instant before the car hit the wall, Laura clasped her hands over her head and bent low over her knees.

High-pitched human screams. Metal crunched and bones and muscles broke and tore. Glass shattered, glittering pieces spraying. The world became a smoke-clouded cartwheel, spinning, spinning.

Deathly silence followed as the cloud slowly settled.

When Gabe and Larry arrived at the scene of the accident, the truck driver and his friend were already pulling bodies from the wreck.

Julio, Jorge and Juan were laid out on the sidewalk. Gabe wasted one glance on them before rushing to the mangled metal, its wheels slowly turning on top. It seemed impossible that anyone could still be alive inside the twisted heap of smoking hell.

In that moment, Gabe knew how he felt about Laura. The revelation that he loved this woman above anything else was like a searing pain. He crouched next to Larry's legs, which were sticking out from the open door. "Can you get to her?" His voice was hoarse.

"She's buckled in." Larry's breathless voice gave him some hope.

Gabe wanted to shove Larry aside and crawl into the hole and stop his world from spinning, but he was too big for the opening. "Is she alive?"

"I think so. Don't know yet." Seconds later, Larry cried, "I'm getting a pulse. It's weak, but steady."

A lifetime later, Laura was freed from the wreckage.

Her clothes were covered with glass and blood. Someone else's, Gabe quickly concluded after carefully running his hands over her slim body searching for injuries. Except for a few minor cuts and abrasions, he found none. Her pulse was low and steady. Her pupils contracted evenly. At the back of her head he felt a bump the size of a golf ball.

When Gabe lifted her in his arms to carry her to the ambulance someone had called, Laura groaned and opened her eyes, fighting for the breath that had been knocked out of her.

"Lie still." Gabe's arms tightened around her. "You were in a car wreck, but you're all right."

Laura closed her eyes against the bright world spinning around her. When the whirling stopped, she opened them again. "What about the others?" she asked, memory returning.

Larry helped Gabe lift Laura into the ambulance. "Vasquez is alive. His men are dead. We're taking you both to the hospital."

"Take care of Peter," Laura whispered, and fainted before Gabe could reassure her.

Two days later, Laura said goodbye to Gabe in front of the small private plane that was flying him and Gino to the Houston Medical Center.

She had seen little of him since the accident. He had brought Peter to visit her at the ABC hospital where she had spent one night under observation. Even last night, Gabe had not come to her. Laura had lain awake, listening to the muted sounds coming from his room, despair spreading like desert dust, choking the ever-struggling spark of hope.

"I guess this is goodbye," she said softly, her eyes hungrily studying each of his features, memorizing them.

Gabe cupped her face with his rough hands, caressing the smooth, pale skin. Her eyes glittered with unshed tears.

"Take care of yourself, darlin'," he said huskily, his voice barely audible above the screams of jet engines. "You're quite a lady. I couldn't have had a better partner."

Laura's lips twisted with sharp pain. The only partnership she wanted was out of her reach. Forever. Julio's deeds rose like a thick cloud of dust between them, a wailing song of loss. He saw her lips quiver and bent his head, drawing from her mouth enough love to carry with him through the lonely days and nights to come. If she had asked him to take her with him, he would have lifted her into the plane. But she didn't. Because he loved her, he tore himself out of her arms and climbed into the plane that would take him back to the land he loved—the land where roses shriveled and died.

Laura smiled, keeping the promise she had made herself so long ago, until Gabe could not see her any longer. With her fingers pressed against her lips and tears streaming down her face, Laura watched the small plane taxi, surge forward and finally leap smoothly into the smog-gray sky. A long time later, she turned back toward the car where Edith and Herb were waiting with Peter.

She wished that she, too, could leave Mexico, where everything reminded her of Gabe and the bitter pain of her loss, and return to the familiar surroundings of her life. But as long as Julio's life hung on a thread, she felt an obligation to stay. Dona Elena loved Peter and sought solace in his presence. Laura found that she was unable to deprive the woman of the few glimpses of sunshine peeking through the dark clouds surrounding her.

For his wife's sake, Don Emilio tolerated the gringo wife he had always rejected. But he did not conceal the fact that he blamed Laura for Julio's excesses and his accident.

Julio died the night of Gabe's departure.

For his funeral Laura flew down to Acapulco, then spent the following two weeks getting to know her son again—and gently weaning him from the influence of the Vasquez family.

They were two weeks of both joy and sadness. She missed Gabe terribly. Often, when Peter finally dropped off to sleep after a day spent swimming, sailing and snorkeling, she was tempted to pick up the phone and call Houston.

But she never did.

One day she drove with Peter to the village of Santa Ana to thank Padre Fernando and to donate funds to his church.

At the end of the two weeks, on her way back to New York, Laura stopped over in Mexico City.

Edith met her at the airport. "Things are looking up, Laura. Gino is responding to treatment and is walking around. He's already had plastic surgery on his face. Gabe said that he refused to have the other scars operated on."

At the sound of Gabe's name, longing welled up in Laura, strong and passionate and painful. "How is Gabe?" Laura asked huskily.

Edith's brown eyes softened. "Quiet and lonely, the stubborn fool. He needs you, Laura. Won't you go to him?"

Laura's lips twisted with bitterness. "It would never work."

"Why not?" Edith asked sharply. "He loves you, and I think you love him. You'd get used to the ranch life, and to the heat and the tumbleweed. You're not a person to fear dust storms and flash floods."

"No," Laura agreed. She had found strength in the desert and the mountains and love in Gabe's arms. But even the newly strong and fearless woman she had become could not fight the shadows of the past. "As much as I regret it, I was Vasquez's wife."

"Don't tell me you feel responsible for his actions," Edith protested. "You were as much a victim as Gino."

"Some mistakes you never stop paying for," Laura said soberly. "Edith, I know you mean well, but I know what I'm talking about. That day, after we visited Gino at the hospital, Gabe could not bear to look at me. And Gabe cares. Gino doesn't know me. How do you think he would react if Gabe took in Vasquez's widow and child?''

Edith shook her head firmly. "Gino is very much like Gabe. He wouldn't blame you any more than his uncle does." She looked at Peter, who was busy painting trails of ketchup on the plate and licking off his fingers. When he stuffed a handful of French fries into his mouth and began chewing them with obvious delight, she added, "As to blaming that adorable child for what his father did—I'll never believe that of either of them."

Hope welled up in Laura. Edith sounded so certain. And she had known Gabe and Gino for a long time. On the other hand, Gabe had warned her that Edith had tried to matchmake for years. In her desire to see Gabe married, his friend might easily minimize the obstacles.

"I'll see what happens," she said evasively. "For right now, I'm returning to New York. My mother will be waiting for us there. Gabe knows where to find me if he changes his mind."

Edith swallowed a protest and shrugged her shoulders. Both she and Herb planned to spend the following week, Thanksgiving, with their children at the ranch. It would be a splendid opportunity to sound out Gino and observe Gabe. "We won't lose contact," she promised softly. "Ever heard of dust songs?" When Laura shook her head, she explained. "When the wind blows dust across the range, it has an eerie, mournful sound. As a child, Gino called them dust songs. They've always had an odd effect on me. I feel lonely, even inside the house and surrounded by people." She smiled. "They affect Gabe the same way. The dust songs will bring him to you."

"Mama, can I open the package now?" Peter asked, pulling on the strings of the parcel that had arrived from Mexico that morning.

"May I," Laura corrected, stretching high to put the angel on top of the Christmas tree. December winds were blowing through the city's canyons, whipping slush at the windows. She looked at her mother, sitting in a high-backed chair near the fireplace. "How does that look?"

"May I? Please?" Peter interrupted.

"It's a little crooked," Colleen Foster said. "Laura, let him open the package. He's going to pester you until you do."

Laura adjusted the angel and looked down at her son. Even after seven weeks, she was reluctant to let him out of her sight. "Persistent little devil, aren't you?" she said, loving him with her eyes.

Peter grinned his gap-toothed smile. "May I?"

She sighed. "Yes, you may." She could deny him nothing, a fact she knew would have to change. After Christmas, she promised herself. When things returned to normal and her mother returned to Ireland, because she was almost as bad as Laura, spoiling him rotten. When Peter went to preschool there would be plenty of time to start with a little discipline.

"Thanks." Peter reached for the scissors lying next to him, fitting his stubby fingers into the loops. His tongue came out as he concentrated on the task of snipping the string. Laura wanted to reach out and hug him.

Instead she turned to the box of ornaments standing on top of the ladder, picking up a gingerbread house that had been her favorite when she had been Peter's age. "It still looks like new," she said to her mother, admiring the minute details of the red windows and the almond-studded roof.

"I paid a fortune for it," her mother recalled dryly. "But you absolutely had to have it."

Reaching for one of the top branches, Laura stepped too far to the left. The ladder tilted sideways, then straightened when she redistributed her weight.

"Laura, be careful," her mother pleaded. "You shouldn't even climb ladders in your condition."

Peter stopped shredding the wrapping paper and looked at his mother. "What's a condition?"

Before Laura could think of an answer that would satisfy her son, the door chimes rang. "Saved by the bell," she grinned, shaking her head at her mother. Her Christmas present had come early. A few days ago, she had found out that she was carrying Gabe's child. She had shared her joy with her mother, but she wanted to put off telling Peter until her pregnancy showed. While her son had adjusted well to the changes, he still felt an occasional sense of insecurity.

Edith had only called once after Thanksgiving. She had talked a great deal about her children and very little about Gabe and Gino. Laura had drawn her own conclusion from that call. Nothing had changed. She doubted that it ever would.

Climbing down the steps, she smoothed the thick blue-and-black sweater over her black pants. "I'm sure it's Karen. She said she would drop by for an Irish coffee."

"Or that hairy ape, Fred, from next door, wanting to borrow another cup of sugar. If it's him, let him hang up the ornaments," her mother called after her.

Chuckling, Laura went into the foyer. Fred was a dear. Laura didn't mind him borrowing the odd cup of sugar, coffee or milk. She was only annoyed when he rang after midnight to borrow some gin. As she raised the peephole cover, the chimes rang impatiently.

"Who is it?" she asked, peering into the hall.

She saw him the moment his deep voice drawled, "Gabe."

With her face pressed against the door, she feasted her eyes on him before the vision, clad in an unfamiliar rusty tweed jacket, blue shirt and red tie, would disappear, leaving nothing but emptiness.

It wasn't the first time her eyes had tricked her. Twice she had run after a man with Gabe's height and thick, tawny hair. But neither man had had the bronzed skin, golden eyes and slow, dazzling smile that had haunted her.

"Darlin', I've come a long way. Will you open the door or do I have to try one of my tricks?"

Laughter gurgled in her throat, and tears shimmered in her eyes. "These locks better take longer to open than a flick of the wrist," Laura said, "or I want my money back." Her shaking hands fumbled with the knobs of the best security locks money could buy, and pulled at the door.

"Damn," she swore when nothing moved. "Don't go away," she pleaded with a voice that was half exasperation and half laughing sobs, wiping her wet palms on her pants. The next time she concentrated and succeeded. She threw the door open and hurled herself at Gabe.

When his strong arms closed around her, she felt complete. At this moment, it didn't matter why he had come. She didn't care that he had left her without hope. She didn't care if he planned to leave her again. He had come to her. It was a beginning. Her hands reached up and cupped his jaw. "I missed you," she whispered, unable to say any more.

Gabe held her as if he would never let her go. He stared at the face, a face more poignantly beautiful even than his memories. Then he kissed her as if he had wandered the dusty desert for days in search of water and finally found it.

"Laura, what is taking so long?" Colleen Foster walked into the foyer and stopped at the sight of a stranger kissing her daughter in the middle of the hallway.

Reluctantly, Laura turned within the circle of his arms. "This is Gabe," she said. The three simple words and the deep blue sparkle in her eyes told her mother that this was the man Laura loved enough to want his child.

Until now Colleen had been afraid that Laura had fallen in love with a man as superficially charming as Julio. But one look into those steady eyes and at his face, and she breathed a sigh of relief. She saw no weakness, only solid strength and a loving gentleness that brought a lump to her throat.

"Come in," she said, her voice lilting with happiness. "You're just in time to help us dress the tree."

Gabe looked at the small, slender woman who might have been Laura's sister except for a few wrinkles and the gray streaks in her short, stylish hair. "Thank you," he said, accepting the invitation to enter the house and the family.

"I'm the tallest one in my family. I always get the job of putting up the star."

"You're too late for that," Laura said, laughing. "But don't worry, there are lots of tall branches still bare. At least I can put the ladder away."

Peter was emptying the box filled with gaily wrapped presents. At their entrance he looked up, saying, "These are all for me. You only got one." When he noticed Gabe, his eyes widened, then narrowed cautiously. Scrambling to his feet, he said with a formal politeness that startled Laura, "How are you, Mr. Borga?"

Frowning, Laura looked from Peter to Gabe. Was it insecurity that turned the child who knew few strangers into this reserved young boy?

Gabe ignored Peter's reaction. "Fine. And how are you, Peter?" He lowered his tall body to the child's level and smilingly pointed at the packages. "I see you got quite a few presents already. Do they rattle?"

"This one does." Peter picked up a long narrow box and shook it, but refused to hand it to Gabe. "How long are you staying?" Laura opened her mouth to protest her son's rudeness. But a look from Gabe kept her silent. She held her breath, listening intently for his answer. It would be hours before Peter went to bed and her mother retired. Until then she would have no opportunity to talk to Gabe privately, to ask him herself why he had come or how long he would stay.

"I don't know yet," Gabe said quietly, standing up with the fluid grace she remembered so well. Shrugging out of his jacket, he laid it across a chair. Rolling up his sleeves, he said, "How about helping us decorate the tree?"

Peter hesitated, clutching the package like a shield, raking the big man in front of him with eyes as wary as his mother's had been when Gabe had first stood before her. Then he slowly stacked the packages with the other presents. "Will you lift me up so I can reach the top? Mama put the angel on crooked."

With a lump in her throat, Laura watched Gabe lift her son with gentle hands. Squeezing her arm, her mother whispered, "He's going to be all right."

Hours later, Laura said good-night to her son and slowly made her way to the living room, where Gabe waited for her, sitting in front of the fire on the soft leather couch.

She hesitated at the door, now wishing that her mother had not tactfully withdrawn. The last few hours had been happy ones, filled with shared smiles and Peter's laughter, teasing her with a vision of a life she desperately wanted but dared not hope for.

"Why did you come?" she asked across the space of the room.

Gabe stared expressionless at her face, wishing he could read the thoughts hidden behind it. She looked so fragile in that voluminous sweater, the silky curtain of the midnight-black waves cascading down her back. He had almost forgotten how slender she was. In the weeks past, he had mostly remembered her beauty and her strength and the warmth of sharing his sleeping bag. He almost got up to walk away from her.

Then he remembered the loneliness that had been with him since he had left her, the sense of loss that grew with each dust song. "I couldn't stay away." He had needed to find out if she meant those words torn from her when she had been lost and vulnerable.

He rose to his feet, picked up a log from the shining brass bucket and laid it on top of the glowing embers, afraid of what her answer would be. He had given her time for the excitement that had sent her into his arms to wear off. What if she had found out that it hadn't been love that she had felt for him but a mixture of affection, newly awakened desire and gratitude?

"It's time we talked," he said, swiftly getting to his feet, facing her across the space. "When we met, you were desperate. I've seen desperation change people. Under even less pressing circumstances, for the sake of their families, I've seen honest men become crooks and virtuous women prostitute themselves. I wanted you and I took advantage of your fears."

"That's not true," Laura protested urgently. "I wanted you to make love to me. I all but propositioned you."

Gabe shook his head, his face hard and distant. "You had just been run down by a helicopter, had escaped two of Vasquez's men and had seen your son for the first time in a year. You were off balance and not responsible for your actions. I have no excuses for mine."

Laura paled, her hands clenching at her sides. Was it guilt that had brought him to New York, and the need to reassure himself that she was all right? Briefly she wished he had not come to breathe new heat into the cooling embers of hope.

"That accounts for the first night," Laura said, her voice rising with quiet determination to coddle the small flame. "I fell in love with you then. I haven't changed since."

Gabe's hard face softened. He raised his arms, only to drop them again. "Love has many faces. Gratitude is one of them. Friendship another." He searched her face and flinched at the raw pain darkening her eyes. Still he pressed on, because he had to be sure that what she felt for him was strong enough to withstand the erosion of dust and heat and drought. "The most common one, of course, is sexual gratification."

"No." Her bitter voice cut through his clinical dissection. "It was never that for me." She wrapped her arms across her belly, even now swelling with the child conceived out of her love for him. "I fell in love with you in the cave. Perhaps I was off balance then, because my defenses were down. But that doesn't make my feelings any less real. I loved you then. I love you now. If you still doubt me, come back in ten years and my answer will be the same."

Suppressed sobs shook her body, and tears filled her eyes. She knew she could stop this torture by telling him she carried his child. Gabe's strong sense of responsibility would not let him walk away from her then. But, like Gabe, she did not want to build their future on a shaky foundation.

Through the mist of her tears, she saw Gabe change. Slowly, like a ray of warm sunshine piercing dark clouds, his smile softened the harsh lines of his face. He crossed the space between them with that smooth gait she remembered so well and drew her into his strong, powerful embrace.

"Laura, be very, very sure," he said, his voice rough and urgent. "Once I have you, I won't let you go."

Her arms closed around him, and she trembled with the force of her emotions, sobs racking her slim body. "It was you who walked away from me," she cried.

Gabe laughed roughly before he kissed her. As he drank from her tender lips, he felt her soften against him, clinging to him. Her sweet tears melted away his last lingering doubts.

"What about Gino?" Laura asked when she finally emerged from the kiss, breathless and glowing with happiness. "Won't he resent the fact that I'm Vasquez's widow?"

Smiling, Gabe shook his tawny head. "I almost came up to New York when Edith told me about that bit of nonsense." His eyes glowed golden with laughter and happiness. "Gino's response wasn't quite as subdued."

"I wish you had," Laura sighed, framing his face, thinking of the lonely nights when tears had wet her pillow.

"You needed time," Gabe said soberly. "We all did."

Laura put her fingers on his lips to stop his words. They had a lifetime to talk about the past, about others, and about the future.

This moment was theirs alone.

She drew his head down and kissed him. "I love you, guardian angel, partner, father of my child."

Gabe went very still, understanding the complete meaning of her words. And then he kissed her with a reverence and gentleness that brought fresh tears to her eyes. "I love you, my woman."

* * * * *

*...and now an exciting short story
from Silhouette Books.*

*

HEATHER GRAHAM POZZESSERE
Shadows on the Nile

CHAPTER ONE

Alex could tell that the woman was very nervous. Her fingers were wound tightly about the arm rests, and she had been staring straight ahead since the flight began. Who was she? Why was she flying alone? Why to Egypt? She was a small woman, fine-boned, with classical features and porcelain skin. Her hair was golden blond, and she had blue-gray eyes that were slightly tilted at the corners, giving her a sensual and exotic appeal.

And she smelled divine. He had been sitting there, glancing through the flight magazine, and her scent had reached him, filling him like something rushing through his bloodstream, and before he had looked at her he had known that she would be beautiful.

John was frowning at him. His gaze clearly said that this was not the time for Alex to become interested in a woman. Alex lowered his head, grinning. Nuts to John. He was the one who had made the reservations so late that there was already another passenger between them in their row. Alex couldn't have remained silent anyway; he was certain that he could ease the flight for her. Besides, he had to know her name, had to see if her eyes would turn silver when she smiled. Even though he should, he couldn't ignore her.

"Alex," John said warningly.

Maybe John was wrong, Alex thought. Maybe this was precisely the right time for him to get involved. A woman would be the perfect shield, in case anyone was interested in his business in Cairo.

The two men should have been sitting next to each other, Jillian decided. She didn't know why she had wound up sandwiched between the two of them, but she couldn't do a thing about it. Frankly, she was far too nervous to do much of anything.

"It's really not so bad," a voice said sympathetically. It came from her right. It was the younger of the two men, the one next to the window. "How about a drink? That might help."

Jillian took a deep, steadying breath, then managed to answer. "Yes . . . please. Thank you."

His fingers curled over hers. Long, very strong fingers, nicely tanned. She had noticed him when she had taken her seat—he was difficult not to notice. There was an arresting quality about him. He had a certain look: high-powered, confident, self-reliant. He was medium tall and medium built, with shoulders that nicely filled out his suit jacket, dark brown eyes, and sandy hair that seemed to defy any effort at combing it. And he had a wonderful voice, deep and compelling. It broke through her fear and actually soothed her. Or perhaps it was the warmth of his hand over hers that did it.

"Your first trip to Egypt?" he asked. She managed a brief nod, but was saved from having to comment when the stewardess came by. Her companion ordered her a white wine, then began to converse with her quite normally, as if unaware that her fear of flying had nearly rendered her speechless. He asked her what she did for a living, and she heard herself tell him that she was a music teacher at a junior college. He responded easily to everything she said, his voice warm and concerned each time he asked another question. She didn't think; she simply answered him, because flying had become easier the moment he touched her. She even told him that she was a widow, that her husband had been killed in a car accident four years ago, and that she was here now to fulfill a long-held dream, because she had always longed to see the pyramids, the Nile and all the ancient wonders Egypt held.

She had loved her husband, Alex thought, watching as pain briefly darkened her eyes. Her voice held a thread of sadness when she mentioned her husband's name. Out of nowhere, he wondered how it would feel to be loved by such a woman.

Alex noticed that even John was listening, commenting on things now and then. How interesting, Alex thought, looking across at his friend and associate.

The stewardess came with the wine. Alex took it for her, chatting casually with the woman as he paid. Charmer, Jillian thought ruefully. She flushed, realizing that it was his charm that had led her to tell him so much about her life.

Her fingers trembled when she took the wineglass. "I'm sorry," she murmured. "I don't really like to fly."

Alex—he had introduced himself as Alex, but without telling her his last name—laughed and said that was the understatement of the year. He pointed out the window to the clear blue sky—an omen of good things to come, he said—then assured her that the airline had an excellent safety record. His friend, the older man with the haggard, world-weary face, eventually introduced himself as John. He joked and tried to reassure her, too, and eventually their efforts paid off. Once she felt a little calmer, she offered to move, so they could converse without her in the way.

Alex tightened his fingers around hers, and she felt the startling warmth in his eyes. His gaze was appreciative and sensual, without being insulting. She felt a rush of sweet heat swirl within her, and she realized with surprise that it was excitement, that she was enjoying his company the way a woman enjoyed the company of a man who attracted her. She had thought she would never feel that way again.

"I wouldn't move for all the gold in ancient Egypt," he said with a grin, "and I doubt that John would, either." He touched her cheek. "I might lose track of you, and I don't even know your name."

"Jillian," she said, meeting his eyes. "Jillian Jacoby."

He repeated her name softly, as if to commit it to memory, then went on to talk about Cairo, the pyramids at Giza, the Valley of the Kings, and the beauty of the nights when the sun set over the desert in a riot of blazing red.

And then the plane was landing. To her amazement, the flight had ended. Once she was on solid ground again, Jillian realized that Alex knew all sorts of things about her, while she didn't know a thing about him or John—not even their full names.

They went through customs together. Jillian was immediately fascinated, in love with the colorful atmosphere of Cairo, and not at all dismayed by the waiting and the bureaucracy. When they finally reached the street she fell head over heels in love with the exotic land. The heat shimmered in the air, and taxi drivers in long burnooses lined up for fares. She could hear the soft singsong of their language, and she was thrilled to realize that the dream she had harbored for so long was finally coming true.

She didn't realize that two men had followed them from the airport to the street. Alex, however, did. He saw the men behind him, and his jaw tightened as he nodded to John to stay put and hurried after Jillian.

"Where are you staying?" he asked her.

"The Hilton," she told him, pleased at his interest. Maybe her dream was going to turn out to have some unexpected aspects.

He whistled for a taxi. Then, as the driver opened the door, Jillian looked up to find Alex staring at her. She felt . . . something. A fleeting magic raced along her spine, as if she knew what he was about to do. Knew, and should have protested, but couldn't.

Alex slipped his arm around her. One hand fell to her waist, the other cupped her nape, and he kissed her. His mouth was hot, his touch firm, persuasive. She was filled with heat; she trembled . . . and then she broke away at last, staring at him, the look in her eyes more eloquent than any words. Confused, she turned away and stepped into the taxi.

As soon as she was seated she turned to stare after him, but he was already gone, a part of the crowd.

She touched her lips as the taxi sped toward the heart of the city. She shouldn't have allowed the kiss; she barely knew him. But she couldn't forget him.

She was still thinking about him when she reached the Hilton. She checked in quickly, but she was too late to acquire a guide for the day. The manager suggested that she stop by the Kahil bazaar, not far from the hotel. She dropped her bags in her room, then took another taxi to the bazaar. Once again she was enchanted. She loved everything: the noise, the people, the donkey carts that blocked the narrow streets, the shops with their beaded entryways and beautiful wares in silver and stone, copper and brass. Old men smoking water pipes sat on mats drinking tea, while younger men shouted out their wares from stalls and doorways. Jillian began walking slowly, trying to take it all in. She was occasionally jostled, but she kept her hand on her purse and sidestepped quickly. She was just congratulating herself on her competence when she was suddenly dragged into an alley by two Arabs swaddled in burnooses.

"What—" she gasped, but then her voice suddenly fled. The alley was empty and shadowed, and night was coming. One man had a scar on his cheek, and held a long, curved knife; the other carried a switchblade.

"Where is it?" the first demanded.

"Where is what?" she asked frantically.

The one with the scar compressed his lips grimly. He set his knife against her cheek, then stroked the flat side down to her throat. She could feel the deadly coolness of the steel blade.

"Where is it? Tell me now!"

Her knees were trembling, and she tried to find the breath to speak. Suddenly she noticed a shadow emerging from the darkness behind her attackers. She gasped, stunned, as the man drew nearer. It was Alex.

Alex...silent, stealthy, his features taut and grim. Her heart seemed to stop. Had he come to her rescue? Or was he allied with her attackers, there to threaten, even destroy, her?

*   *   *   *   *

Watch for Chapter Two of SHADOWS ON THE NILE coming next month—only in Silhouette Intimate Moments.

Starting in October . . .

SHADOWS ON THE NILE

by

Heather Graham Pozzessere

A romantic short story in six installments from best-selling author Heather Graham Pozzessere.

The first chapter of this intriguing romance will appear in all Silhouette titles published in October. The remaining five chapters will appear, one per month, in Silhouette Intimate Moments' titles for November through March '88.

Don't miss *"Shadows on the Nile"*—a special treat, coming to you in October. Only from Silhouette Books.

Be There!

IMSS-1

In response
to last year's outstanding success,
Silhouette Brings You:

Silhouette Christmas Stories 1987

Specially chosen for you in a delightful volume celebrating the holiday season, four original romantic stories written by four of your favorite Silhouette authors.

Dixie Browning—*Henry the Ninth*
Ginna Gray—*Season of Miracles*
Linda Howard—*Bluebird Winter*
Diana Palmer—*The Humbug Man*

Each of these bestselling authors will enchant you with their unforgettable stories, exuding the magic of Christmas and the wonder of falling in love.

A heartwarming Christmas gift during the holiday season... indulge yourself and give this book to a special friend!

Available November 1987

XM87-1